I0606587

This whole thing had felt wrong from the get-go. But the only important thing now was the missing girl…

Andy thought about calling Joey and telling him about Harley but decided to leave that to the police. Unfortunately, Carlyle needed to be told. He owed him that.

"What do you mean you almost had her?" Carlyle shouted.

Andy pulled the cell away. "There were three girls. I didn't have a chance to make a positive ID. Things went down too fast, then the girls disappeared."

"You incompetent bastard. You let them take my granddaughter?"

"I don't know if anyone snatched them, or if they got scared and bolted."

"I wasted my goddamn money and time on you," Carlyle said. "I want Beyer back on this. Where are you now?"

"I can handle it without him."

"Quiet. I want you to meet up with Beyer. Brief him on everything you have. After that, go back to selling rides."

"Bullshit."

"As of right now, I'm canceling the credit card. Your services are no longer required," he said. "Now tell me where you are so I can send Beyer."

"Fuck you. Let your flunky dig up his own information." Andy slapped the cell shut. The hell with him. He was committed to finding Emily, money or no money.

The man who telephoned him implied he wants to do business with amusement ride rep Andy Zartanian, and Andy seriously needs to do some business. When they meet, it is clear within moments that the man doesn't know Chance's Aviator from the Log Flume. Annoyed at having his time wasted, Andy turns to go. The man hurries to explain he's there on behalf of a wealthy Bostonian whose granddaughter was last seen with a carnie on a Virginia midway. His employer, the man says, is offering a handsome compensation package to Andy. All he has to do is track down the young woman and bring her home. Suspicious, but drawn to the financial upside, Andy signs on and starts refreshing his carnie contacts. But as Andy suspected from the get-go, it's much more complex than simply extracting young Emily from her newfound companions. As he fights his way through the seamy backside of sparkling midways and festive crowds, Andy is reminded why his grandfather always said carnie life was the devil's sandbox.

KUDOS for *Possum Belly Queen*

In *Possum Belly Queen* by Robert O'Hanneson, Andy Zartanian is a carnival ride salesman who is hired by a wealthy grandfather to find his granddaughter who was last seen with some "carnies" before she disappeared. Andy doesn't want to take the job, but he is desperate for cash to save his business, and the grandfather makes him an offer that is too good to refuse. But as Andy starts looking for the granddaughter, he uncovers a darker side of carnie life that he had no idea existed and is soon in over his head. And as he suspected from the beginning, things are not what they seem. O'Hanneson is an excellent storyteller, crafting an unusual plot in a fascinating setting. His characters are involved and very well developed. You'll be riveted from the very first word. ~ *Taylor Jones, Reviewer*

Possum Belly Queen by Robert O'Hanneson is the story of missing girls associated with carnivals. The unlikely hero, Andy Zartanian, is asked to help find one of these girls for her grandfather. Andy is suspicious, but he's also in need of cash, so against his better judgment, he accepts the commission. It doesn't take him long to find out that he should have listened to his instincts, but by that time, he is committed to finding not one but several missing girls—even at the risk of his own life. *Possum Belly Queen* is a superbly crafted story. The unique setting, fast-paced action, and plot surprises will keep you turning pages from beginning to end. This one's a keeper, folks. ~ *Regan Murphy, Reviewer*

ACKNOWLEDGEMENTS

To Bonnie Hearn Hill for brilliant editing and continual support. You are reading this book because of her and the Tuesday night writers.

To my friend, Bill McCarthy who helped with the carnie jargon and set me straight when I got it wrong.

To retired Sergeant Jon Buehler, Modesto Police Department for his firearms expertise.

To our sons, Dave, Steve, Greg, Geoff and their wives and our seven grandchildren, Courtney, Lauren, Alexis, Kasi, Gage, Addie, and Lily. I'm not sure whether you understood what I was doing daily, but I was really writing.

To David Glaister for his photography and enthusiasm.

To all the hardworking carnies and show owners who run safe operations and dedicate their lives to making people of all ages scream, laugh and smile. The characters in the book are fictional and do not represent the wonderful people I have met during the thousands of hours I have spent on carnival midways and in amusement parks worldwide.

And finally to Lauri Wellington, Faith Caminski, and Jack Jackson at Black Opal Books who worked behind the scenes to get this book published.

Possum Belly Queen

Robert O'Hanneson

A Black Opal Books Publication

DEDICATION

*To Carol O'Hanneson,
my wife, best friend, and captain of the ship,
who never gave up and helped steer me to port.*

Chapter 1

Even though Pop loved the carnie life, he used to call it the devil's sandbox. He could never understand why Andy didn't feel the same way.

Amusement parks turned silent and eerie when the lights were off. Standing among the metal beasts, Andy got the same feeling in the pit of his stomach he had in the army when he was on a mission and hit a blind spot. No way out until it was finished. Couldn't discuss it then, couldn't forget it now.

He made his way down the Santa Cruz boardwalk past the Roundup and Paratrooper then headed toward the Log Flume and a potential 90 Gs that would save his sorry ass. Wood groaned above him. The Giant Dipper. Steel coasters didn't make that sound. He stopped and looked up. A maintenance man maneuvered across the top of the structure.

A motor whined, then the chain-dogs engaged. A steady mechanical drone of metal against metal grew louder. The test run for the day. The coaster hesitated at the top of the lift, then plunged down the drop and whipped around the first turn.

"Would you ever get on that ride?" A clipped, almost British accent startled him from behind.

He recognized that ninety-thousand-dollar voice, turned, and extended his hand. "I've ridden every coaster in the country but wouldn't step foot on a round ride," Andy said. "Stomach can't take it."

The man was a couple of inches taller than him, maybe six-two, lean, and wore tailored threads. This wasn't amusement business attire. Hell, his shoes probably cost more than one of Andy's suits.

"Mr. Zartanian I take it," the man said and shook his hand. "Stephen Beyer. I'm glad you agreed to meet with me."

Andy tried not to look as wary as he felt about this guy. "You said you wanted to talk about a Mack Himalaya and some other pieces of iron."

"Iron?"

"Rides." Damn, the *dukmar* didn't even know the jargon. "You must not be in the business."

"Right, the rides," Beyer said with a wide grin.

"I know most of the equipment on the market," Andy said. "No one can get you a better deal."

"That's what I've been told." He tugged on his French cuffs.

"Unfortunately, the exchange rate has made everything a little tight with foreign equipment," Andy said. "What type of pieces are you looking for? Chance's Aviator is an incredible ride. Their Revolution 32 is kicking butt. Great rider capacity."

When the coaster entered the station, a blast of air and the screech of metal erupted.

Beyer glanced around then looked back at him. "Brake system," he said. "Well, I'm not exactly interested in any rides."

"Not exactly?" Andy repeated. "What the hell is that supposed to mean?"

Beyer's body stiffened. "I apologize if I misled you in any way, Mr. Zartanian, but the reason for our meeting isn't about purchasing amusement equipment."

Andy should have known the minute he saw the man. Andy's head felt like it was about to explode. Had he driven over the hill for nothing? "Look," he said. "I sell rides to parks and carnivals for big-ticket money. You're wasting my time if you're not here to purchase a piece."

He pulled the pack of Marlboros out of his jacket pocket, tapped out a cigarette, then lit it with Pop's old Zippo.

Beyer wrinkled his nose. "I'd appreciate it if you wouldn't do that," he said.

"You've got some pretty big ones, getting me out here on the pretense of doing business, then asking me not to smoke," Andy said. "I don't like being jerked around."

Beyer's face flushed, and his jaw tightened like a pitcher ready throw his best fastball. "Mr. Zartanian, the reason I'm here is worth considerably more than what you would have made selling me a ride."

"Keep talking." Andy took a long drag, trying to decide whether he should believe him, his words as sharp as his facial features.

Beyer moved around to his other side, upwind from the smoke. "I represent Jonathan Carlyle. You may have heard of him."

"Not that I recall. And when I'm finished with this cigarette, I'm out of here."

"Mr. Carlyle is head of Carlyle Precious Metals out of Boston," he said. "Fifth generation."

"You want me to be impressed?" Andy saw ninety

grand and his life drifting away like the smoke he exhaled. "Yeah, and he's probably personal friends with the Kennedys. If this guy is interested in developing an amusement park somewhere, you've got my attention. If not, we're through talking."

"I think not." Beyer's tone hardened. "Mr. Carlyle wants to engage your services to help find his granddaughter Emily."

Andy flicked the cigarette butt on the damp boards and snuffed it out with the sole of his Topsider. "You're kidding, right? Why would I want to do that?" he asked. "Hell, I wouldn't do it if you paid me the ninety thousand I would have made selling you a ride. Either you're out of your mind, or you have me confused with someone else."

"Oh, I have the right person," Beyer said. "Andy Zartanian, forty-one, currently living in Los Gatos. Grew up in San Francisco, raised by your Armenian grandmother." He knew he had Andy's attention. "Divorced. A daughter, Julie, who lives with your ex, Marie, in Virginia Beach."

Beyer's unflinching gaze and steel-blue eyes made Andy as nervous as the personal information he was spewing out. What else did this cocky son-of-a-bitch know?

"So you've done your homework."

"Mr. Carlyle is extremely thorough." Beyer paused long enough to let the words sink in. "As I said, he wants to find his granddaughter. She's around the same age as Julie."

Hearing him mention his daughter's name again hit a raw nerve. Andy hadn't seen her in months, only talked to her a few times on the phone. He reached for the pack again, then felt Beyer's hand clasp onto his wrist.

"Smoke really bothers me, Mr. Zartanian. Have all the cigarettes you want once we're done."

Andy shook free. "What have the police or FBI dug up?"

"We haven't called them because she ran away and wasn't kidnapped," he said. "Mr. Carlyle doesn't want his granddaughter's picture smeared on the front page of newspapers and tabloids. It's her future he's thinking about."

"When did she disappear?"

"A week ago. The last time her friends saw her, she was with a carnival worker."

"A carnie?" Andy couldn't help thinking how he'd feel if it were Julie who was missing.

Beyer nodded. "No one has seen her since. I'm sure you know what those carnival people are like."

This guy had a way of pissing Andy off. "Most are honest, hardworking people, blue collar. Some are close friends. Boston's a big city. Go find your boss a high-priced PI."

"I'm talking to you because we need someone with a faster inside track," Beyer said. "Someone the carnies will talk to."

"There's dozens of guys out there with the same background."

"But not all of them spent six years in the army, involved in what you were, and know the business the way you do."

"Years I'd like to forget," Andy said. "What's the army got to do with it?"

This guy didn't know the whole story. Images flooded in like a bad dream. Women and children laying in pools of blood surrounded by body parts. Rarely a night passed when Andy didn't awaken soaked in perspiration.

Beyer didn't answer. "You recently sold Joey Conner a giant wheel in Gibtown. The man paid a million dollars for it. Right?"

"Close enough." Andy was no longer shocked at anything he or his minions had dug up on him.

"Your commission was a hundred thousand," he said, "but that's not why I'm here. I've made a reservation for you in first class on United Flight 172, leaving SFO at 8:45 tomorrow morning. I'll meet you in the Red Carpet Club at 7:15. Mr. Carlyle will provide you with the details tomorrow night over dinner."

Andy's patience was gone. "I'm not interested," he said and started to leave. Beyer grabbed him by the arm. He shook loose. "Don't ever do that again," he told him. "I don't do business with people I can't trust. Find someone else."

"I have no doubt you'll be on that flight," Beyer said. "No one is asking you to do this gratis. If my information is accurate, and it usually is, you earned just under one hundred fifty thousand last year." He said it without expression, as if he reeled off financial histories of strangers every day. "You need more than that to bail yourself out and keep the business going. On top of that, your ex-wife is bleeding you dry."

"No amount of money is enough for her. She'll do the same to the next guy."

"And then there's the matter of your daughter's education."

The hair on the back of Andy's neck stood up. "Leave her out of this."

"Julie's a gifted child." Beyer's thin smile seemed to underline the words. "Good education can be expensive."

Andy shoved his hands into his pants pockets. "You think I don't know that?"

"You Armenians are a stubborn lot, aren't you?" Beyer pulled out an envelope and held it up. "This will change your mind. Inside, there's information on a wire transfer being deposited into your account the day after tomorrow. One hundred fifty thousand. You'll receive a matching amount when Mr. Carlyle's granddaughter is safely returned."

The offer stopped Andy cold. "You're telling me this guy, Carlyle, is willing to pay me three hundred grand to find his kid? A runaway?"

"Plus expenses," he said. "She's not just any kid. Emily's his life. Do we have a deal?" Beyer looked at him. Didn't blink.

Andy said nothing, walked over to the wall, then stared down at the waves lapping onto the sand below. His gaze swung right toward Steamer Lane, waters he'd surfed as a teenager.

Turning back, he swallowed hard, then took the envelope. Trying to salvage what was left of his self-esteem, he said, "One last thing."

"What's that?"

"What happens if I don't find her?"

"We both know that's not going to happen." Beyer's amused indifference widened into a grin. "Wear a suit and tie and lose the Topsiders," he said as he scanned Andy's clothes. "Mr. Carlyle is extremely fastidious."

And with that he turned and walked down the midway.

Son of a bitch, Andy thought. In spite of what he'd promised himself, he was back in the game.

Chapter 2

The girl ran down the beach toward the sound of splashing water. She stopped, rubbed her eyes, and tried to bring her surroundings into focus but only saw shimmers of light bouncing off the whitecaps. Still in a deep fog, she continued along the water's edge. Something bad had happened, but she couldn't remember what, not anything, not even her name. She felt dizzy as her legs moved in slow motion until they became heavy and stuck in the sand, causing her to fall forward. Her nails clawed at the tiny granules, as sounds from the waves began to fade, and the salty foam touched her lips.

⁂

Andy couldn't believe he was doing this. All he could see was the image of Julie and how he'd feel if she'd disappeared with a carnie, and, admit it, this was all about the money. If the job was what it appeared to be, the money could bail him out, maybe help pay for Julie's education. But there was always a catch, a potential hook that could drag him down. Careful.

Pop's memorabilia filled most of Andy's office. The door was constructed of wind-worn boards from Casino Pier's boardwalk. He'd turned an Eli Bridge Ferris Wheel car into a rocker. Framed photographs of him with owners of family-owned parks long gone—Harry Batt at Pontchartrain Beach, Larry Stone at Paragon Park, Roger Shaheen at Shaheen's Fun-o-rama—filled one wall. Photos of carnivals hung on the opposite wall, the most impressive, Royal American Shows that moved on rail cars. He had known everyone in the business, everything about what worked, and what didn't.

And had dedicated another wall to his military family. Six years of his life he'd spent in the army's most proficient unit until the incident that earned him a Purple Heart and an honorable discharge.

His lifelong friend, his godfather, came to mind. Doctor Agopian could help. He punched in the numbers.

"Armenian International Group," she said.

"Doctor Agopian, please. Tell him it's Andreas Zartanian."

"One moment please."

This well-respected man was head of a clandestine group of Armenians located in Boston and connected Andy back to his great-grandfather and the cause for which he'd given his life, a genocide the Turks still denied had happened.

"Andreas, my boy, it is good to hear from you," Agopian said, his voice thick with accent and hoarse from asthma. "It's been far too long."

"I know. We'll get together soon. I promise." Andy paused. "I need your help."

"May I ask what this is about?"

"There's a man in Boston by the name of Jonathan Carlyle. He owns Carlyle Precious Metals. I need whatever information you can gather on his background."

Andy waited until the doctor stopped coughing. "I'm meeting with him tomorrow and want to know what I'm up against."

"Ah, so you'll visit Rose and me in Watertown, maybe dinner?"

"Sorry. I'll only be there briefly," Andy said, feeling guilty. "I'd really appreciate it if you could get one of your people to check him out for me."

"I'll take care of it personally the moment we hang up," Agopian said. "It's short notice. Call me tomorrow night or first thing the following morning."

As far back as Andy could remember, this man had treated him like family, and he reminded himself that because of their bond, they were. Once this job was over, he'd return and spend some time with him and Rose. He owed them that much before age or health prevented that from happening.

∞

Beyer showed up precisely at seven, dressed in another dark gray, tailored suit and burgundy silk tie. "You were wise to accept Mr. Carlyle's offer," he said, tugging at his cuffs. "He doesn't take well to being turned down."

"I didn't have much of a choice, did I?" How long was it going to take to find this girl? Until then, business was on hold. Hell, his whole life was on hold. Andy had enough money to live on, but not enough for more than a month or two before he boarded the office's front door.

"I spoke with Mr. Carlyle last night," Beyer said. "Unfortunately, other matters require his immediate attention. He'll meet with you at his club but won't be able to join you for dinner."

"Dinner with Carlyle doesn't mean squat to me," Andy said. "The sole reason for this trip is to get information on Emily. The sooner I do, the sooner I get back to my normal life." He'd lied. Nothing about his life was normal, never had been.

Beyer scanned him from head to toe. "If you recall, I said suit and tie."

"Sport coat, slacks, tie and loafers is as far as I go."

Once they reached the gate, Beyer handed the officer on duty a slip of paper. He pulled back his jacket and exposed a holstered weapon. The rules had suddenly changed. Andy's pieces, a SIG-Sauer P226R DAK and a Beretta 32 cal. Tomcat, along with three magazines for each were in the baggage he'd checked. Only authorized police officers and government agents were allowed to board aircraft with firearms. Who in the hell was this guy?

Beyer sat across from him in first class and sipped a cup of coffee.

"Are you going to tell me what happened back there with security?"

Beyer looked over at Andy, then put his seat back, and closed his eyes. Silence was his answer.

Andy disliked this guy more now than when he first told him that he wasn't going to buy a ride. If Beyer was this much of an asshole, what would Carlyle be like?

Andy slipped out his wallet and flipped it open. His fingers brushed across Julie's picture. She was beautiful at just fifteen.

God, he missed her. As soon as he was through with this mess, he would fly her out to California for however long Marie would let her stay.

The photo next to hers was *Mamig*. Grandma always wore black during Martyr's Week, still in mourning from losing her father to the Turks. Her face held the softness he remembered as a child. "My little Andreas," she would say when he climbed onto her lap. He remembered the warm breath of the oven, the *lavash,* and the feel of her kisses against his cheek. He closed his eyes and tried to shut out all the screw-ups he'd made—mistakes that managed to settle in on him and squeeze back the memories.

⋇

A tailwind landed them at Logan ahead of schedule. Stephen Beyer didn't like small talk. He certainly didn't share anymore on the flight than he had the day before.

The limo exited Logan Tunnel then threaded its way through traffic until it pulled into the circular driveway in front of a large brownstone. Hung above the enormous double doors was a bronze plaque with raised polished letters. "Bell Tower Men's Club."

"Good to see you, Mr. Beyer," the doorman said, opening his side.

"Good evening, Mick." Beyer stepped out and turned toward Andy. "This way."

The imposing interior reminded Andy of a room he'd seen at Hearst Castle, only much older. They weaved their way across the mahogany-paneled salon. Men, dressed in suits, smoked cigars and sat in huddled conversations, drinking out of engraved tumblers and oversized martini glasses.

Not wanting to let the opportunity pass, Andy tapped Beyer's shoulder. "I thought smoke bothered you."

He didn't respond and led him to a table on the far side of the room where an elderly gentleman sat alone in a wing-back, leather chair. As they approached, he remained seated and extended his hand.

"Mr. Zartanian. Jonathan Carlyle," he said. "How was your flight?"

"Fine." He looked as Andy had expected him to, in

his seventies with thick, wavy, gray hair, meticulously groomed, and a well-trimmed mustache. Monogrammed cuffs extended from light pinstripes. Although Andy knew nothing about cigars, the one Carlyle smoked looked expensive.

"Please." Carlyle motioned. "Have a seat."

The chair slid back with Beyer's help. "I'll be in the library," he said then turned and left.

"May I offer you a drink? Perhaps a brandy. No, Bombay on the rocks with a twist, or is that up?"

This guy liked to play head games. How much more did he know about Andy than what Beyer had shared?

"Your information isn't all that accurate," Andy said. "I got rid of the hard stuff a while ago before it got me. These days, I stick to wine and an occasional beer."

Carlyle motioned to a man in a black tuxedo. "Bring Mr. Zartanian a glass of your Haut Brion Bordeaux." He turned back to him. "Cigar?"

"I'll pass." Andy lit a cigarette, then took a long drag.

"By the way, I've made arrangements for you to stay in the JFK Suite at the Fairmont," he said. "It's my retreat when I want to get away and think. Quite sumptuous and comfortable."

"With all due respect, Mr. Carlyle, I'm here to talk."

Carlyle sat back in his chair and studied him. "Mr. Zartanian, let me make one thing eminently clear from the start. You're being paid handsomely to find my granddaughter. I expect this to be handled effectually and quickly."

Andy didn't flinch from his gaze. "I never renege on a deal. If she's with some carnie, I'll find her."

Carlyle grabbed a glossy black presentation folder, embossed with a gold CPM logo from the chair next to him, and slid it across the table. "That contains all of the information you'll need, including recent photographs."

Andy opened the dossier and slipped out the contents. Emily Carlyle, a sweet looking sixteen-year-old, didn't appear to be the type who would run away. In one picture, she was dressed in jeans and a green sweatshirt with Harper Girls School printed across the front. The second showed her on a pier leaning against a railing. She was dressed in white shorts, a blue sleeveless T-shirt, and flip-flops.

"Well? Carlyle said.

"It looks thorough. Her stats, pictures, even the books she reads." A smile crossed Andy's face. He hesitated when he saw where she had disappeared. That's where Julie lived now. "There's one thing that bothers me."

"What's that, Mr. Zartanian?"

Andy ran his fingers back over the dates. "Where she was last seen?"

"I don't understand."

"What was Emily doing in Virginia Beach during a time when school was normally in session?"

Carlyle sipped his brandy. "A religious retreat required her school to close from Friday through Monday," he said. "Emily's aunt has a condo there and thought it might be fun for the two of them to fly down and spend a couple of days together."

"That's not in here." Andy's index finger tapped the open page.

"An oversight," Carlyle said. "I spoke to Grace myself to see if she remembered anything that could help."

"Is Grace here in Boston?"

"No." Carlyle rolled his cigar between his fingertips. "She's in Europe on a buying trip. Antiques. She travels across the pond several times a year."

"Isn't that a little strange?" Andy asked. "Her niece

disappears, then she's off to Europe. Come on, Mr. Carlyle."

"Your insinuation is offensive," Carlyle said then stamped out his cigar in the ashtray. "My sister runs a well-known antique gallery in Boston. Her trip had been planned months in advance. Let's move on."

"What about Emily's friends in Virginia Beach?"

"Stephen already spoke to them but turned up nothing," Carlyle said. "I don't want you to waste your time."

Andy was starting to get frustrated. "I guess if I'm going to be the one responsible for finding her, I'll be the judge of what's a waste of time and what's not."

Carlyle reached inside his jacket pocket and removed a platinum card and envelope then pushed the card across the table. "This is for your expenses. Airfares, car rentals, hotels, food, and any other incidentals." He did the same with the envelope. "Five thousand in cash to get you started. Is there anything else?"

The waiter returned with a large wine goblet, then placed it on a coaster to his right. "Will there be anything else, sir?"

"That's all for now," the elderly man said.

Andy lifted the glass, swirled it, inhaled the contents, then tasted it. "Very nice."

"It's one of the finest in our cellars," Carlyle said then grabbed the edge of the table and shifted his position again. "I take it you have everything you need."

"There is one more thing."

Carlyle took in a deep breath. "Go on."

"I don't see anything in here about her parents."

The color in Carlyle's face drained, and his jaw tightened. "My daughter died shortly after Emily was born. She meant everything to me. All I have now is her, my only grandchild. You must find her."

The mention of the mother dying hit close to home. "What about her father?"

"He worked for me until late last year. That's all you need to know."

"Is there a possibility he might be involved?" Andy picked up the photographs and studied them again to see if he'd missed anything.

"He's never given a damn about her. Then or now." Carlyle spit out the words then took a long swig.

"Emily's last name. You said it's Carlyle. What's the father's?"

Carlyle slammed his fist on the table with such force that it caused his drink to splash and heads turn. "It doesn't matter. He's out of her life. She's a Carlyle now," he said then sank back in his chair. "The bastard knows me well enough to stay away from her." He motioned with his hand. The waiter hurried to their table.

"Tell Mr. Beyer I'm ready," Carlyle said. His cold eyes met Andy's. "My patience is wearing thin. If I were you, I'd start with the carnival that played Virginia Beach the weekend she disappeared. I want an update every day by 6 P.M. Is that clear?"

Beyer arrived with a wheelchair and stared down at him.

"I'm not finished," Andy said.

Carlyle's eyes narrowed. "What now?"

"I fly back to San Francisco tonight if I don't get straight answers to my questions." Andy shoved the folder toward him then slid the chair back. "Hire someone else."

"You're making a big mistake," Beyer said.

"Quiet," Carlyle shouted. "Go on."

"Emily could have run off with a carnie, or something else could have happened." Andy picked his words carefully. "You said her biological father's alive but doesn't give a damn about her."

"That's right."

"And he probably hates you as much as you hate him."

"I'm sure the feeling's mutual," Carlyle said. "Get to the point."

"Then he could be involved. We have a deal when I get his name and address," Andy said. "I also want the contact information for the people you talked with in Virginia Beach."

Beyer pulled open his jacket enough to expose the holstered gun.

Carlyle's hand shook as he reached for Beyer's arm. The veins on his neck bulged. "James Armstrong," he said. "Stephen will give you his contact information and the other names you requested."

"Then we have a deal." Andy couldn't believe he'd said it, but he had, and they did have a deal.

"The driver will take you to the Copley Plaza," Beyer said then helped Carlyle into the wheel chair.

Andy slipped the envelope into the folder then stood as Beyer pushed the frail man away from the table. He turned his head back toward him. "Don't disappoint him."

"So what if I don't get the other hundred fifty grand?"

"You fail to understand," he said. "You won't need the first."

Chapter 3

T he girl's eyes blinked open as the sun was about to rise. Water lapped around her, then a small wave washed over her body. She struggled to her feet and tried to brush away the wet sand. Pain erupted in her palms and feet. She'd reopened the wounds. The voice in her head grew louder. She had to keep running. Get away from the house. Her life depended on it.

❧❧❧

It was apparent why they called this place the JFK Library and Museum Suite—early sixties everywhere. Framed photographs of Kennedy and his family, before and during his presidency, hung among an opulence that made Andy uncomfortable. Even though he was exhausted, having American royalty stare at him made for a restless night's sleep.

Showered and dressed for what he hoped would be a quick assignment, Andy held up Emily's pictures and studied both, every single detail, the same way he'd studied plans for missions the government never acknowledged. Blonde hair that fell to her shoulders appeared soft, but her ice-blue eyes lacked the luster of a happy sixteen-year-old. A facial expression of children programmed from birth to fit their parents' life template. He looked out at the Charles River. "Where are you? Talk to me, Emily. Talk to me. *Heyhoyel,* no more cigarettes." He crumpled the pack and threw it across the room. "I'm done with this crap."

He moved to the desk, sat, opened his laptop, and clicked favorites, then Amusement Business. The expansive site covered amusement parks, carnivals, entertainers, and arenas throughout the country. He focused on the section with scheduled fairs and still dates. Conner Royal Midways had played Virginia Beach during the time of her disappearance. The same unit was now in Williamsburg. He pressed the numbers on his cell, got the receptionist, and waited for Doctor Agopian.

"Andreas, my son, I apologize for not being able to get the information to you sooner. I'm still waiting for more. Mr. Carlyle is an interesting man." He paused. "The family goes back several generations here in Boston."

"I'm aware of that."

Agopian cleared his throat. "You are truly Dajad's son, and just as impatient," he said. "This man is a very astute business man, sometimes brutal. He's crushed the lives of many who have gotten in his way. Ironically, the family is known for their philanthropic work."

"I appreciate you getting the information for me," he said, glancing at his watch. "I—"

"One more thing. His club."

"I met him there last night. Bell Tower Men's Club."

"Yes. Very stuffy. Its members share a great deal of wealth and power. Old money. I'll keep checking and see what else I can find out."

The doctor's words left Andy hanging. The mention of his father opened the door to memories of a mother he had barely known before she died when he was three and the hours he'd spent with *Mamig* at St. John's Armenian Church in San Francisco. *Hayr* Mihran, the priest at the time, had acted as a surrogate father when Pop was out of town, which seemed like most of the time. The reverend father did his best to mix lessons of religion with life in an attempt to keep Andy focused on the beliefs of the Armenian Apostolic Church. But when *Mamig* died, Andy began to stray and never looked back. Today, he wished he hadn't.

℗℗℗

Andy was about to board his flight to Norfolk when his cell vibrated.

"What in the world's going on?" Mia Nakano, his personal assistant said.

She made excuses for him and had a knack for bailing him out whenever he screwed up. Most men would call this Eurasian beauty eye-candy. Customers loved her. Maybe he did too.

"Good morning to you, too," he said. "Hope you enjoyed the extra days off."

"They were okay," she said. "But where in the world did we get the hundred and fifty thousand that landed in our account this morning?"

"Do I detect a bit of a 'tude?" he asked.

"A hundred and fifty thousand isn't attitude."

"It's a long story. I'll explain later and call you when I get to Williamsburg," he told her. "Trust me, there's a nice bonus in this for you. I'm going to need your help in running down a few people."

"Like with a car?"

"Can the wisecracks," he said. "Information. I have to go now."

First class gave him the room he needed to transfer the information from Carlyle's dossier into his laptop and post the still dates he'd downloaded from Amusement Business. Conner Royal Midways had three units out, the red, white and blue.

After landing in Norfolk, he rented a car then pointed the black Hertz Mustang toward Williamsburg. Though it served the purpose, it paled in power compared to his '69 fastback.

Joey's blue unit was easy to find like any other carnival in the country—all members of a culture Andy had been born into, thanks to Pop.

That crusty Armenian never had an unexpressed thought and worked harder than any man he'd ever known. Andy needed his old-world advice and thick-fingered thump on the back of the head about now. The car accident still troubled him, never made sense. He missed him. With no parents, grandparents, or siblings, the Zartanian name would die with him unless he married and fathered a boy.

Andy spotted the office trailer at the end of the midway, a forty-foot fortress where business was conducted and money counted, some on the books, some not. He made his way toward it. Colored lights flashed and chased as they prepared to open. Hip-hop had replaced rock and roll. A loud bang startled him and caused him to turn in the direction of a nearby storage trailer.

"You SOB," a man yelled. "No one goes south on me."

Andy recognized that gruff voice. A young kid flew out the back and bounced onto the dirt. Joey jumped down and landed a foot jam to his gut. He kicked him several more times then jerked him up by the collar and slammed him against the side of the trailer, squeezing his throat. Reaching inside the kid's pants pocket, he grabbed a wad of bills and threw it to the ground. "You fucking tweaker. You have five minutes to get your stuff and ass out of here," he said. "You won't be able to walk if I see your ugly puss around here again." He reached down, picked up the carnie roll then turned and walked toward the office.

"Hey Joey," Andy shouted.

Joey's six-foot-plus frame spun around, and dark brown eyes flared, ready to take on the next in line. He was sporting a sun-bleached buzz cut.

"I thought flattops went out with the Edsel."

When Joey saw him, he dropped the scowl. "What the hell are you doing here, you crazy-ass Armenian?"

"Came to kick your butt."

Joey laughed. "In your wildest dreams. Come on, I'll buy you a cup of coffee." He grabbed his shoulder, pulled Andy to him, then wrapped him in a headlock and messed his hair. "Where's your goddamn camel?" he asked.

Andy pulled loose. "Traded it in for a Mustang at Hertz."

"The two-bit punk tried to scam me out of three hundred bucks working the Hoopla Blocks. Kid's on meth," he said. "I'll kill that bastard if I catch him around here again."

"Tell me the truth," Andy said. "Have you ever killed anyone?"

The look Joey shot back was his answer. Joey punched the alarm code on the keypad next to the door then turned the handle.

Inside, Joey sat behind his desk, stacks of bills on his left and a .357 magnum, long barrel next to them. Andy was sure he kept money in sight to remind him of how far he'd come, and the gun to intimidate anyone who dared threaten him. Framed carnival and circus posters were slapped across the walls. Andy had known Joey for only five years but could tell he had a rough start. He sank into an overstuffed chair across from the big man. Steam rose from a pot of carnie coffee that sat on a burner on a credenza behind him. Thick and burned. Carnies called it Deadhead's Brew.

"You haven't delivered my Giant Wheel, so I know you ain't here for money," Joey said then relit the cigar in his ashtray.

"No. The down payment makes us even so far." Andy smiled. "I'll be back in August or September when you stop returning my calls."

"Like every year, Andy. It's a game," Joey said. "You fuck me over with an overpriced ride. I return the favor and not pay you. You add outrageous late fees and add on interest, something I still don't understand but always pay."

"Bullshit. You shell out, even though you piss and moan, because you make a fortune with the rides I sell you." Andy reminded him.

"It's not like the old days," Joey said. "Damn cheating fair boards suck up most of the profit now. I gotta ice the bagman just to keep them off my back. Then there's patch money for the fucking cops. Used to be, we all made a buck or two. Then they all got greedy. Every one of those bastards take their cut without blinking. Fucking crooks."

"So you gaff a few joints. Make it up on rigged games and concessions the Feds know nothing about."

"Have to survive." Joey leaned forward. "Now tell me the real reason you're here."

"I'm chasing down a young girl who appears to have hooked up with one of your ride jocks." Andy pulled out the photos and tossed them on the desk. "The information I was given said it happened about a week ago at the beach."

Joey picked them up. "She got a name?"

"Emily Carlyle."

Joey paused and studied each one then dumped the ashes of his cigar close to the ashtray.

"Have you seen her?"

"I'd remember this one if she was shacking up with one of my guys," Joey said.

"You've had underage girls sleeping in the possum bellies of ride trailers before. You're telling me you re-member all of the lot lizards?"

"Nah, but I keep a closer eye on them now. No hard habits. Police and sheriff deputies spot-check." Joey paused. "Tell me, what show hasn't had its share of young stuff? Ride jocks pick them up then dump them when we tear down and move on. There's always plenty of fresh meat in the next town."

Andy felt his blood pressure rising. "I have a fifteen-year-old daughter, Joey. If anyone referred to her as fresh meat, I'd shoot the bastard."

"Sorry, man. Don't get all whacked out," Joey said. "Think about it. Every girl you've looked at or done is someone's daughter, too."

Joey was right. Making this personal wasn't going to get Andy anywhere. "What about your other units?"

"Nick's got the red up in Richmond at the coliseum. White's in Nags Head," Joey said. "Why you looking for this girl?"

"Her grandfather hired me," Andy said. "You men-tioned that Nick's in Richmond? I thought he and your sister got a divorce. Word is she caught him coming out of a hotel with another woman."

"You mean slut. Everybody's got a story." Joey

picked up a pile of twenties and slammed them back down on the desk. "This is what Nick Pappas does. Makes me money. Lots of it. He knows the business inside out. All sis ever does is spend it."

"I'm going to need to talk to some of your help," Andy said.

"Be my guest. If you're going to be around tonight, I'll let you buy me dinner. Maybe get a game of Liar's Dice going in the G-Top and clean your ass like I did in the Showtown Bar last year."

Andy remembered the night well. Gibsonton, Florida, the heartbeat of carnivals and circuses, a place where some of its citizens are considered freaks by the rest of society. Joey had taken a little over three hundred from him, then laughed, stuffed a c-note into Andy's shirt pocket, and slapped him on the back. "Easiest mark in town," Joey said loud enough for everyone in the smoke-filled bar to hear. They laughed.

"Thanks for the stimulating conversation."

"Anytime."

Andy scooped up the photos then stood to leave. "Think I'll head up to Richmond and talk to Nick."

Joey shook his hand and squeezed his shoulder. "Good luck. Make sure the Giant Wheel is delivered to me when I set up in Dayton. It's in my contract with the fair board," he said. "If I'm stuck with a penalty for not having it, it's coming out of your pocket."

"You worry too much, Joey," Andy said. "The piece will be there on time."

"Just covering my ass." Joey winked. "You know how I like busting your balls. If I see the girl, you'll be the first one I call."

Andy stepped down onto the midway and followed the smell of grease to the cookhouse. A tricked-out food trailer was fronted by a shaded area with white plastic tables and chairs, the official carnie dining room.

Andy approached a young male sitting by himself, his head hung between his hands and stringy hair, dripping wet. He appeared to be suffering from too much partying.

Andy slapped a photo of Emily on the table in front of him. "Seen her around?"

The kid looked up through swollen, red eyes, the same look he'd seen on druggies hanging out at sugar shacks on hundreds of midways. His blank stare met Andy's.

"I asked if you've seen her around? Maybe Virginia Beach?"

The kid glanced down, then up again. "Nope," he said then stood and lumbered to another table with four ride jocks.

Showing the photo to several others in the cookhouse got him nowhere. Andy checked the table next to him, to make sure it would hold his weight, then jumped up on top and held Emily's picture above his head so everyone could see it.

"You say you don't know this girl. Never seen her around," he shouted. "I don't believe it and have a grand that says you have. Ten crisp C-notes for the one who points me in her direction." He paused. "Well?"

A tattooed, bearded, thick-necked goon stood and walked toward him. Even though Andy could cut the guy's feet out from under him in a second, he didn't want to waste valuable time with someone whose arms were as big as his thighs. But he would if he had to. A chain that hung from the guy's belt was attached to a thick, black wallet that poked out of his front pocket. Why not the rear like most people?

"No one knows nothin'. Make it two Gs, and they still know nothin'. Got that, asshole?"

"Why are you speaking for them? You scared of something?" Andy said then jumped down. Damn, he was doing exactly the opposite of what he wanted.

Fur-face gave him a two-finger shove to the chest, turned to the others, and laughed. They joined in. He turned back. "Man, do I look like the type who scares easy?"

"Cool it," Andy said. *Maintain. Focus on the mission.* "All I'm trying to do is find this girl."

"I told you, no one knows nothin'. Now get the hell out of here. You're cutting into our free time."

Andy moved out of the cookhouse then walked past the Spider and Tilt. As he headed toward the Mustang, he heard a female's voice call out in a hushed tone.

"Hey." It was coming from behind a dog-on-a-stick joint. "Don't stop," she said. "Keep walking. Check the unit in Richmond if you want to find that girl you're looking for."

Chapter 4

The girl's voice damned near stopped him in his tracks, but Andy kept walking. Someone did know something. Fear was keeping them silent.

He needed to move on to Richmond and talk with Nick Pappas, but first he had to talk to the person who could break the carnie code of silence.

Sprocket, a wiry biker pushing sixty, lived in Virginia Beach. Pop had gotten him his first job with a carnival after his discharge from the army. He'd still be on the road if he hadn't met Gabby, a young Latina beauty. Despite settling down at the beach with a steady job, he kept in close contact with carnies who worked the eastern seaboard.

After several minutes of Andy pleading his case, coupled with the promise of five hundred dollars, Sprocket agreed to run up to Williamsburg and talk with the crew. He told him that fur-face's name was Harley.

It took him a little over an hour to reach the Richmond Coliseum. When Andy drove into the parking lot, he saw the Bungee Tower sitting stoic against a blue sky, watching over his iron friends. The high-pitched whine of motors and flashing lights told him the show was open.

Andy passed several food joints. The smell of corn-dogs, caramel, and popcorn merged and wafted throughout the midway. Ride jocks and grinders moved into position. Game booths lined the other side. Gaffs inside straightened slum, brightly colored stuffed animals that hung above on all four sides. Balloons popped and buzzers and bells exploded inside the cubicles. The signature orange and yellow canvas tops distinguished this show from others in the country.

Nick's crew wore powder-blue Conner Royal Midways Polo shirts and black jeans. Some heads were shaven. Others had stringy, unkempt hair—same attitude, just different ways of expressing it. He'd known enough carnies to understand that most weren't bad. But each had a hole in his or her life that had led them into this transient world with its own set of rules. He spotted the cookhouse, where an older man dressed in a tee and denim overalls stood behind the well-worn yellow, Formica counter, hunched over a large pot, stirring it with a wooden paddle. Thin gray hair was a little more than a buzz cut.

He looked up and smiled through missing teeth. "Help you, buddy?"

"What's today's special?"

"Who's asking?"

His crotchety voice reminded Andy of Pop's. Maybe that's what the amusement business did to some people, made them surly.

"Andy Zartanian. Zartanian Rides."

"You ain't Daj's son, are you?"

"Sure am."

"The guy was pure gold," the man said. "Sorry to hear about what happened to him."

Everyone in the industry knew, but Andy wasn't in the mood to get into a discussion about how his father lived, or worse yet, died. "Thanks, but it's getting hungry out."

The old guy laughed. "Rube's goulash over rice and red beans. Best you'll ever taste." The sweet aroma of paprika drifted from the pot.

"Is Nick Pappas around?"

"No. Took off earlier," the cook said and kept stirring the thick mixture. "Usually's back by the time the rides crank up."

Andy placed the picture of Emily dressed in the sweatshirt on the Formica counter in front of him. "Have you seen this girl around here?"

The old guy picked up the photo, held it close to his face, and squinted. "Can't say that I have. Them young kids come and go. Think they know everything at that age." He handed it back to him. "Strange."

"What's strange?"

"Last week down in Charlotte." The man paused and looked at the photo again. "Another guy came by looking for a girl. Said she was somebody's granddaughter I think. But this picture ain't the same."

Andy pulled out the other photo. "Like this?"

Rube squinted again. "Yeah, could be her."

"What did he look like?"

"Don't quite remember. Eyes ain't like they used to be."

"Tall? Muscular? Thick head of hair?" Andy asked.

"Yeah. Dressed in a fancy suit. A man don't wear his church clothes to no carnival."

"This girl disappeared in Virginia Beach."

"We played there with Joey," he said. "Not enough marks for all of us to stay, so we split up and took this unit to Charlotte before coming here."

"I'll take some of that goulash," Andy said and laid two fives on the counter. "Keep the change."

It appeared Carlyle had Beyer searching for the girl and had come up with zip. Andy was plan B. Maybe that was the reason Beyer resented him.

Andy sat at one of the tables and bolted down the eye-watering food. Either Rube was right about his goulash, or Andy was hungry, probably a little of both.

Two large fans kept the air tolerable but did nothing to curb the circling flies' appetites.

A late model, black 350 Ford dually with an extended cab pulled alongside an office trailer similar to Joey's. Nick Pappas stepped out and strutted toward the cookhouse, spit-shined cowboy boots crunching against the asphalt. He was dressed in laundry-pressed jeans, a crisp western style shirt, and a wide, leather belt with a silver buckle the size of a CD.

Andy stood. "Hey, Nick," he shouted.

Pappas turned and took a second look. It had been awhile since he'd seen him. "Andy," he shouted while he walked toward him. "Joey called and told me I'd be seeing you." He shook his hand, exposing a gold nugget band and diamond-faced watch. "He mentioned something about you looking for some chick," he said. "Ride sales must be in a slump for you to be out stumping for some young thing."

Andy ignored the comment, pulled out both photos, then handed them to him. "Does she look familiar?"

"Man, they're here one day and gone the next," Nick said. "This one's pretty hot. I'd definitely remember her."

His comment rubbed Andy the wrong way, the same as Joey's had. He tightened his jaw and kept his cool. "Are you sure you haven't seen her?"

"Yeah." Nick handed the photos back to him. "She hasn't been around this show."

Andy motioned to his bowl. "Care to join me?"

"Already ate," Nick said. "How long you going to be

in town?" He placed one boot on one of the chairs, pulled a paper napkin from a shiny metal holder, then ran it over the expensive leather.

"Not quite sure," Andy said. "Nice boots. Tony Lama's?"

Nick laughed. "I see you don't know your leather. These babies are Blutcher's. Made in Beggs, Oklahoma. I flew there for a fitting. Best damn alligator on the market."

"Sounds expensive."

"Cost me a grand and change. Doesn't include airfare," Nick said. "Hey, man, I'd love to shoot the shit, but I've got to take care of some business. Catch you later if you're around." He walked away with the usual, cocky swagger.

Andy never liked the guy before and liked him less now. He went back and polished off a second helping, then began showing the photos to help hanging around the cookhouse. They were more receptive than the crew in Williamsburg, but the answers still came up the same. No one recognized her.

A girl in her mid-to-late teens sat by herself at a round, plastic table that backed up to the side of an old Kilinski Super Slide. Bottled-black hair, heavy makeup, and piercings rounded out her weary Goth look. A fresh trail of hickies ran down one side of her neck.

"Excuse me." He laid both photos side by side on the table. "Have you seen this girl around?"

She stared blankly at him, then lowered her head. "Her?" she said and tapped a black painted nail on the picture of Emily dressed in the green sweatshirt.

"Yes."

"No," she said.

"Are you sure?"

"Don't you understand what no means? You're invading my space," she said. "Get the fuck away."

"You're a little testy for such a simple question." Her hair reeked of weed.

She tilted her head back then moved it left and right. "I see nothing in your eyes. And the more I see the less I like," she sang.

"What the hell does that mean?"

"'Breath' by Breaking Benjamin, asshole." She shoved the photos back toward him, stood, and walked away with a one-finger-salute waving high above her head.

Something about that look and her attitude bothered him even more than the fact that she was probably tripping on an illegal substance. Goth knew more. She walked past the Flying Bobs, looked back, then ducked around the Mitt Camp. Slivered moons and astrological signs glittered across the canvas front.

Andy ran after her and rounded the corner. Muscular fingers clamped onto his shoulders and pinched the nerves, dropping him to the ground. A whack to the back of the head was the last thing he remembered.

He opened his eyes slowly, then closed them. A throbbing pain in his neck and head came in waves. It took several seconds before things came back into focus. Then he realized the black metal above him was the ceiling of a van.

Two men wearing black ski masks, black jackets, and gloves stared down at him.

"One warning only," the larger guy said, his voice hoarse. "Stay away from here. Is that clear?"

"I'm only looking for a runaway," Andy said and started to sit up when a backhand from the smaller one collided with his chest and knocked him back.

"Look somewhere else. Whoever you're searching for ain't here."

"Got it," Andy said.

Someone was going to great lengths to stop him from finding the girl. It wasn't worth it to push now. He'd square it with these two later.

The smaller one yanked open the side door, and the other rolled him out of the van into an empty lot. By the time his head cleared, the black van had sped around the corner and disappeared.

Andy brushed away dirt and gravel from his pants and shirt, then ran his hands through his hair. The coliseum loomed on the horizon about a quarter of a mile away. He reached into his pockets. The wallet and wad of cash were still there.

As he headed back toward the parking lot to retrieve his car, a police cruiser pulled in and screeched to a stop. Two patrol cars followed and encircled him. What the hell was going on? Officers jumped out, gripped their weapons with both hands, and pointed them at him.

"Hands up and turn around," the cop said, motioning with the barrel of his gun.

"What's this about, officer?"

"Do it, now," he shouted.

Andy saw the younger cop's hand shaking. Damn rookies. He couldn't risk the guy overreacting with a nervous trigger finger. "I didn't do anything, officer," he shouted. "Name's Andy Zartanian. I'm from California."

"Down on your knees," he ordered. "Keep your hands above your head." The cop yanked Andy's right arm down and cuffed it. Then he felt the bracelet tightening around his left wrist. The cop grabbed his collar and jerked him to his feet.

"You've got me mixed up with someone else," Andy said.

"I doubt it. One of the carnies at the coliseum phoned 911. You're a real close match to the description and location they called in," he said. "Pricks like you don't do well in jail."

"What am I being charged with?"

"You don't know?" He grabbed the cuffs, lifted his arms and shoved Andy toward the cruiser. "You're a suspect in an attempted rape."

Chapter 5

Sprocket set the receiver back in its cradle. There was plenty of time to get up to Williamsburg and back before dark. He would have done it for free but let Andy do the talking. Five hundred wasn't bad pay for three or four hours work.

He grabbed the camo vest off the back of the chair, slipped his inked arms through the openings, then adjusted the medal pinned chest high on the right. The Purple Heart he'd earned in 'Nam's Tan An Delta.

Gabby walked into the room. "Where do you think you're going?"

Not many people dared talk to him the way she did. The tradeoff was the thirty-year age difference and Brazilian passion.

"Andy Z called. Wants me to run up to Williamsburg and poke around Conner's midway."

She placed her hands on her hips. "I thought you were going back to the boatyard," she said. "We need the money."

"Hold dinner for me," he said, then opened the door, and walked out.

"Like hell," she shouted, then continued in Spanish as he slammed the door behind him.

Sprocket picked up the German-style helmet that sat on the black gas tank of his Hog, placed it on his head, then straightened his salt and pepper ponytail so it fell over the back of his vest.

Exhaust blasted. He let out the clutch, then rubber screeched against pavement as he headed down the street. Once he hit the highway, he accelerated to seventy and kept it steady. The afternoon breeze rushed past. It wouldn't be long before it turned into a blast furnace.

He was here because of Daj, the iron-fisted Armenian who'd found him running aimlessly after his discharge. The midway or jail had been his choices.

The lot was quiet with only a few townies milling around on the midway. He'd worked for Joey on and off for years. The big man was tough but fair and ran a clean operation.

"Hey, Sprock," a female yelled.

He turned. Molly came out of the cookhouse trailer. "Tell me, your love life went to shit and you're looking for a job, right?"

He laughed. He liked her, always had. She served good food and plenty of it. They met halfway, then hugged.

"Don't know if you saw anything, but a buddy of mine was up here asking around about a young girl," Sprock said. "Guess Harley ran him off."

"Saw it all. But you know how it goes. Ain't seen nothin'."

He placed his arm around her. "You wouldn't have a cold brewski hiding back there, would you?"

"Sure do," she said, then grabbed his arm, and walked briskly toward the cookhouse. "Slap your ass down on one of those benches while I get it."

He sat under the thin netting that offered minimal protection from the harsh sun. If it wasn't for Gabby, he'd be back here in a heartbeat. Carnie life was the sawdust in his blood.

She returned with a large red plastic cup. "Disguised the longneck for you," she said. "Ain't proper having open containers on the lot."

He laughed. Memories of eating her food and the good times flooded back. But it was time to deal with the business at hand.

"My friend told me that a big guy with a thick beard ran him off. It was Harley, wasn't it?"

"Guessed right." She looked around, nervous. "Harley means well, maybe a little too cautious. Doesn't like strangers prying."

"Guy's a friend. He's trying to find a missing girl," Sprocket said. "Is there something going on you're not telling me?"

Her expression changed. "You know me better than that."

"I'm not saying it's you. Only asking if you know anything."

"Know what?" a husky voice said from behind.

He spun around on the bench. "You get uglier every time I see you."

Harley extended his right hand then slapped Sprocket's. "The old lady let you out of your cage?"

"Yeah. Got a pass for a few hours," Sprocket said. "What's with the leathers? You going someplace?"

"Headed out to take care of some business." Harley glanced at his watch mounted on a wide leather band. "Saw you here and wanted to say hello before I split."

"Word is you gave a buddy of mine a hard time."

He laughed. "You talking about that pussy looking for that girl?"

"It's a good thing you didn't call him that to his face," Sprocket said. "He'd rip your arm off and shove it up your ass."

Harley's jowls tightened. "Send him back. Or maybe that's why you're here."

"Damn, you're wound tight. What the hell's going on?"

Harley glanced at Molly then back at him. "This is family. We don't like outsiders poking their noses where they don't belong." He looked back at Molly. "You haven't seen any missing girls, have you?"

Sprocket stepped forward. "Don't try and intimidate her," he said. "Talk to me. I was part of this family before your probation officer was born. So why all this hush-hush bullshit?"

"None of your goddamn business," Harley said, then turned, and walked away.

Sprocket stared at Molly. "Is he losing it? Harley's always been cool with me."

She shook her head. "Don't know, but he's been edgy like that for the past couple of days."

There wasn't much more he could do there. He hugged her, then headed toward the back of the lot. Sitting on his bike's leather seat, he pulled out a joint, lit it, then thought about Harley's behavior that was totally out of character. He knew something about the missing girl.

With his helmet on and joint hanging from the side of his mouth, he eased out of the parking lot and onto a back road that led to the highway. About to make a left turn, the high-pitched whine of a rice-rocket erupted on his right. A lime green streak shot past, then something hit him from the left. He went down, slid on his side, and came to a stop on the shoulder. A blurred image of a white pickup disappeared around the corner. Then the engine's sputter faded to silence.

Chapter 6

Andy sat on the edge of a paper-thin mattress in a small, dank holding cell. A stainless toilet and sink hung from the rear wall. Steel bars separated him from the next cell, a larger one, where honorary members of the Loser Men's Club were being held. Odors of urine and vomit that filled the holding tank next to him made him gag. This was the first time he'd been arrested. Or as the officer called it, held in protective detention. Isolation was their way of separating him from criminals who had little use for men who raped women. Bullshit. He'd been set up and had to get out of there.

"Zartarian," a large sergeant shouted.

Andy stood and stepped toward the cell door. "That's me."

"Today's your lucky day. You're free to go." A buzzer sounded, then the cop slid open the bars. "It appears there's been a mistake."

"That's what I've been telling everyone," Andy said. "What the hell changed your minds?"

"The 911 operator said the call was made from a phone booth across from the coliseum," he said. "We haven't been able to locate the person who called it in. Officers checked the carnival and concluded it was all a prank."

"A prank?"

The cop's face tightened. "Shit happens." The officer led him through steel doors. "You'll have to sign for your personal belongings."

The words echoed in Andy's ears. That's all he could say? Deciding to keep his mouth shut was probably the one thing he'd done right since arriving in Richmond.

All it had taken was a phone call to put him on the wrong side of the bars. He had always believed in the law that protected the people, been willing to die for it. Now, he didn't know.

⁊∙⁊

Andy found himself back at square one with sore muscles and a throbbing headache. The Mustang was just as he'd left it. He reached over and unzipped the small, faux-leather suitcase on the passenger seat. Packed in a weapons case at the bottom were his 9 millimeter SIG and .32 caliber Beretta, each with several magazines. Pancake and ankle holsters lay next to them. He loaded the Beretta, slid it into the nylon and Velcro, then secured it to the inside of his right ankle. The 9mil fit snuggly under his right arm. He pulled out of the Coliseum lot, joined the flow of traffic, then drove down to a strip mall, and parked. Had he become a mercenary, or was he doing all of this for the right reasons? The answer he conjured up bothered him.

The first call was to Carlyle. He told him what had happened and the reason he hadn't called before six. He left out the information about Beyer chasing down the girl in Charlotte. The bastard pushed the same as always.

When he mentioned Julie's name again, Andy flipped the phone closed.

He knew Mia would still be in the office.

"When are you going to tell me what's going on?" she said. "You're in trouble, aren't you? I just know it."

He asked her to call her future brother-in-law, one of Santa Clara County's ADA's, and do background checks on Nick Pappas and James Armstrong. She kept asking if he was nuts.

"You're scaring me, Andy," she said before he cut her off.

As soon as he hung up, his cell rang. Sprocket's wife Gabby screamed at him, wanting to know what he'd gotten her husband into.

"He ran up to Williamsburg for me to check on something."

"I know that. Something's wrong," she said. "He told me he'd only be gone for a little while. He always calls. It's been over six hours."

"He probably got hung up," he said. "I'm in Richmond. I should be at your place before nine. Let me know if he gets home before I get there."

Less than two hours later, he pulled up in front of Sprocket and Gabby's house, a green-trimmed, white, two-bedroom bungalow. A large, yellow tow truck bearing a local gas station's name on its doors sat in the driveway with a crunched chopper laying flat in its bed.

As he reached for the doorbell, the front door opened. Gabriella stood there, eyes glaring at him. She turned her head back and pointed.

"He just got home. See for yourself," she said and pulled the door all the way open. "No thanks to you, he could have been killed."

Andy walked inside and saw Sprocket lying on the sofa. His right arm was propped on a pillow and wrapped in bandages from his shoulder to his wrist. Road-rash covered his left cheek and forehead. He must have gone down hard. His ponytail was a little grayer than the last time he'd seen him. Though Andy knew his left eye was glass from a malfunction with a grenade launcher, he could have sworn that thing winked at him.

"What the hell happened?" he asked.

"I laid it down. Ate it big time." Sprocket rubbed the bandages. "Could have been worse."

"You're too good a rider."

"Not when some fucking idiot runs you off the road," Sprocket said. "I'd just pulled out of the show's lot and was ready to make a left when this fucking Jap rice-rocket hauled ass past me on the right. The next thing I knew was a white pickup hit me on the left. I slid off the road and landed on the shoulder."

A male in his mid-to-late twenties walked out of the kitchen, a hardcore biker if Andy'd ever seen one. His jeans were covered with grease, and a leather vest barely fit over heavily inked iron-pumped pecks.

"Lil' Mike, meet Z."

He shook Andy's hand with a crushing grip. "Heard good shit about you," he said then turned to Sprocket. "Got to split, man. I'll unload the bike and put it in the garage."

"Thanks for everything, man."

"So you think it was intentional?" Andy asked.

Sprocket looked at Gabby, then back at him. "Damn right."

"Someone tried to kill you?" She knelt next to the sofa, looking every bit of thirty years his junior. "Why are you doing this? You have a good job at the boatyard. We don't need the extra cash." She stood and turned toward Andy. "This is all your fault."

"Gabby," Sprocket said.

"No." She put her hands on her hips, then faced Andy, her eyes still defiant. "I lost Mama and Papa to thugs. I'm not losing him too."

"Did you get a look at him?" Andy asked, ignoring Gabby's tirade.

"No. Happened too fast."

Andy dropped Emily's photos on the coffee table. "This is the girl who's missing."

"Gabby, bring me and Z a couple of beers," Sprocket said. She looked down at the pictures then back at him. "Gabby," he repeated, "the beers."

Andy walked over to him. "She's right. I'm real sorry for dragging you into this mess."

"Sorry, hell. I'm the one who made the decision to do it." Sprocket lowered his voice. "I had a chance to talk to Harley. The dude's really upset about something."

Andy squatted next to the sofa. "Did you press him?"

"Yeah, and got squat."

"Damn, I'd hoped you'd get something out of them."

Gabby walked back into the room, a bottle of Heineken in each hand. She slammed them on the marred wood table, plopped down on an overstuffed chair, and crossed her arms.

Sprocket shot her a look of irritation then glanced up at Andy. "Not all is bad. I picked up a little chatter about several girls disappearing since the show left winter quarters at the beginning of the year." He paused. "Could be somebody's pedaling flesh."

"Do you think Harley's involved?"

"After what happened today, I don't know. He's a rough dude. A fully patched badass. Not a guy I'd want to piss off." Sprocket turned on his side and moved closer to him. "Smokes a little weed and drinks too many Buds now and then but that's about it."

"Maybe some extra cash turned him."

Sprocket said nothing.

"If someone in that unit is connected to trafficking young girls, I have to know. Can you dig deeper?"

"Yeah," he said. "I'll do what I can from here and make a few calls."

"I'm not sure whether I should run back up to Richmond or head down to Nags Head and take a look at the other unit in the morning," Andy said.

"Whatever you do, watch your back, man." Sprocket shook his head. "From what I hear, these guys play pretty rough."

Andy peeled off five hundred dollar bills. "I appreciate all you've done. Send me your medical bills and whatever it costs to get the bike put back together," he said. "If you need anything, I'll be at the Sheraton on the beach tonight."

Gabby walked him to the door. "I feel bad about that girl, but Sprock's all I've got," she said. "Please, keep him out of this. I know you might find it hard to believe, but I really love my old man."

He left, wishing someone loved him that much. Since Marie left, one-night-stands were all he could handle. Mia could be the exception.

His cell rang.

"You owe me big time," Mia said.

"Knock off the owe-me's," he said. "Just tell me what you have. This hasn't been my best day."

"He made another call and found out that Carlyle's daughter died like fifteen years ago."

"That's what he told me," Andy said. "What about Armstrong?"

"It appears he worked for Carlyle until last year. Can't find anything on him since," she said, "But this Nick guy is bad news."

"Go on."

"Pappas has a long rap sheet that goes back to when he was thirteen," she said. "He was arrested twelve times for drugs, petty theft, burglary, and shoplifting, but for some reason he was always set loose." She paused. "You're not going to believe this."

"What?"

"He only did two plus years for manslaughter at Joliet," she said. "Tyler told me there was a notation that connected him to a New Jersey crime family. But the real strange thing is a tickler on his jacket."

"Whew," came out in a low whistle. "Check on a Stephen Beyer in Boston. That's Stephen with a p-h. Call me the minute you get something on him or more on Armstrong." He cut her off. Pappas' background was more checkered than he'd expected. What the hell was he into? And did it have anything to do with Emily?

Later that night on the balcony of his room, it came to him. He had a good idea what the tickler in Nick's file meant, and only a select few were privy to the information.

❧❧❧

The fog started to lift, and Emily was able to think more clearly. She remembered who she was but still wasn't sure what had happened. A big house with men dressed in suits, their faces still blurred. No, the yellow bungalow. It was safe. Wherever it was, she knew she needed to find it. All the streets looked the same. Why were people staring at her? "No," she screamed, then ran as fast as she could.

Chapter 7

It was early Thursday morning when Andy jogged down the beach. The urgency to find Emily had escalated in the last twenty-four hours. He couldn't afford to lose anymore time but needed to clear his head. Chasing down her friends was key. After that, he'd head back up to Richmond and once more try to find out what the Goth chick knew. There had to be a way to squeeze information out of her.

He showered and was about to shave when he looked in the mirror. A barely receding full head of dark brown hair and a day's stubble stared back. A change in his appearance might help. He rinsed the foam off his face and dressed in khakis, burgundy Polo, and his usual Topsiders without socks.

The addresses Beyer had given him turned out to be weekly rentals, both vacant. He called the real estate office listed on the sign in front of the cottages and was told they weren't allowed to give out personal information on tenants.

Glancing down at Emily's picture, he wondered why a girl with her background would willingly choose the carnie lifestyle. If, instead, she had been kidnapped, he knew that scum-of-the-earth jerks prostituted innocent girls like her to sexual perpetrators.

He wasn't sure but thought he'd heard or read that the age for consensual sex was legislated by the individual states. Back in his room, he flipped open his laptop and Googled, "Age of Consensual Sex in the USA." Virginia was eighteen, which made any sexual acts with Emily illegal. He was astounded to learn that over half the states listed sixteen as the legal age, and Iowa and South Carolina listed fourteen. A footnote stated that Canadian females were legal at fourteen and in Mexico at twelve. This disturbing bit of information only managed to further piss him off.

Andy stared at the cell in his hand for several minutes and questioned whether he should call. God, he wanted to but knew the answer to his question. He punched in the numbers.

"Marie, it's me," he said. "I'm in town on business, and I'd like to see Julie."

"No way. The agreement is that you are to give me two weeks' notice. And the final decision is mine."

How had he fallen for her? "I didn't even know I'd be here until yesterday."

"That's your problem, not mine." She hesitated. "What's it worth to you?"

"I can't afford what I'm paying you now."

"Then the answer is still no." The line went dead.

After checking out of the hotel, he hit the highway and called Sprocket to make sure he was okay. Andy kept the needle at seventy and landed in Richmond around noon. Mia hadn't gotten back to him with more information on Emily's father or Beyer. Patience was never one of his strong suits and less so today.

He called her and learned that she had nothing new. "Have him dig up anything he can on a Jonathan Carlyle." Even though Doctor Agopian was probing into Carlyle's background, backup never hurt. He snapped the cell shut before she asked more questions.

A billboard for Paradise Island came into focus on the opposite side of the highway. It was a club where judges and businessmen sat alongside average stiffs, stuffing g-strings with bills. A year ago, he'd met Al Lexington, a Bush Gardens V.P., there and cemented contracts for a monster and a kiddie coaster over several Heinekens, crab-cake sandwiches, and sizzling strippers. He was unsure which of those had closed the deal.

Andy sat at a table in the rear and watched flesh spiral up and down a brass pole, the fantasy of every man there except him. All he could see was Emily's face floating in the smoke-filled room.

A waitress with long legs and cleavage that begged to escape her tightly cinched bustier bent over and placed a cocktail napkin in front of him. "Can I get you something to drink?"

"Does Crystal still work here?" he asked.

"Left a few months ago." Her skin was untouched by the sun, and her soft features contrasted with the hardness of the place. "Something to drink? Cigarettes?"

"I don't smoke." At least he hadn't for the last few days.

"So what's that you're clicking?"

He glanced down. Pop's lighter. "An old habit. Just bring me an ice tea, please."

She grinned. "You want to make that a double?"

He passed her the laminated menu. "Number three."

She returned balancing several drinks on a tray, then set the tumbler down in front of him.

"Do you have a name?" he asked.

"Kitten."

He refrained from making some glib remark that he

was sure she'd heard a thousand times from customers. Andy wanted to know her real name, the one on her birth certificate.

"Is there any way I could get a hold of Crystal?" He dropped a creased twenty on the tray. "Anyone here stay in touch with her?"

She stared at him. "Why do you want to know?"

"She's a friend," he said. "Name's Andy Zartanian. I sell amusement rides."

"Rides? Like whirly-gigs at carnivals?"

"Never heard them called that. But yeah." He pulled out a card and dropped it next to the folded bill. "Back to Crystal."

She picked up the twenty and slid it in her bustier, then looked at the card. "I'll make a call and see what I can find out while they're building your sandwich."

Another glistening body took the stage and pulled herself up the brass pole, then spiraled down. The noise of the crowd rose, and the catcalls grew louder as the dancer clung to the stage's hardwood floor, then slid across it like a snake with her tongue extended and ass raised. Kitten returned and placed the stacked sandwich in front of him. "Enjoy."

"Crystal?" he said.

"Still working on it." She turned and left.

The way she walked reminded him of Crystal, a learned trait in this business that assured larger tips. He remembered the night he'd spent with her after that sale to Al. They'd connected, met later, and opened up to each other. He tried to unload some of his baggage and drown sorrows over the divorce and distance between Julie and him. Her story was different. She told him about her miserable childhood, a rebellious teenager who had taken life's fast track and run away, eventually ending up here, a thousand miles from home. He trusted her honesty and respected her courage to share so much. If they were moving girls through the club, Crystal would know.

The sandwich was even better than he remembered. Washing it down with ice tea, he watched the next girl jump up onto the stage and wondered how she'd gotten her start. Runaways usually ended up in sleazy places they hadn't dreamed existed. No picket fences or PTA meetings.

She came back to the table. "Sorry. No luck. I have your card. I'll give you a call if something turns up. Crystal was good people. You staying in town?"

"My numbers are on the card. You can always reach me on the cell. More than likely I'll land at the Marriott."

He caught a glimpse of the bouncer slapping a guy on the back when he entered the club. Shit, Nick Pappas. Another shaved head wrapped him in a bear hug.

"Does he come in here often?" he asked and nodded toward the door.

"You mean the dapper cowboy with the dye job?" she said and laughed. "Thought it was Wayne Newton the first time he came into the place."

Andy hadn't seen the resemblance in the past, but did now. "Yeah."

"That's Nick Pappas," she said as a waitress rushed to him with a Bud longneck in one hand and a three-finger shot in the other. A dancer came from the other side of the room, threw her arms around his neck, then planted kisses on his cheek. "Comes in when he's in town. Big tipper."

"What can you tell me about him?" he asked, moving the chair around with his back to Nick.

"Always looks the same," she said with indifference. "Usually picks up one of the girls for the night."

He put another twenty on her tray. "Since Crystal's not around, maybe you could help me."

"Sorry," she said and handed him back the bill. "Don't date the clientele."

"No, wait," he said and touched her arm as she started to leave. "That's not what I meant. I'm only after information."

"What kind?"

"About a runaway," he said. "Can we meet somewhere after you get off work?" She flashed a look of distrust. "A public place where we can talk. You pick it." He glanced back. The oily, tanned head moved across the room toward his table.

"Everything okay, Kitten?" he asked and cracked his knuckles.

A neatly trimmed crop of black hair hung under his lower lip. His shirt collar opened to a hairless chest and a thick gold chain. Tattooed on his right hand was a snake with a severed head and a saber in between.

"Everything's fine."

The bouncer grabbed her by the arm and squeezed then let go. "That table over there needs another round." He looked down at him. "You want action. Sit your ass down in front of the stage and fill the g-strings or pay for a lap dance in one of the back rooms." He stood looking down at him with his arms crossed, as if begging him to do something.

Andy smiled. "Might just do that. But first I'm eating my sandwich."

Oily head smirked, then walked away.

When he finished, Andy grabbed the ticket next to the ice tea, pulled out two twenties, and tucked them under the tumbler. He stood and was about to leave when his cell rang.

"I get off at six," Kitten said. "Meet me in the Onyx Bar at the Marriott."

Chapter 8

Getting back onto the lot would be easy. Breaking down Goth to give him answers he needed wouldn't. Any information Andy could gather, coupled with what Kitten might know, would at least be a starting point.

He jumped into the Mustang, drove back toward the coliseum, turned right a block before, and worked his way up and down adjacent streets, noting businesses and flophouses. He kept one eye glued to the rearview mirror. The game had taken some ugly turns, with too many people not talking, and he wanted to make sure no one was tailing him. He pulled into the garage behind the Marriott, checked in, and requested a room on one of the lower floors.

After settling in, he got a hold of Mia.

"Nothing more on Armstrong yet," she said, "but Beyer is an ex-Massachusetts State Trooper."

That explained how he'd boarded the aircraft with a weapon, and why Carlyle had used him initially to search for Emily.

Andy left his room, took the stairwell at the end of the hall down to the rear exit and into the garage, then left through the back alley. He combed the streets to get a better feel of the surrounding area. Escape routes if it came to that. On his way to the hotel, he'd spotted a Goodwill store a few blocks to the east.

Wandering between the racks of tired clothing, he found two pairs of faded jeans, a denim shirt, two T-shirts, a well-worn Atlanta Braves baseball cap, brown boots, and a U.S. Army sweatshirt. As he walked toward the register, he noticed a black and red canvass sport's bag the same colors as the one he had when he played high school ball. It would work.

He made a quick stop in the drugstore next-door, then headed back to the hotel.

Stripping down to his boxers, he stared in the mirror. "You dumb shit," he said. "You're getting in way over your head." He picked up the scissors, then stopped. Kitten. He had to meet with her first.

Andy dialed Carlyle's number and briefed him on only what he thought he needed to know.

"Find that girl and make her talk," Carlyle said. "My granddaughter's safety is paramount. If you can't, I know someone who can."

"I'm sure you do, but there are better ways than bamboo under fingernails," Andy said. "I'll handle it."

There was no doubt that Beyer was the man Carlyle had in mind for the dirty job.

After dressing and securing the ankle holster in place, he headed downstairs and waited in the Onyx Bar. This was the first chance he'd had to pull the pieces together. Though it had been awhile since the hard stuff, tonight he needed something stronger.

"Bombay on the rocks with a twist," he said. "Make it a double."

Andy jotted notes on a cocktail napkin, then glanced up into the mirror behind the bar, and saw a female coming toward him. He almost didn't recognize her but swiveled on the stool and saw Kitten walk toward him. She was dressed in jeans, wedged sandals, green sleeveless sweater, and a green William and Mary baseball hat with her blonde ponytail pulled through the back. Her face looked freshly scrubbed with only a hint of makeup and fear written all over it.

"You look different," he said.

"Better or worse?"

"Better but scared."

"I am." She glanced around the bar. "I almost didn't come, but right now it looks like you're the only one who can help me."

"I don't understand," he said.

"We need to go someplace else. I'll explain when we get there."

"Why?" he asked as he slid off the barstool.

She looked back at the doorway and bit her lip as if she expected to see someone. "Bear with me, okay?"

He downed half the gin, signed the tab, and turned back to her. "Ready?"

She clutched his arm, and they hurried out the rear entrance.

"Where are we going?" he asked.

"A place where I know I'll be safe. By the way, my real name's Sarah Walkovitz. Grew up in Brooklyn."

"Sarah's much nicer than Kitten," he said. "You're shaking."

"Just keep moving." After the third block, they turned down an alley where a small neon sign hung above the door. "The Treadmill."

It took a while for his eyes to adjust. The long bar to the left was empty with the exception of a female bartender slicing lemons. Only women occupied the scattered round tables and booths that lined the walls. He looked at her.

"Yes, I am," she said. "Surprised?"

"Blown away is more like it," he said. Being the only male in the place, he felt as if all eyes were lasers aimed at him.

"Let's grab a couple of stools over there," she said and pointed to the far end of the bar.

"The usual, Sarah?" the perky redhead said. "And you?"

He scanned the bottles of wine displayed on the back bar. "I'll take a glass of that Toad Hollow."

After her Chardonnay and his Sauvignon Blanc came, he finally asked. "Is the shaved head that interrupted us at the club the reason we came here?"

"Yes." She bit her lip again. "Leon manages the place for a piece of the action. Real owners live in upstate New York."

"Mob?"

"Could be." She sipped the wine. "He asked about you after you left."

"What did you tell him?"

"Nothing at first. Later he called me into his office and asked what we were talking about." Her hands fidgeted with the napkin. "When I didn't tell him, he slapped me, then wrapped his fingers around my throat. I finally broke down and told him you were asking about Crystal."

"Then what?"

"I said that was all I knew. I guess he finally believed me, because he told me to get the hell out of his office," she said, touching her fingers to her throat. "One thing I've learned in this business is not to ask a lot of questions, then you don't have to cough up a bunch of answers." She turned her attention to the glass of wine.

"Why did you agree to meet with me?" he asked.

"Crissy's a nice person." Her eyes locked onto his. "She said you were, too. She trusted you. Right now, I need someone I can trust." She reached into the right rear pocket of her jeans and pulled out a folded bill. "Here's your twenty back."

"Keep it."

She threw it on the bar. "Then the drinks are on me."

"Thanks." He was stuck on her comment and stuttered before the words came out. "W—when did she say this?

She smiled and touched the top of his hand. "One night when we were sitting around, you know, girl talk. We were close. Crissy said you were honest and listened to her. Believed in her. She had a lot of grief growing up. A mother who loved booze more than her own daughter. And a father who only managed to visit when he was out on parole. The timing with you was wrong." She hesitated and swallowed hard. "I'm glad it didn't work out for you two."

"What do you mean?"

"I loved her." Tears welled. "Still do."

"What happened to her?" he asked.

"One day when she didn't show up for work. I asked Leon if she'd called in sick. He said she quit and was headed back to Texas."

"Maybe that's what happened," he said, even though his gut told him different.

"Bullshit." Her hand slapped the top of the bar. "The bastard lied. I would have been the first, and probably the only person she would have told if she was leaving."

"So you think Leon was behind this?"

"Had to be." She ran her fingers up and down the stem of the glass. "That day I left work early and went to her apartment. The place was trashed. All of her things were gone. I know she didn't leave on her own." She paused and squeezed her lips tightly. "We were getting ready to move in together. I know something awful's happened to her."

"Was she into anything?" he hesitated. "Maybe drugs?"

"No way. She didn't even drink."

Andy remembered that. She'd asked him not to smoke or drink anymore that night. "How did she get along with Leon?"

"Leon gave her a lot of slack at first. She was a master at working the bar but wouldn't step foot on stage," she said. "He wanted a lot more from her."

"Like what?"

"Private parties."

"Go on," he said.

She took another large gulp. "If Leon finds out I'm talking to you about this, I'm as good as dead."

"He won't." He reached over and placed his hand on hers. "Promise."

"Paradise Island has a Platinum List. Patrons they invite to special private parties," she said. "They're usually held in suites at hotels like the Jefferson. Leon takes his top of the line girls and decks them out for a wild night. These guys pay several thousand each to attend."

"Does he use dancers from the club?"

"Some," she said. "Others, he brings in from different clubs I think. A few from out of town from what I've heard."

"Did Crystal ever attend these parties?"

"One time," she said. "Leon forced her to go. She got real upset when she was there to do more than serve drinks. It was in the Jefferson's Presidential Suite. The place has a piano and spiral staircase. You know, the whole nine yards. Goes for close to two grand a night just for the room."

"What happened?"

"Crystal told me that she'd only been there about twenty minutes when some creep started to grope her." She twisted the napkin. "Said she slapped the bastard, then tore out of the place."

"That must have pissed off Leon."

"Damn right it did. She didn't work for two weeks," she said. "She had to wait for the swelling to go down and bruises to fade enough for makeup to cover them."

"Has he ever asked you to do that?"

"Yeah. He's tried everything to get me to go. I think he finally got it through his thick head that I wouldn't," she said. "I made it clear that all I wanted was to wait tables. No dancing. After Crystal disappeared, I've tried to leave, but Leon won't let me."

"He can't stop you."

She pulled her hand away. "The hell he can't. You don't know him. He has connections." Her fingers tightened around the stem of the glass. "He's threatened me before. He told me he'd use them if and find me anywhere I went. I have no doubt he would."

"Did Leon know that you and Crystal were an item?"

"No way," she said. "If he had, he would have forced us into doing a lesbian act at parties. Guys like that sort of stuff, two girls doing each other."

Her demeanor stiffened, so he changed the subject. "Do you know if Nick Pappas ever attended one of these parties?"

She looked at him with a puzzled expression. "Why are you so curious about Nick? I thought you didn't know the guy."

"I never said that. Only asked about him," he said. "He could be involved in something else. Tell me what you know."

"I'm not really sure, but I guess he could be into lots

of crap." She ordered another round. "That comes with the territory when you're friends with Leon."

"Any signs of him running young girls through the club?"

"I don't think so," she said. "Makeup hides a lot. Fifteen. Sixteen. Eighteen. Can't tell the difference anymore. I'm sure a few lie and get by with phony IDs."

He reached inside his jacket pocket and pulled out the two photographs. "What about this one? Have you seen her around?"

She studied both. "No. Even with a ton of makeup, it would take a lot to turn her into a twenty-one-year-old," she said. "Leon would never risk getting shut down."

"What about the parties?" he said. "I'm sure he panders to special requests, and no one there would complain if one or two of the girls happened to be underage."

She rolled the paper napkin between the index and thumbs of both hands. "I don't know. I only hear what the girls talk about. No one's ever mentioned underage girls."

"Young, white, blonde, and blue eyes brings top dollar from what I've been told," Andy said. "They're better than cocaine."

"What do you mean?"

"An ounce of cocaine on the wholesale market goes for a hell of a lot. But a young girl can generate two to three times the going price in a night tricking for these animals. Multiply that by seven days a week over a period of three years."

"That's sick." She shifted uncomfortably. "What do you want from me?"

"Keep your eyes and ears open. Chat with the girls. See what else you can find out, especially about Pappas and possible connections to the club or Leon. Any juice at all you can dig up might help."

She hesitated. "Deal. Now it's my turn to ask you for a favor."

"What's that?"

"Help me get away from Leon and find Crissy," she said. "When you leave town, I want to go with you."

"What?"

"You heard me." She squeezed his wrist. "You may be my only way out."

"I sell rides." She didn't know he was already in up to his eyeballs.

Her hand moved to his shirt and caught the hair underneath. "I'll do anything you ask. Please, just take me with you."

The fear in her eyes was real. Suddenly, she looked like a scared child.

"I don't know if I can." What was he going to do with her while he chased down Emily? "Give me a few days to take care of some business, a week at the most."

Her lips widened into a smile of relief, the first time he'd seen her relax. "You don't know how good it feels that I'm going to be screwing over Leon."

"You really care for Crystal, don't you?" he said.

"Care? I told you I love her." She paused. "From the beginning, she treated me with respect. My first day on the job, she took me under her wing." She put her hand back on his arm. "She knew I'd lied to Leon about working in a club but kept quiet. No one ever believed in me like that."

Before he left, Sarah gave him her cell number, home number, and address.

"Be careful. Don't get in Leon's way. He carries a knife, and he isn't afraid to use it. Switchblade's tucked in the waistband of his pants. You know, in the small of the back."

"Don't worry," he said. "I can take care of myself."

She grimaced and he patted her shoulder. "Have you ever seen him cut anyone?"

"Not exactly," she said. "But I saw him toss someone into the alley. Two days later, the guy was found on the other side of town with his throat slit."

"How about if I give you a ride home?" He threw another twenty on the bar.

She pushed it back toward him. "Thanks, but you go on ahead. I'm going to hang around here for a while."

"Call if you need me." He stood to leave. "Anytime. It doesn't matter. Twenty-four-seven. Just call."

She spun around on the barstool, stood, and tucked the bill into his shirt pocket. "I will." She brushed a kiss across his cheek.

As Andy walked toward the entrance, he wondered how he'd gotten himself in so deep in less than a week. He shoved open the door and stepped outside. A black Mercedes was parked across the street. Two men stared in his direction. He didn't recognize the driver, but he knew Leon's shaved head.

Chapter 9

Emily shivered as the night air closed in. The big house became clearer, but the men's faces were still a blur. The short one with the accent had scared her. She couldn't think of him now.

Her movements were slow and painful. The rocks. That's how she'd cut herself. How long had she been out here? She turned down the next street and saw it, then ran toward the little house. She twisted the doorknob and found it locked. "Open up. It's me, Emily," she shouted and pounded on the weathered wood. "Hurry." She heard footsteps, then the latch. It opened.

"Who are you?" a thin, elderly man with glasses asked.

She shook. Unable to speak, she looked past him. This wasn't the bungalow.

∪∫∪∫

Andy rushed back inside, bent over, and yanked the Beretta out of his ankle holster. "Leon's out front. Where's the back door?"

The bartender pointed. "That way past the re-strooms."

"Come on Sarah." He grabbed her by the arm. "Let's get the hell out of here."

He opened the door, looked in both directions, then bolted down the alleyway, one hand hanging onto Sarah, the other with his finger on the trigger.

"You saw Leon?" she said, her voice breathless.

"Yeah, in a black Mercedes with another guy. Is there another way to the Marriott?"

"Where'd they go?" Leon yelled from inside the bar.

"The back door," a male voice said. "Out there."

She kicked off her shoes and ran along side him to the corner and around a building. He didn't look back. The front entrance of the hotel was straight ahead, but he led her around back and up the stairs, two at a time to his room on the third floor.

Both sat on the bed, trying to catch their breaths.

"I'm sure no one saw us enter the hotel."

"What am I going to do?" she said, then burst into tears.

"You're staying here for now. I'll think of something." He holstered the gun, went into the closet, retrieved his SIG from the drag bag, then slipped on the shoulder holster.

"Who are you?" she asked.

"You know who I am."

"Salesmen don't carry." She grabbed his arm and shook. "Damn it, tell me the truth."

"Calm down." Her breathing quieted. She let go. "I carry a gun because I collect money. Carnies generally pay in cash. I've had as much as a couple of hundred-grand in my briefcase at any given time."

"I'm screwed." She lowered her head. "Royally fucked."

"No you're not. I'll get you out of here. But first you're going to have to calm down." She flopped back on the bed, her forearms covering her face. He touched her arm. "I'm ordering room service."

"I can't eat."

"You have to. It may be quite a while before we get another chance."

After ordering the food, he threw the shirts and sweater he'd purchased at Goodwill on the bed. "Pick out something to wear."

She hesitated, grabbed a couple and held them up, then gave him a puzzled look. "I don't get it."

"You will," he said. "Come into the bathroom."

"What?"

"Just do it." He reached into the plastic Walgreen's bag and placed scissors and a bottle of hair dye on the counter. "There's probably enough here for both of us."

"You're serious, aren't you?"

"Very." He closed the bathroom door then paced. A knock at the door startled him.

"Room service."

Andy let the waiter in. He placed the tray on the table and handed him the check. Since it was Carlyle's money, he added a thirty percent tip. Shortly after the waiter left, Sarah came out with one towel draped over her shoulders and dabbing dots of dye off her face with another, long blond locks gone.

"Are you going to tell me what you have in mind?"

Over burgers and fries, he laid out his plan, which seemed to help calm her. He offered the only hope she had.

She pushed her plate away. "Your turn," she said with too much enthusiasm. They walked into the bathroom. "Take off your shirt and sit on the edge of the tub." She cut his hair, then applied the dye. Even though she followed the instructions that came in the box of Loreal's Iced Moca, his scalp and the area under his chin burned like hell.

He looked in the mirror. "It's different. Lighter than I expected." He tossed her the tanning cream.

Sarah pulled the sweater over her head and stepped out of her jeans, exposing lacy, black lingerie. She spread the cream in her hands, then rubbed it over her body. He felt like he should look away but couldn't.

She flashed a smile, then tossed the tube back to him. "This should be interesting with your olive complexion."

He covered his face, neck, hands and arms with two coats. The effect was almost too dark.

"Do you really think all of this is necessary?" she asked.

What wasn't she getting? "We've gone through all of that. I agreed to get you out of here and put everything else on hold," he said then threw the stained towels, empty bottle of dye, and tube of tanning lotion into the duffle bag. After cleaning the bathroom, making sure no traces of what they'd done remained, he led her into the bedroom.

"You're going to have to do what I ask without questioning me. We have to move on instinct. My instinct."

Andy changed into the worn jeans, checked the holster around his ankle, then picked up the cell.

"What are you doing?" she said.

"Calling a friend." He punched the buttons. "You'll be safe at his house." Misgivings washed over her face. "He and his wife live in Virginia Beach."

"No. Everything I own is in my apartment," she said. "I need to get my stuff."

"Your life's worth more than your stuff." He felt irritated at wasting so much time. "Don't you think Leon's expecting you to do just that? Hell, he's probably got his goons all over that apartment building."

Gabby answered the phone.

"I need to talk to Sprock."

"Maybe you forgot what I said. He's done with you. He's not going to help you anymore."

"Gabby, wait," he said, hoping she wouldn't hang up. "I need a small favor. A place for a friend of mine to stay for a few days. That's all."

A few seconds elapsed. "We don't need any more trouble from you," she said. "Don't bother coming here. Stay away."

Sprocket got on the phone. "Z, get your ass down here. We'll talk then." She protested in the background. "Goddamn, Gabby. Shut up, his dad saved my life," he said. "See you when you get here, man."

"Should be no later than midnight," Andy said into the dead phone.

Sarah slipped on the black T-shirt and threw the Army sweater over her shoulders, then stared in the mirror.

"I look ridiculous."

She had a shabby waif look. "You can pick up some clothes and shoes tomorrow in Virginia Beach," he said, then pulled out a wad of money, peeled off three hundred-dollar-bills and handed them to her. "Right now, we need to get out of here."

"What if Leon has someone waiting outside?" She bit her lip. "He's pure evil."

"He doesn't know I'm staying here. And I'm pretty sure no one followed us."

"You don't know Leon," she said. "He could sniff out a bloodhound." She walked over to the window, pulled the curtain to the side, almost afraid to look out.

"Do you know how to use a gun?"

She looked back. "Not since I was a teenager. My

dad forced me to go with him to the firing range. Wanted to make sure I'd be safe growing up. What a laugh."

He slipped out the Beretta. "Take this. Keep it hidden. I'm going to get the car. It's a black Mustang."

"No," she protested. "I want to go with you."

"Listen to me." He grabbed her by the shoulders. "When I know it's clear, I'll call the room. You haul ass downstairs to the garage."

He closed the door behind him. His hand tightened on the SIG under the denim shirt as he moved down the hall toward the stairwell. The elevator door opened, and an elderly couple stepped out and stared, then hurried past. From their reaction, it was obvious he didn't fit the image of a Marriott guest.

Hollow echoes of boots clicking against concrete steps filled the stairwell above him. He leaned over the railing and looked up. The sound stopped, then a door slammed. He quickly made his way to the garage level and looked through the glass on the fire door. No headlights or people. He pulled it open, listened, then sprinted to the car and started the engine.

Andy dialed the room. "Hurry."

Seconds felt like minutes as the engine idled alongside the curb. Why was it taking this long for her to get downstairs? Something must have happened.

A car whipped into the far end of the garage.

"Shit," he said.

The oncoming headlights temporarily blinded him. He was about to jump out when Sarah opened the fire door and limped toward the car.

"Get in," he yelled. The door slammed. He accelerated out the exit. "What the hell happened?"

Tears poured down her cheeks. "I heard noises, then caught my foot on the stair," she said. "Twisted my ankle and scraped my knee."

He pulled his right pant leg up, slipped the gun out of her hand and placed it back in the holster.

She slept most of the way to Virginia Beach until he slowed to turn down Sprocket's street.

The curtain in the window next to the door moved to the side, and Sprocket's bearded face peered out.

"It's me, Andy," he yelled.

Sprocket threw open the door. "What the fuck did you do to yourself?" he said then slapped Andy on the back with his good arm. "You look like shit."

"This is Sarah."

Gabby stood in the doorway with her arms folded. He knew he was going to have to do a lot of convincing.

Two cups of coffee later, and after a lengthy discussion, Gabby agreed to let Sarah stay with them. Maybe she softened when she saw how frightened Sarah was. For the time being, one of Andy's problems was temporarily on hold.

Chapter 10

The "Do Not Disturb," sign hung on Andy's door at the Marriott. Getting to bed at 4 a.m. hadn't been his routine since the service.

It was close to noon when he got himself together and headed back down to the garage. He hid his laptop and the 9 mm with extra magazines under the spare tire in the Mustang's trunk and walked to the Webster Hotel, a flophouse he'd spotted a few blocks from the coliseum. It would serve as a safe haven until he got the information he needed.

The clerk snored in his wooden office chair, legs crossed on a marred desk.

"Hey," Andy shouted. "Got any rooms."

The desk clerked jumped up then shook his head awake. "By the day, week, or month?" he asked as he looked over his bifocals.

"Day with bath."

"By the day is the most expensive. Be thirty." He held his gaze. "Cash only," he said, breath sour from booze.

Andy knew he'd been ripped off when he saw the room on the second floor. It faced the street. The seedy dump's double bed listed toward the window. A lamp with a dated shade sat on a stained nightstand next to it. The only other piece of furniture, a stick chair, rested under three wooden pegs that protruded from the wall, the closet. The hotel's marquee hung outside the window. Good luck getting any sleep.

He made a quick call to Mia and left a message. "Leave word on my voicemail where you can be reached this weekend. My cell will be off."

Andy killed two hours walking the streets until he knew the midway would be jammed with people. When the time came, he pulled the ball cap down and walked toward the blasting speakers, then stopped in front of a large brick planter and rubbed his hands in the dirt, making sure most of it stayed under his fingernails.

Families slathered down funnel cakes, and kids plucked at the pink fairy floss. Teenagers, lot lice, punks looking for trouble, and girls showing way too much skin, milled around the asphalt. Spine-cracking rides roared and splashed the blue cloud-covered sky with blasts of color from strobes and chasers. Music from one ride rolled over to the next. Marks lined up in front of games, trying to win carnie currency, stuffed animals for their dates.

Andy scanned the area for Goth. Females usually worked the games and food concessions, and in rare instances, kiddie rides. Carnivals belonged to men. A man's world that used females.

Nick stood outside his office with a shit-eating grin, talking to a girl, who despite her makeup, looked like she was barely eighteen. Andy moved to a good vantage point between a hotdog trailer and popcorn wagon.

"Give me a dog loaded," he said, "and a large diet coke."

"The fixin's are on that table," the woman said and nodded to the side.

The areas around the games swelled as gaffs taunted and teased passersby's to get them to play. Rings flew over crates of Coke bottles, none looping the necks. Once in a while a basketball made it through a hoop that sounded a bell.

The hotdog had a snap to it, the kind he liked. He wasn't getting anywhere sitting in one spot and was about to get up and check the action farther down the midway when Goth appeared and walked over to the Milk Can Toss. Tight, black jeans were tucked into laced, black boots with thick soles. She wore the show's trademark shirt. Her hair had changed. She'd added streaks of purple and red that oddly seemed to have softened her look.

She knew how to turn the tip better than most of her counterparts and baited people into taking a free toss, then closed for bigger bucks. The girl hiding behind the mask smiled and laughed unlike when he'd first met her.

"Dude, you a townie?" a voice said from behind.

Andy turned. "Just passing through."

The young ride jock had a full head of black hair pulled back in a ponytail. He wore a leather vest with elongated openings over his midway uniform. A stringy, braided goatee hung from leathered skin, and his eyetooth shined gold. He had a full sleeve of tats on his right arm and few on the left.

"She puts out a good dog, but if you're looking for something that's money, try Tony's down the midway," he said. "Sausage smothered with jalapeños and onions in a crusty bun."

"Thanks. I'll keep that in mind."

"Looks like it could be a good night." The jock scanned the area, taking in all the action.

"Which ride's yours?" Andy asked.

"Himalaya. Set it up and tear it down with my eyes closed," he said. "The best in the business."

"Modest, too."

The guy slurped down hot coffee. "Friends call me J.T."

"Danny Blake." The name slipped out of Andy's mouth effortlessly.

"Ask anyone here who's the best Himalaya man," J.T. said. "I stir the soup like no one else, make the crowd go crazy." He took another sip. "Hey, if you're still here, come by in about fifteen minutes and check it out."

"I might just do that. You been with the show long?"

"Couple of years. Bounced around a little before Conner. It's a good gig. Like the route." J.T. paused. "You're not a greenie. Sounds like you know a little about the biz."

"Years ago. Way before your time, I worked on a couple of West Coast shows," Andy said. "Landed a truck-driving job in Sacramento at the state fair. Been doing it ever since."

J.T. chuckled. "I might do that when I decide to settle down. Right now, there's too much action here."

He was right about the number of lot lizards available to carnies. Far too many runaways. Everyone was someone's daughter.

"Gotta run, dude. Don't forget to check out my gig." J.T. stood and walked over to the Milk Can Toss. The smile on Goth's face widened. He kissed her hard on the lips, then patted her ass and walked away. Shit. *He must have been one of the guys who turned out my lights.*

Andy hung back, next to the generator trailer that powered the midway, and watched him work the crowd, yelling, "Faster?"

The riders screamed back in chaotic bursts. J.T. turned up the music, the rap, and controlled the ride like a pro. Strobes shot across the backdrop and mirror ball. Two crewmembers jumped on and off the rotating cars like circus performers, a stunt OSHA would frown on.

When it stopped, riders got off, waving their hands and yelling. It immediately filled again. This was one of the best run Himalaya operations he'd ever seen. J.T. was good, and had to be making a killing for Conner Shows.

Andy walked toward the ride as it slowed. "Real nice," he yelled and shot him a thumbs up.

"Thanks, dude. Give you a freebee if you want."

"Not even if you pay me. Stomach can't handle it." It still boggled Andy's mind how people liked the damn round rides. Getting sick and throwing up wasn't his cup of tea.

At least he'd made some headway and connected with one person who could possibly help him find Emily.

He started past Goth, then stopped.

She flashed that come on sucker smile. "Try your luck? It's easy. I'll even throw in a couple of freebies."

"And when I win that large bear, who do I give it to?" She laughed. Thought she had another mark. "There's plenty of girls here who'd love one. Could get lucky," she said. "Tell you what. I'll make it three free balls."

He slapped down a five and grabbed one of the balls. Carefully aiming, he tossed it in a low arc with a backspin. It came close.

"Nice," she said.

The next one hit the rim and fell into the can.

"Wow. You're good. Which one do you want?"

He picked a black and white bear then tossed three more balls.

"You have one left," she said. The fourth hit again. "Damn it, no one's ever done that."

Two teenage girls, just about Julie's age, strolled down the midway toward him.

"Hey, catch," he said and threw one to each of them.

Andy spent the next two hours circling the midway. He stopped at vantage points and familiarized himself with every detail until he could close his eyes and visualize the layout. The army had taught him to know the enemy well. His was somewhere close by.

Without warning, a thunderous clap shattered the night sounds, and the black sky opened up. The downpour pummeled the coliseum, drenching everyone. Soaked patrons scrambled in every direction like escaped animals running for freedom. He ducked under the overhang of a ticket booth and looked up at the chain driven winch under the coaster as it shut down. Bolts of light zapped the sky, followed by thunderous roars. It didn't appear the storm would let up soon. Lights around the show went down like falling stars. Rain could turn the midway into a graveyard in a matter of minutes.

J.T. sprinted toward him. "Hey, dude, don't just stand there," he shouted as he slowed, his vest pulled over his head. "Come on down to the cook shack."

Andy followed him into the shelter of the canopy. "Damn, that storm came out of nowhere," he said.

"Shit like this happens in Virginia all the time." J.T. laughed. "Get yourself a coffee. Rube'll take care of you," he said. "Better yet, got a cooler in the back of the camper filled with Buds."

"Put my name on one," Andy shouted then sat back in the plastic chair and watched. A male and female lifted the canvas skirt on one of the ride trailers, opened a door, and climbed inside, their home on the road.

A good ten minutes had passed when J.T. strolled back into the cookhouse. Andy shuddered. Harley followed. What the hell was he doing here?

"Danny, meet Harley," he said.

Harley grabbed his hand and shook it hard. "Seems like I seen you around," he said. "You look awful familiar."

"Maybe on the midway tonight."

Harley's gaze burned into Andy's eyes. "Nah." He shook his head. "Somewhere else. I never forget a face. You a roughie?"

"No. Gave up the business years ago," Andy said. "Just got into town. Dumped a load and waiting for another one."

"Long hauls?" Harley asked.

"Yeah. Coast to coast. Border to border." Andy twisted the cap and took a long swig. It was hard to act nonchalant under Harley's constant gaze.

"Like I said, never forget a face." Harley kept studying him. "Seen you somewhere before."

"Give the guy a fucking break," J.T. said. He lifted his bottle of beer and clinked it against Andy's then Harley's. "To the shit-ass weather breaking before tomorrow."

Goth came toward them and planted a wet one on J.T.'s lips. "Got one for me, baby?" Even with the makeup, she looked a few years shy of twenty-one.

He reached for a Bud on the table, popped the cap, and handed it to her, then pointed toward Andy. "Dude's Danny Blake."

"We've already met," she said. "The fucking sharpie took me for two large bears, then gave them to two young thangs."

J.T. laughed. "Meet my main squeeze, Tori."

Her eyes widened and her face reminded him of a devil before she attacked. "Beware, I'm coming inside, feeding you lies to fuck with your mind," she sang then laughed. "'Make You Believe,' by Insect."

"Knock it off," J.T. said. "She's heavy into that alternative Goth shit. Sings it all the time."

Andy tilted his head back and emptied the rest of the Bud. "Got another?"

They sat back and threw down three rounds, exchanging their best carnie stories. It soon became obvious Harley wasn't buying that they'd never met. Tori clung to J.T., a classic possum belly queen.

Not about to let up, Harley shifted the conversation back to Andy and truck-driving. "Where's your rig?" he asked. Andy ignored the question. "Your rig. Where's it parked?"

Andy remembered a truck stop on the outskirts of town. "Skill…no, Skeller's. Left it there for servicing."

"Whadda you drive?"

Andy hated this cat and mouse game of twenty questions. Keep it short.

"Peterbuilt 387 with a sleeper. Belongs to a buddy of mine."

Harley unlocked his gaze and turned to J.T. "We got business to do before I head back."

"Yeah. Sorry to cut you off, dude," J.T. said. "Stop back tomorrow if you're still in town."

"Might do that."

"Later," Tori said.

Andy downed the rest of the Bud then started to leave. The thunderous rainstorm had transformed over the last hour into a mild shower.

"Hey," a voice shouted from behind.

He turned and saw Rube motioning. "You calling me?"

"Old Rube's been around a long time," he whispered. "I'm surprised those clowns didn't recognize you. Your getup ain't foolin' me one bit."

"What the hell's going on around here?" Andy asked.

Rube looked around then leaned in closer. "Can't say for sure, but you best not get caught. Seen more than one person snooping around here disappear. You don't want that to happen to you now, do you?"

"You got something for me on the girl?"

Rube glanced around. "Maybe. Memory ain't what it used to be. Came to me after you left. She was here for a day. Bunked with that Tori in the Super Slide's possum belly," he said. "Never saw her after that morning. She just up and disappeared."

"Do you think Nick knew about her being here?"

"Could be. But can't say for sure. Don't know any more than that. Don't want to," Rube said. "But there's something else."

"What's that?"

"That big, fancy guy was here again this morning. Wore them tan trousers and a short sleeved shirt instead of that Sunday suit. Sure don't like someone I can't trust, if you know what I mean."

Damn it. What the hell was Beyer doing back in town?

Chapter 11

Emily spotted the pizza parlor that she'd eaten at with Tori and Megan. The bungalow was around the corner. "Finally." She hurried down the street then up the walkway and opened the front door.

"Tori. Megan. It's me," she shouted then caught herself. Tori hadn't been there for days, maybe more. She'd been trippin', lost in a fog. She sorta remembered seeing Megan. And some guy Tori talked about but not his name. The carnival. That's the last time she saw her. Yeah. They were there when everything started to get fuzzy. It happened more than once with explosions of pain somewhere in the mix. And needles. She pulled up her sleeve. Tracks. She'd been on drugs. The men in the big house were out to rape her. Kill her.

❧

It was clear now that Andy had to make sure there were no run-ins with Beyer.

In order to dig deeper, he went back to the coliseum lot early Saturday morning. Clear skies and a forecast high of ninety-five. Despite the heat and thick humidity, the midway would be packed by early afternoon.

No one but Rube was in the cookhouse when he arrived.

"You still hanging around?" Rube asked.

"Couldn't wait to get a cup of your special brew."

"You bullshitting old Rube?" he asked and leaned over the counter. "Remember what I told you last night. Be careful. You never know when that fancy guy will show up."

"Got it."

"Want something to eat? Maybe a little biscuits and gravy? It's loaded with spicy sausage."

"Are you certain that you only saw her that one time?" Andy said.

"Keep your voice down." Rube grabbed Andy's wrist. "I told you. It was like she was never here. She and Tori had breakfast, then split."

"Anything else you remember?"

"I remember a lot. But nothing about that girl."

Andy sat in a plastic chair that gave him a clear view of the midway and back lot where motor homes and pickups with campers sat motionless next to the boss' mobile living quarters. Nick's truck was parked in the same place it was last night. Two sleeping bags stirred inside the Super Slide's belly.

Andy stood, went back to Rube, and nodded. "Is that J.T. and Tori?"

Rube laughed. "J.T. has a pickup and camper. Tori's sleeping first class now," he said. "Kid who works the slide and his girl moved in."

He'd seen it hundreds of times. Teenagers who'd traded a life in a middle-class home for a metal enclosure under a trailer. Damned if he knew what was so attractive about this nomadic life for these young kids.

People lumbered out of their L.Q.'s as he downed Rube's biscuits and gravy. The extra sausage and red pepper flakes were nice touches. J.T. stumbled into the shower trailer, one of three Andy had sold Joey in Gibtown a little over a year ago. Each had one side for females and the other for males. Separate showerheads and benches were partitioned with shower curtains.

Ten minutes later, J.T. walked into the cookhouse with a towel draped around his neck and shaving kit tucked under his arm. "Didn't expect to see you," he said then rubbed his face with the towel.

"Still waiting on a load." It was hard to tell how old this guy was. Working the rides and moving around aged a person fast. "Thought a cup of Rube's brew would jolt me awake."

"Got that right." J.T. stroked his wet hair with one hand. "Damn, that shower sure felt good."

"Can I buy you a cup of coffee?" Andy asked.

"Sure." They walked over to the counter. "Going to be a kick-ass day with this weather," J.T. said.

"Your girl sleeping in?"

"Nah. Hitched a ride with Harley to Williamsburg," he said. "Then she's hitchhiking to Vah Beach. Sister lives there."

For some reason, only locals referred to Virginia Beach as Vah, which meant that he'd spent some time there. He said sister. Emily?

"The beach should be packed today," Andy said. "I'll bet the two of them are going to get toasted."

"She's not into catching rays," he said. "Hooked on games, mostly Skeeball. Gets off on watching those tickets spit out. The arcade at Raging Rapids is where she hangs out. Works her ass off, then drops all her coin on those fuckin' games."

"You tearing down tomorrow night?"

"Nah. The date up in Baltimore got fucked up because some asshole politician got sideways with the fair board," he said. "Nick's got us here for another week."

Baltimore was the first big date in the season that generated serious money. So big, Joey brought three units to town, along with booking independent operators. "What about the other units?" Andy asked.

"Word I got from Nick is that everyone's staying put. Cost too much to tear down and move," he said. "Fucking diesel and gas prices have shot through the roof."

"Tell me," Andy said, trying to keep him talking. "The damn rig costs me a small fortune to fill up."

"Harley swears he knows you," J.T. said. "Kept mentioning your name after we left."

"As far as I know, our paths have never crossed." Andy turned toward the midway and his eyes locked onto the guy leaning against the Hurricane's railing. Beyer stared in his direction. Andy pulled the bill of his Braves hat down, turned, then took another bite. "What was it you did when you were in the biz? Rides?" he asked.

"Started as a roughie, setting up and tearing down. Got a hold of some cash and bought a couple of food joints. Pizza and hot dog on the stick," J.T. said. "Stashed enough away to build a Punk Rack, Swinger, and Milk Can Toss. Then sold it all and hit the road. Had enough of the hassle."

"So that's how you took Tori."

J.T. smiled. "My games were mostly legit. Gaffed a few by making it difficult as hell to win," he said. "Take the Punk Rack. Every so often I'd face one of the cats in the opposite direction, making it impossible to knock off the rack."

"I know how it works," Andy said. "That's where I started, scamming the marks."

Beyer came toward them. Andy hunched over his plate with his eyes down.

"Excuse me, gentlemen," he said and placed Emily's photo on the table. "Either of you seen this girl hanging around?"

Careful not to look up, Andy reached out, looked at it, then shoved it back and shook his head.

"You her father or something?" J.T. snapped.

"No," Beyer said. "I asked if you've seen her?"

"For all I know, you could be some pervert." J.T. was ready to take him on. Why didn't he just shut up so Beyer would go away?

"Could be, but I'm not," Beyer said, grabbed J.T. by the shirt, and yanked him out of the chair.

"Fuck you." He struggled to break free.

Andy reached down, glided the Beretta from the holster, then moved behind Beyer, and shoved it into his side. "Let him go." Beyer started to turn. "Don't even think about it," Andy said in a low whisper. "Get your sorry ass out of here, now."

Beyer hesitated for a second as if he was going to make a move. Andy jabbed him harder with the gun.

"Okay?" Beyer started out of the cookhouse, then turned. "Both of you just fucked with the wrong guy."

⌘

He unlocked the gate, stepped back inside the pickup, then drove down the desolate road. Large magnolia trees reached across from both sides, forming an arch just before he reached the circular driveway in front of the tired mansion.

White paint peeled from the clapboard siding, railings, and four columns.

Two men, one with a scruffy beard, stood guard at

the top of the marble steps, each with an automatic weapon slung over his shoulder.

"He's been expecting you," the taller guard said.

The man entered through the front door into a vacant foyer, and heels clicked against the hardwood as he walked into a large unadorned great room. Patches of missing wall plaster exposed lathe underneath. Yellow stained areas on walls marked where paintings once hung.

Sitting at a table across the room with three guards surrounding him, Angel glanced up from the cards in his hand. "Good to see you, *Jefe*."

He walked over and clamped his hand onto his shoulder. "We need to talk."

Angel nodded toward the others. "Get lost. Check on the girls or take a piss. How 'bout a drink, boss?"

"No. Just got word three more are coming in this afternoon. One's Mexican. The others, who knows?" he said.

"I'll let you know how they do after a day or two," Angel said. "Do you want to see the new one?"

"Goddamn idiot. That's why I'm here, *cabron*." He pulled out his knife and stuck it into the table. "We have ten downstairs, right?"

"I think so."

"What the fuck do you mean you think so?"

"*Si. Diaz.*" Angel walked over to the stairwell and shouted. "Rita, bring the new one up."

"Make sure there's room for the three coming in." He removed the knife and ran the tip of the blade under his fingernail.

Rita, a firm body with a flawless olive complexion was in her late thirties. The ex-call girl had elevated herself to the house's madam. She trained new arrivals and handled them on the outside when the women were moved around in executive motor homes, always with at least one armed guard.

She grasped on to the new girl by her elbow and pushed her into the room.

"Lea understands what she's supposed to do," Rita said and let go of her grip.

"Turn around," he said. She rotated slowly until she faced him again. "How old are you."

She shivered, crossed her arms, and rubbed both with her fingertips, her nails bitten to their quick. "Seventeen," she slurred.

Lea's face was caked with heavy makeup, eyes lined in black and mascara, lips red and puffy. Long, black hair hung over her right shoulder. She wore a body-hugging red teddy, a matching thong and black stiletto mules.

"Show us what you can do," Angel said.

Lea looked at Rita and shrugged.

Rita shoved her forward. "Do what I told you."

He and Angel leaned back in their chairs as the girl danced slowly. After coaching from Rita, her moves became more seductive.

"Unwrap the package," he said.

"Now," Angel shouted.

Lea acknowledged the nod from Rita and slipped the teddy over her head then pulled the panties down and stepped out of them. She continued dancing with her eyes closed.

"I've seen enough," he said. "Come here. Closer." She hesitated then stood in front of him. He ran his fingers over her arms, stomach, and ass then cupped her breasts. "Nice."

He touched the skin under her upper arm, then squeezed it between his thumb and index finger until she screamed and tried to pull away.

Tears ran down her face as she pleaded. "Stop it. You're hurting me. No."

He let go. "Next time, act like you enjoy it." He looked at Rita. "This one still needs work."

Chapter 12

ndy had just saved J.T.'s ass. Judging by his reaction to Beyer's questions and the photo, he'd recognized Emily. A kernel of opportunity presented itself, and Andy didn't want to blow it. A thousand to one, Tori's trip to Virginia Beach had something to do with Emily's disappearance. If she was there, he'd find her.

"Holy fuck, dude. That was something," J.T. said. "Didn't know you were packin'. Why didn't you cap the bastard?"

"That wouldn't have been very smart. What the hell was that all about?" Andy asked. "Do you know that chick?"

J.T. threw the rest of his coffee on the ground. "Maybe. Maybe not. The guy's a jerk."

"If she's a runaway, she could be in trouble."

"Let's just drop it," J.T. said. "I need to check out a few things on the ride before we open. You gonna stick around?"

"Not sure, yet. If I do, I'll drop by later. Maybe we can throw back a few beers."

J.T. wandered off past the fried dough joint and disappeared behind the Paratrooper. The carnie had given him his first lead. Andy had to get to Virginia Beach fast.

ငာင

Residents milled around the lobby of the flophouse, a few still glued to the flickering screen. Musty air thickened from the heat and humidity. The clerk smiled when he saw three twenties hit the cracked marble counter.

"Two days," Andy said then left and worked his way over to the Marriott garage, using plate glass windows as mirrors. Whether or not it was necessary, he wanted to make sure he wasn't being followed.

He retrieved the SIG from the Mustang's trunk, jumped inside, and headed east. He punched numbers into his cell. Sprocket answered on the second ring and said he'd wait for him. Andy asked him to line up a bike.

Three messages from Mia troubled him. The edge in her voice told him of a growing concern for his safety. He owed her at least a partial explanation. He called her home and woke her. They talked for a few minutes until she was satisfied he was okay. It felt good that someone cared about him. The eighteen-year difference in their ages bothered him but not enough to end it. He had feelings for her, feelings that could get in the way down the road, depending on how far he went.

Andy pulled up in front of Sprocket's and found him hunched over the bike with a wrench.

"What the hell are you doing?" Andy said. "Get the damn thing fixed. I'm paying for it."

"What did you get yourself into now?"

"Were you able to get that bike?"

Sprocket limped toward him. "Got a chopper coming. How long's it been since you've ridden?"

"Bought a Ness Bulldog last year," Andy said. "I'm sure I can handle whatever you've got."

"Want me to come along?"

"In your condition?" He had to be kidding. "No. I'm taking Sarah."

"A little road-rash, that's all. You need me, you call, got it?"

The Jeep pulled up and parked in front of the house. Gabby's expression changed when she got out and slammed the door. "Don't even dare drag Sprocket back into this."

"I'm not. We're only talking."

She was becoming a real pain in the ass.

"Come on you two," Sarah said. "Lighten up."

"I think Emily's here with a girl from the carnival," Andy said. "There's a good possibility they'll be hanging out at Raging Rapids this weekend."

"Is that the girl you told me about?" Sprocket asked. "Won't she recognize you?"

"Yeah. But not Sarah."

"What?" Sarah said.

"The beach is going to be packed today and tomorrow. We'll cruise Atlantic and Pacific Aves, then ride over to the water park," Andy said. "Sprock's getting me a bike."

"No way." She threw up her hands. "I'm terrified of motorcycles."

"Settle down. No highways. Twenty-five, thirty miles-per-hour max around town."

"You don't understand." Her eyes filled with tears. "My brother died on one of those damn things."

"I'm sorry." Another part of her life he didn't know about bubbled to the surface. Anything he said right now would sound hollow.

She wiped her eyes with the back of her hand and

stared at him. "I guess I owe it to you for getting me away from Leon."

He reached over and squeezed her shoulder. "The girl's name is Tori. Loves the arcade, and she's hooked on Skeeball. There's a good chance Emily could be with her."

"What if she isn't?"

"Then we follow Tori."

"Hey, man, you definitely need me now." Sprocket said. "No one knows this place better than me. Let me help."

"Over my dead body," Gabby shot back. "You're in no shape to ride a bike."

"She's right." Andy looked at Gabby and gave her a thin smile, trying to bridge the growing gap. "Besides, Sarah will blend in better with the young beach crowd." He turned to her. "You ready?" She nodded reluctantly, her expression all too revealing. "Leon's not going to be here if that's what you're worried about."

Lil' Mike pulled up in the yellow tow truck with a black chopper harnessed to the bed. "Sprock, you sure you trust this guy?" He said, looking at Andy. "Bike's worth twenty big ones."

"Say's he can ride." Sprocket laughed. "Let him run up and down the street a few times and check him out yourself."

Andy sat back in the leather, started it, then shot down the street and back, convincing Lil' Mike the bike was in good hands. "Ready Sarah?"

She hesitated, threw her leg over, and wrapped her arms around his waist.

"Not so tight," he said. "Relax." He took off, drove to the end of the street, and almost laid it down on the curve. "Shit. Don't fight it. Stay upright. I'll do the leaning."

"Okay. Don't get all pissy," she said. "You're lucky I'm on this damn thing at all."

"I hate the new helmet law, but I guess we better go back and pick them up," he said. "We're burning daylight."

Sprocket's fit. It was the first time Andy had worn a German-style brain bucket. Gabby's was a little snug on Sarah.

Andy described the girls again as he pulled one of the photos out of his shirt pocket. "Since she's trying to hide, she could have changed her hair. Cut it. Dyed it." He tapped the photo. "The key to finding her is finding Tori."

It wasn't long before the heavy traffic came to a standstill had them sucking up exhaust fumes. Frustrated, he raced the engine and accelerated past several cars.

"Shit. Slow down," she shouted. Her arms tightened. She pressed her head against his shoulder. "You're going to get us killed."

"Keep your eyes glued to the sidewalk on the right." He nudged her with his shoulder. "I'll watch the left."

"No way." She jerked her head up. "Keep your eyes on the damn road. I'll watch both sides." Her sharp voice pierced his ear.

"Fine, but turn your head left and right, not your body."

Shops with bright-colored awnings lined both sides of the street. A few had kiosks out front, selling the usual tourist junk. T-shirts, postcards, beachwear, sunglasses, and suntan lotion. By-the-slice pizza joints ran a close second. The white sand and breaking waves were visible between oceanfront hotels that dotted Atlantic Avenue. Crowds swarmed the sidewalks.

"Let's head down to the arcade," he said.

"Your call." Her grip began to relax.

Andy drove under the *Raging Waters* sign and into the parking lot then passed twisting tubes filled with rushing water. Riders screamed as they wound their way down the slides. Heartier souls bodysurfed in the giant wave pool. Sounds of whining engines and screeching tires came from go-karts in the rear of the complex. Dozens of motorcycles lined the front of the arcade, their rear tires angled against the curb. One empty space remained at the end.

Sarah yanked off her helmet, shook her new short crop of hair, and ran her fingers through it. "Now I know why bikers don't like wearing these things."

"I'll wait here. Go inside," he said and pulled out the photo again. "See if you can spot her or Goth."

"Then what?"

"Let me know. I'll take care of the rest."

Water parks were no different than amusement parks and carnivals. Good operations were laid out to entertain customers, maximize their spending, then send them out the gate with ear-to-ear smiles. Only carnies referred to them as marks.

Waiting wasn't easy. Fifteen minutes felt like an hour. Finally, Sarah reappeared in the doorway and nodded as she moved toward me. "They aren't in there."

"Let's give it another hour," he said. "Then we'll go back, drag the gut, and try to find them."

She glanced down at his hand. "You're driving me crazy with that frickin' lighter."

"Sorry," he said and dropped it into his shirt pocket.

Thirty-five minutes had passed when three girls walked down the sidewalk toward the arcade, one with jet-black, spiked hair.

"That's her," Andy said. "The one in the middle's Tori."

They were an odd contrast. She wore a leather dog

collar with steel studs and matching wristbands. The other two wore T's and shorts with baseball hats that hid most of their faces. The all-American-girl look. "I'll bet one of them is Emily." Another hundred and fifty thousand was still on the line with this girl.

"What do you want to do?" she asked.

"Follow them inside. Buy some tokens and stay close. Try to ID Emily."

It was starting to come together. All he had to do was find out where they were staying and call Carlyle. He knew Beyer was close by, somewhere between here and Richmond. Once he handed her over, the money would be transferred, then he'd make another attempt at seeing Julie. After that, he would board a flight back to San Francisco and get his life back on track.

A little more than two hours had passed when Tori strolled out with only one of the girls. Sarah followed.

"Where's the other one?" he asked.

"Inside. Can't say for sure, but I think the one with Tori is Emily." She stood next to the bike. "I got a pretty good look at her."

"Go back inside and stay with the other girl. I'll tail these two."

When the girls were outside the gate and walking toward Pacific Avenue, he revved the engine and kicked it into gear.

They were still on Pacific when the girls stopped and turned. Tori stared at him. Damn, keep moving. He accelerated past them and parked in front of Giovanni's Pizza.

When they turned down Eighteenth, he ran back to the corner and saw them slip inside a yellow bungalow, third from the end. He had to make sure it was her before he made the call.

He returned to the bike then coasted to a stop on the

opposite side of the street, a few doors down. Something felt odd. Closed windows and drawn curtains didn't make sense in this heat and humidity.

Andy punched in Sprocket's number. He answered on the first ring.

"I need your help," he said. "Followed the girls to a place on Eighteenth just off Pacific. You okay to drive?"

"Be there in five."

The lime-green '56 Ford pickup rolled to a stop behind the chopper.

"They're in there." Andy pointed toward the yellow Nantucket.

"Whadda you want to do?"

"We have to get a look," Andy said and started to cross the street.

Sprocket limped behind him. A scream came from inside.

"Holy shit." Andy ran across the street and up the stoop with his Beretta drawn. He rapped on the door with the butt of the gun, then twisted the handle. "Damn thing's locked."

The flimsy jam shattered on the second try when he forced it open with his shoulder.

With the gun pointed, he swung to the left, then panned right. Someone had trashed the inside. The coffee table lay upside down with a broken lamp next to it, papers scattered everywhere. Small bloodstained footprints faded from the front door toward the rear of the cottage.

He inched his way around the corner and eased down the hallway. The toe of his shoe pushed open the first door on the left, a bathroom. Andy pointed with his index finger to the door opposite him. He twisted the knob, shoved it open, then stepped back. An empty bedroom. Only one room remained, the door barely ajar.

With the nose of the Beretta's barrel, he nudged it

open. "Shit," he yelled and threw Sprocket the cell. "It's Harley. Someone slit his throat. Call 911. Hurry."

✌◌✌◌

Bells, buzzers, lights, and music filled the arcade as Sarah squeezed past shouting and screaming kids. The girl tore coupons from the slot of a coin-drop, then took off her cap and stuffed them inside. She wasn't Emily.

Sarah watched her leave the building, then followed a safe distance behind. When she turned down Eighteenth, sirens screamed in her direction. The girl froze across the street from a yellow bungalow, then bolted. About to follow, she saw Andy run out onto the front porch.

A patrol car screeched to a halt in front, and an officer jumped out with her gun drawn. "Place that piece on the ground in front of you," she shouted, "then turn around and get your hands above your head."

Chapter 13

Harley's motionless body lay like a fallen beast on the floor between the bed and dresser. Blood pooled beneath his unruly beard. Andy moved closer, careful not to disturb anything. His throat gaped open.

"Shit, someone filleted the poor bastard."

Sprocket came closer and bent over him. "Jesus. Dude's tough. Not many people could get close enough to do that kind of damage."

Andy stepped back. "J.T. told me Harley was staying in Williamsburg."

"What do you think happened to the girls?" he asked.

"Someone must have snatched them and hauled ass out of here."

Sprocket kneeled next to Harley's lifeless body. "Maybe they aren't as innocent as you think."

The contents of two backpacks were scattered across the bed next to him. "They wouldn't have left their things behind. Stuff is important to teenagers."

As Andy walked out the front door, a police car screeched to a stop at the curb. Two officers jumped out with their weapons drawn.

"Place that piece on the ground in front of you," the female cop shouted, "then turn around and get your hands above your head."

Sarah stood across the street with her hand clasped over her mouth. How in the hell had she found them?

"Now," the officer yelled again.

He tossed the piece on the lawn then lifted his arms above his head. Shit, another delay, explaining his way out of this mess to the cops.

"We're the ones who called," he shouted then realized Sprocket was still inside. "There's two of us."

"Shut up," she said. "Stay where you are."

As if he had a choice. Where did they expect him to go with two guns aimed at him?

"I said turn around. Keep those hands above your head," she shouted.

"A man's been murdered. He's in the back bedroom. Throat's been slit."

"I've got him covered. Hook him up," she said.

The other officer slapped on handcuffs, pulled him across the lawn, then sat him on the curb. She moved to the porch and cuffed Sprocket's good arm to a downspout.

Sarah bolted across the street. "What are you doing?" she screamed.

Two more patrol cars pulled up, and an officer grabbed her.

"Let go of me," she yelled, trying to wrench free.

"Officer, there's a permit in my wallet. Name's Andy Zartanian. By the way, there's also a 9 mm holstered under my right arm."

The cops looked at each other, then at the female who'd put the bracelets on him. The wiry cop stepped forward, reached inside his opened shirt, and pulled out the piece.

Thirty minutes later, Detective Weaver removed the cuffs. He wasn't the type of person one would pick out of a crowd as being a homicide detective. He wore a white shirtsleeve with a button-down collar and a dated paisley tie. Horn-rimmed glasses and a buzz cut hinted ex-military. He wasn't buying Andy's reason for being there.

"Everything I told you is the truth. Standing here, answering the same questions over and over isn't going to help find the girls."

"A man's dead." Weaver's thick New Orleans drawl was unmistakable. "I'll tell you when we're finished."

Sarah started to unravel. "It's gotta be Leon. I know it. Oh, God, Andy, he knows I'm here."

Her ill-timed comment about Leon led to another round of questions. It was over three hours before Weaver and his partner finished the questioning and verifying their identities.

"Stay in town and leave your cell on."

Leon had become part of the investigation and would be questioned. Worse of all, he'd learn that Sarah was in Virginia Beach, if he didn't already know.

They hurried back to Sprocket's house and ended up on a collision course with another one of Gabby's tirades, her English becoming more broken the angrier she got.

"Shut the hell up," Sprocket shouted. "These people are our friends, and they're in trouble."

"But—"

"Calm down and listen. We're not turning our backs on them."

"Enough," Andy said. "I have to get Sarah out of here before Leon and his thugs show up."

"Whadda you have in mind?"

"I'm taking her back to the Marriott. She'll be safe there for now."

"No, Andy, I'm scared. You don't know Leon." She

grabbed his arm. "He won't quit until he finds me."

"You have to trust me. He won't find you." He downed the rest of the Heineken. "If anyone tries to tail me, it'll be to the flophouse."

"You still haven't told me what you're going to do," Sprocket said.

"Hell if I know. Thought I'd grab the girl, call her grandfather, and it would all be over by now. Guessed wrong."

"Sarah can stay with us," Gabby said, biting her lower lip.

"I don't want her around here. If Leon thinks she's still in Virginia Beach, the safest place is under his nose in Richmond."

He thought about calling Joey and telling him about Harley but decided to leave that to the police. Unfortunately, Carlyle needed to be told. He owed him that.

"What do you mean you almost had her?" Carlyle shouted.

Andy pulled the cell away. "There were three girls. I didn't have a chance to make a positive ID. Things went down too fast, then the girls disappeared."

"You incompetent bastard. You let them take my granddaughter?"

"I don't know if anyone snatched them, or if they got scared and bolted."

"I wasted my goddamn money and time on you," Carlyle said. "I want Beyer back on this. Where are you now?"

"I can handle it without him."

"Quiet. I want you to meet up with Beyer. Brief him on everything you have. After that, go back to selling rides."

"Bullshit."

"As of right now, I'm canceling the credit card. Your

services are no longer required," he said. "Now tell me where you are so I can send Beyer."

"Fuck you. Let your flunky dig up his own information." Andy slapped the cell shut. The hell with him. He was committed to finding Emily, money or no money.

⌘

Emily and Tori's wrists were bound with duct tape. Wide strips covered each of their mouths. They'd been roughed up, slapped into obedience, and walked reluctantly up the front steps.

This was a different house. The other was modern with a large courtyard and close to the beach. Big cars. Foreign accents.

A man shoved her in front of Tori and jarred her back to the present. He pushed her into a great room where two men sat at a round table at the far end. One had thick, brown hair and wore black slacks and a tight-fitting black polo shirt. The short, heavier one built like a fire hydrant appeared to be Latino and was dressed in faded jeans and a blue, Mexican-style shirt.

"Angel, we have a bonus," the man in black said.

Angel pushed back his chair and walked up to the girls. He smiled. "Out of the country, right?"

"Yeah. Accelerate their orientation. I want them on the shipment leaving at the end of the week."

"I hate to do this," Angel said. "Blondie could bring in some serious cash if we moved her from house to house."

"Shut the fuck up. This isn't your decision. These two are going," he said. "You got a problem with that?"

Angel glared at him. "Rita," he shouted over his shoulder.

A woman emerged at the head of the stairs. "What is it?"

"Two cocktails for our new guests."

She walked behind the bar, bent down, then came back toward them, carrying a towel with two needles on top. "This won't hurt."

She watched the tall man grab Tori from behind, then felt the Mexican's beefy hands jerk her arms back. Emily fought like crazy to free herself, but he tightened his grip. The woman held a syringe in the air, shot a stream of liquid, then plunged it into her thigh. She picked up a second needle, removed a cap, and pushed it into Tori's leg.

"A little GHB will help put the both of you in the mood," she said.

"The bitch will settle down. They all do." He let her go, then grabbed Tori's cheek, and squeezed. "Two choices. Pain or submission." He turned to Rita. "Take them downstairs."

Emily felt dizzy, then remembered the man saying GHB. Maybe that's what they'd given her after they grabbed her before. Tori had told her about taking it at Raves and the great feeling it gave her. She said it helped take the edge off, made life bearable. But it scared Emily. She looked around at the converted basement. Sterile army bunks, lockers, and small tables with mirrors. The cold bunker apartment had a raised concrete curb at the end that kept water in the open bathroom from running into the sleeping quarters. Two exposed toilets sat next to each other with a laundry sink on the opposite side. Two showerheads protruded from a moldy cinderblock wall. This place was different than the other one.

Paranoia set in. The other girls glared at her, or were they just staring? She couldn't tell. For the first time in her life, she wanted to curl up and die. Let Tori kill herself if she wants to, she thought. Maybe she wasn't a friend. Emily felt lightheaded, zoned.

"Those two bunks at the end are yours," the woman said, shoving her forward.

Emily steadied herself then sat quietly until the woman ripped the tape from her mouth. She screamed. The drug-induced calm disappeared then returned in waves.

Tori flinched as the tape came off but didn't make a sound.

"I expect both of you showered by the time I get back." She cut the tape from their wrists then threw a leopard-patterned bra and matching thong on the bottom bed and a red set on the top. "Fight over whichever one you want, but have them on by the time I return." She pointed to a large bookshelf filled with rows of spiked heels. "Find a pair that fit." She turned and went back up the stairs.

Tori flipped her off. "Bitch."

Emily shook her head. Tori's give-a-rat's-ass attitude had returned. "Damn it, we're in enough trouble. Big trouble." Everything moved in slow motion. "You're making it worse. Stop," she screamed. "Just stop."

A girl with bronze skin, barely in her twenties, slipped off her bunk and walked over to them. "Rita meant what she said. You don't want to cross her. Girls who do, don't do it a second time."

"Fuck you," Tori said.

"Listen to her. She's trying to help." Emily's words came out slowly.

"Name's Pilar," she said. "I've been here over a month. They gave you just enough but not too much."

"What do you mean?" Emily asked.

"GHB. You're under their control. Piss them off, and you get a larger dose."

"They said something about shipping us somewhere," Emily said.

"Don't know nothing about that. Just do what they say, and it'll go a lot easier."

"Bullshit." Tori rubbed the red marks on her wrists.

Pilar started to walk away then turned and faced her. "You really don't get it, do you?" She reached out to shove her shoulder, but Tori slapped her hand away. "You're fucking whores. They own your asses." She looked at Emily. "Let your smartass friend do what she wants, but I'd take that shower if I were you before she comes back down to put on your makeup."

Chapter 14

Andy led Sarah up the stairs to the third floor then into his room. "Order room service while I take a shower," he said. "A thick steak, blood-rare, and a Heineken. Get whatever you want."

He felt his identity slipping away, becoming someone he didn't like, someone who would disappoint Pop. Deepened lines on his forehead and the feel of gritty stubble reminded him of how gut wrenching searching for the missing girls had become. This was far bigger than the money and ignited something inside him. He had to think with a clear head. Three people's lives depended on it. Maybe more. Nick's show and Paradise Island held answers that could lead him to solving this bizarre puzzle. But to do that, he had to crack J.T.

"What are we going to do?" she asked. "I can't just sit around here and wait."

"For now you can. Don't step out of this room for any reason. I don't even want a maid to catch a glimpse of you."

"But—"

"I said any reason. You've got room service if you need something while I'm gone," he said. "Have them let themselves in. Stay in the bathroom until they leave. I'm leaving after we eat. Might be back tonight, tomorrow morning at the latest."

Fifteen minutes later, he heard a knock at the door. "Room Service."

"Get in there," he whispered.

The server placed the tray on the table and removed the domed lids. After signing the ticket, Andy handed him a ten-spot.

Sarah came out after the waiter left and plopped down at the table.

"The first thing I'm going to do is head over to the lot and see if word's gotten back to any of the carnies." He cut into the steak. Blood rare. "J.T. knows something. After I get done working him, I'll head over to Paradise Island and poke around."

"What if Leon recognizes you?" She stabbed at the chicken salad and pushed the pieces back and forth.

"He won't. Hell, he might not even be there," he said. "I'll call and let you know what's going on."

With the Beretta secured in place, he slipped the 9 mm SIG in the small of his back then cinched the belt tightly. Even though it was physically uncomfortable, that cold piece felt good next to his skin. So far, it had served him well.

Andy walked a couple of blocks, watching the reflection in store windows, again making sure he wasn't being followed.

He ducked into a drugstore and left through the rear door. Nine o'clock Saturday night in Richmond brought out a motley crew. The closer he got to the coliseum, the stranger they became.

"Look them straight in the eyes and don't flinch. Let them know you aren't going to wait for them to make the first move," Pop always said.

It worked tonight as it had for years when he carried a briefcase filled with money down midways then out into parking lots.

The Giant Wheel glowed against the night sky alongside a Wild Mouse coaster that arched under midway lights. Still a block away, music blared, and smells of freshly fried dough, popcorn, and pizza filled the air. Shrills of laughter, mixed with screeches from riders being tossed upside-down and sideways, grew louder.

He adjusted the denim shirt, making sure the bulge of the gun didn't show, then stepped onto the midway and stayed close to one side. Rube was his first stop.

"What the hell you got in that pot?" he asked.

"The best damn chili in the whole forty-eight," Rube said with a sense of pride.

Andy shook his head. "You old geezer. We made Alaska and Hawaii states years ago."

"Not to me. They ain't touchin' American soil." Rube turned his attention back to the pot. "Never been to either, but have trucked through all forty-eight."

Andy moved closer. "Heard anything?"

"Might have. Always cuttin' up jackpots after hours."

"Yeah, and each time you share stories, they get bigger."

"Wouldn't be carnie like if you didn't add a little. But you wouldn't be asking if I'd heard anything if you didn't already know either."

"You're smarter than I gave you credit for." Andy leaned into him. "Fill me in on what you've got."

"Old boy Harley got wasted."

"That's it?"

Rube flipped two burgers on the grill. "You got more?"

Either Andy trusted him or he didn't. "Saw that girl

and Tori. Then they disappeared," he said. "Did they show up here?"

"No, but J.T.'s been in a foul mood since that Tori girl left."

"How'd you hear about Harley?"

"Nick came down here late this afternoon and broke the news about him. Said his throat was slashed clean through." Rube moved the burgers to the cool side of the grill, then continued to stir the thick chili. "J.T. went ballistic. All he did was yell 'Fuck' over and over."

"Where's he now?"

"Better be at the Himalaya," Rube said.

"Keep your ears and eyes open." Andy threw a twenty on the counter. "I'll check back with you later."

The Himalaya had only a few riders. J.T. was going through the motions, barely blowing his pipes. He acted as if he could care less. When it came to a stop, Andy walked up to the fence.

"Yo," he shouted.

J.T. nodded then jumped down from the control booth. "Still hangin' around?"

"Yeah. Got a load on Monday." Andy's jaw tightened. "Man, what's the matter? You don't sound like your old self."

"Guess you haven't heard." J.T. shifted his weight. "Someone took out Harley. Slit his fuckin' throat."

"Shit. Wasn't your girl with him? Tori. Right?"

J.T. slammed the railing with his fist. "Yeah. Stupid-ass bitch."

"Whadda you mean?" Andy asked.

"I told her. Shit. Never mind. She's fucking history." J.T. kicked the fence. "I hooked up with her in Charlotte. It's time to find some fresh stuff anyway."

"Thought you two were tight."

J.T. slipped a pack of cigarettes out of his shirt pocket and tapped it. "Got a light?"

"Didn't know you smoked." Andy pulled out the lighter.

"Yeah, well, there's a lot you don't know about me."

"You said Tori was going to visit her sister." Andy gauged J.T.'s reaction. "When is she coming back?"

"Why are you so damn interested in that bitch?" J.T. said, ready to square off.

"Hey, man. You got me all wrong." Andy held up his hands, palms facing him. "I'm not into Goth. "I like the sexy stuff. You know long legs and heels. The nastier the better."

J.T. lightened up and laughed. "You want to grab a couple of beers? I'll show you fucking legs. Like real sweet stuff."

"Sure. What about the ride?"

"Lenny's got it. Right Len?" J.T. yelled and waved off the guy in the booth. "Come on." They ducked behind the Himalaya and out back toward his camper. "Wait here."

"Where are we going?"

"I told you. Gonna show you some choice stuff. You'll see." J.T. disappeared inside then came back out. "We'll take the black Explorer," he said dangling the keys. "Nick lets me borrow it. You ever been to Paradise Island?"

"Never heard of it."

"Hop in," J.T. said then pulled a joint from a pack of some cheap brand of cigarettes. "Ganja. Fresh from Jamaica," he said. "The lighter?"

Andy flipped it open and torched the end of the tightly rolled weed as J.T. drew in hard. He held it for a few seconds, then slowly blew out through pursed lips.

"Want a hit?"

"Nah. Swore off that shit along with cigarettes," Andy said. "Where's the show's sugar shack?"

J.T. laughed. "Never heard it called that until I hooked up with Nick."

Andy said nothing and waited for the answer.

"Funnel cake joint has a full menu. Sells to the help as long as they don't get fucked up while the show is open."

J.T. seemed to have found his voice. The conversation distracted him from his frustration with Tori. The weed had him chattering all the way over to the club. He steered clear of discussing their relationship. Andy wanted to probe, knowing she was the linchpin to finding Emily, but listened instead.

When they pulled into the parking space and opened the door, he slipped the SIG out and shoved it under the passenger seat. The ankle piece went from backup to first position.

"With all the time you've spent in Richmond," J.T. said, "I can't believe you've never been here before." He tucked in his shirt. "It's hot, dude. You'll see. These broads are real sweet."

The overgrown goon working the door rippled with muscle. He scanned Andy from top to bottom, then turned to J.T., and nodded. "Dude."

The shaved, shiny black head with a razor-trimmed beard looked familiar. Then it clicked. The Mercedes driver.

"Who's your buddy?"

"Sinbad, meet Danny," he said. "Told him, he'd have a good time here."

"That's up to him. The only guys who don't…well, you know." His eyes continued to size Andy up. "Fucking fags. You one of them?"

Heat rushed to Andy's face. His jaws tightened. He

remembered Pop's words again and shot Sinbad a look to back off. "Do I look like one?"

"You're safe," the bouncer said. "I don't kiss on first dates."

J.T. burst into laughter, but Sinbad didn't. He returned a don't flinch or I'll take you out right here snarl.

Sinbad turned to J.T. "He's okay. Two free passes. Enjoy."

They walked around the four-sided stage to a spot that had a clear view of the front door and ordered two beers.

The silicon-pumped redhead on stage wore a black G-string with glittering sequins and moved in their direction with a smile that accentuated her seductive moves. Her eyes met his, then her gaze drifted toward J.T. She jammed her breasts into his face, while gyrating her ass for everyone sitting on the opposite side of the stage.

She stood and turned, then leaned over and looked back at them between her legs. Firm milky-white thighs came together where a thin strip of black disappeared, completely distracting him from the reason he was here.

Andy slipped a crisp fin out of his pocket and slid between the silk waistband and skin that felt as soft as it looked. J.T. upped him with a double.

"I owe you big-time for introducing me to this place," Andy said. "Nice show. Real nice."

"Best I've seen. Me and the guys come here regularly, then go back and bang some of the bitches on the lot." J.T.'s grin widened. "This shit's foreplay." He laughed.

Another baldhead at the front door drew Andy's attention. Damn. Leon.

J.T. must have caught him staring and motioned with his head. "That's a bad dude. He's tight with the man."

"Nick Pappas?"

"How do you know Nick?" J.T. asked.

Andy scrambled for an answer. "Rube talked about him. So who's the bad dude at the door?"

"Leon. He's heavy into bookies."

"Ponies?" Andy asked.

"Nah. He's no railbird. Sports shit. Every fucking game. Over. Under. Spread. It doesn't matter. College. Pro." J.T. looked back at Leon. "Gets in way over his head sometimes."

"Do you think Nick's making book?"

"Doubt it. But from what I've heard, the boss man loans money for some pretty stiff interest. Why are you so interested in Nick?"

Andy wanted to know more but backed off. Based on his rap sheet, loan-sharking fit. Before he pushed, Andy needed to loosen J.T. up with a few more beers.

Another dancer took the stage and began her three-song-set. Patriotic colors peeled off with each number. In the third, the smallest G-string he'd ever seen stared him in the face. Caught up in her movements, he heard a familiar voice, turned, and saw a hand reach out for J.T.

"Not working tonight?" Leon asked. His beefy paw clamped onto his shoulder.

J.T. winced. "No. Brought my friend over to check out the talent. Danny, meet Leon."

Andy could tell Leon was trying to place the name with his face. His eyes met Andy's and locked. Leon grabbed his hand and squeezed. He couldn't read Leon's expression, couldn't tell if he had put the two together.

Leon nodded, still staring hard. "Do I know you?" Andy prayed he didn't make the connection to Sarah. "Hell, I see a lot of faces around here. After a while they all look the same."

Andy's chest barely let go of the air he'd sucked in.

Leon turned back toward J.T. and slapped his back. "Enjoy yourselves. I just dropped by to see how things were going," he said. "Headed out of town for a day or so. Sinbad's got you covered."

"Thanks, dude." J.T. smiled. "Business or pleasure?"

"A little of both. My business brings me a lot of pleasure." Leon laughed aloud, then walked away.

The police must have talked to him by now. Ten to one, he was headed to the beach. This was the perfect opportunity to follow, but he couldn't.

Dancers came out on stage, set after set, as they downed Budweisers and Heinekens. They'd put away a six-pack each in a little over an hour.

"You want some action?" J.T. asked. "Private lap dances in the backroom."

"Nah."

"Twenty-five bucks. They're good," J.T. said. "Strip down to nothing and rub their tits and ass anywhere you want. Real fuckin' sweet, dude."

"Tempting," Andy said, "but I'm gonna pass."

"Your loss. Let's blow this joint. I'm ready for the real stuff."

Heading back to the lot, J.T. unloaded his life story. The beer had lubricated him more than Andy thought it would. He stopped when he got to Tori and glanced over at him.

"That bitch's stupid. I warned her." He slammed his hand against the steering wheel. "She doesn't listen. Thinks she knows it all, but doesn't know jack-shit."

"About what?"

"Doesn't matter. I need to find a new one and move her in," he said. "The sweet-ass workn' the Punk Rack has been eyen' me. This is her lucky night."

"Thought you liked Goth." Andy waited for his reaction, still trying to push some buttons.

"Yeah, sometimes. Shit, stuffs she's into is wild but weird." J.T.'s fingers tapped the wheel. "You know, fucking kinky. She knows a hell of a lot for her age."

He was just drunk enough for Andy to throw him his fastball right across the middle of the plate. "So where did Tori go?"

"I told you before. Her sister's. She's staying there."

"And not coming back?" he asked.

"No, man," J.T. said. "She's not. It sounds like you want a piece of that."

"I already told you what I like. And Goth ain't it."

"Then fuckin' drop it."

They pulled into the back lot with the show starting to close for the night. Chasers trailed to dark. Music silenced. When the midway shutdown, the rides became iron phantoms.

After J.T. slid out of the driver's seat, Andy reached down and grabbed the piece, then slipped it back under his shirt.

"Think I'll grab a cup of Rube's coffee before I call it a night," Andy said. "You comin'?"

"Nah. Don't wanna wreck a good buzz. Besides, got something else to take care of." J.T. turned and walked toward the office, knocked, then went inside.

Andy inhaled the night air as he walked out onto the midway. Troupers and flatties were scattered around the cookhouse cuttin' up jackpot when he strolled in. Rube spotted him and motioned.

"What the hell's so urgent?" Andy asked.

"That guy. The fancy one," Rube said. "He was here an hour or so ago asking if anyone seen you around."

"Me?"

"No. Both of you. The ride guy, Andy Z, and the one who pulled the piece on him."

Andy liked the fact that Rube was watching his backside. "Yeah, I pissed off his boss. Probably bruised his ego."

"You sure as shit must have. Left me his card and said to call the minute I saw either of you. Told me there'd be five yard-notes in it for me."

"What the hell are you trying to tell me?

Rube leaned closer. "He didn't hide the fact he was packin'. My gut tells me he's lookin' to use it on you."

Chapter 15

Drunks and panhandlers brushed against Andy as he made his way back to the flophouse. He had to work faster and smarter to stay ahead of Beyer. He needed to call Detective Weaver in the morning to see if the investigation had turned up something new. Equally important, he had to decide what to do about Sarah.

At the end of the block, the hotel's neon sign sagged over the doorway and protruded halfway across the sidewalk. That fleabag hotel wasn't a place he wanted to call home for another night.

A sudden motion in a dimly lit alcove startled him. "Shit."

A guy rolled onto his side. He clutched a brown, paper bag with both hands, empty cans of Colt45 scattered around him. The stench of urine slapped Andy in the face.

"Can you spare a buck or two?" the drunk slurred.

Andy started to walk away, then turned back to throw him some change. Beyond the recess, a shadowed movement slipped into an opening. The hell with the drunk. He had to get out of there.

"Thanks a lot, shit head," the bum shouted.

Stay close to the buildings, Andy thought as he headed toward the flophouse. Keep it slow and steady. Don't let the bastard know he'd spotted him.

No one had been in his room. The folded gum wrapper hung between the door and jamb, a handy trick he learned in Special Forces.

His cell was still taped to the bottom of the nightstand. He punched in the numbers and asked for the room.

"It's me," he said. "Did Sprocket call?"

"No. But someone else did. I thought it was you. Whoever it was, hung up."

"When?"

"About ten or fifteen minutes ago. Why?"

His mind raced. "Don't open the door for anyone until I get there."

"What's wrong?" She sounded scared.

He cut her off and slammed the cell shut. Damn it, only Mia and Sprocket knew where he was staying. Even Carlyle didn't know.

Andy reached back and grabbed the SIG, tucked it down the front of his pants, and pulled the army sweater over it. The Braves ball cap hid part of his face.

Three down-on-their-luck residents sat in threadbare chairs watching TV and didn't bother to look up as he passed through the almost deserted lobby, the air stale and humid.

There were only a few people on the street in front of the hotel. Whoever had followed him, more than likely lurked out there, waiting. He needed to get to Sarah but not at the risk of exposing her.

Andy turned right, jaywalked toward the corner, then headed down the street to the Marriott garage. Passing between the large columns and SUVs, he heard footsteps from behind. Damn it, he hadn't lost him. He scanned the open space, then moved toward a red Lincoln Navigator parked next to a concrete support. He crouched and worked his way to a better vantage point.

Footsteps moved in his direction. Then the guy emerged in the middle of the aisle in front of him. Beyer looked in all directions, then started to walk the other way.

"I heard you were looking for me," Andy shouted from the side of the SUV with his 9 mm aimed at him. Beyer spun around. His hand started to reach inside his jacket. "Don't try something stupid, asshole." Beyer stood frozen. "Pull the piece out slowly and place it on the ground in front of you."

"Who the hell are you?" Beyer squinted, trying to see him.

"Do what I said. Now."

Beyer bent over and set his weapon on the ground.

"Kick it toward me." Andy stepped forward, snapped up the gun. "Lift your pant legs."

"I didn't know you were into men's legs."

"Now," Andy shouted.

Beyer complied.

Andy pulled off the hat. "It's me, pea-brain. Andy Zartanian."

"Shit, I should have known. You're the one who pulled the gun on me when that carnie mouthed off." Beyer took a step toward him. "What the fuck do you think you're doing?"

Andy raised the barrel. "Back off."

Beyer stopped. "Tell me what you have on the girl, then catch the next flight back to California while you can."

Adrenalin rushed. "Shut the fuck up."

"You're lucky you're still in one piece," Beyer said.

"Wait until Carlyle finds out you're a loose cannon."

"From where I stand, I'd say I have the upper hand," Andy said. "Shit-can the threats. I'm not working for Carlyle anymore. But I'm sure you already know that."

Beyer took another step forward.

"I told you. Stay where you are."

"I didn't think you were this stupid," Beyer said. "The way I see it, you still owe Mr. Carlyle."

Andy circled around him. "I don't owe that pompous bastard anything. I'll find his granddaughter because I said I would. Only now, it's on my terms."

"You're making a huge mistake," Beyer said.

"Let's see, that's another threat. Gee, you're really scaring the hell out of me." Andy backed toward the garage opening.

Beyer's jaw tightened and face flushed with anger. He stood poised, ready to jump him.

Andy ejected the magazine and slipped it into his pocket, then tossed his 9 mm into the planter. "It's all yours," he yelled, then ran out into the street.

"Sarah, it's me," he panted into the cell. "I was being followed."

"What?" she said.

"Calm down. It's not one of Leon's boys." He tried to catch his breath. "I'll be right there."

From the side of the building, he watched Beyer retrieve the weapon and pull a magazine from his coat pocket. Andy ducked into an alleyway and came out on the main street. After fifteen minutes of backtracking, he was sure he'd lost him.

It came to him. He'd used the credit card Carlyle had given him to check into the Marriott. Son-of-a-bitch, that's how he'd tracked him down. The bastard also had to have the description of the rental car. If Beyer was the one who'd called, he knew there was a woman staying in his room. Andy prayed he didn't know the number, but a twenty to a bellman could get it.

"Sarah, open up," he said, pounding on the door.

"Are you going to tell me what's going on?" She slammed it closed and turned the deadbolt.

"The guy who works for Emily's grandfather is in Richmond." He ripped clothes from the closet and threw them on top of the bed. "We need to get out of here. I've got to find another car."

"Mine's still parked in the hotel garage," she said.

"What?"

"I left it there when I met you downstairs in the bar. How do you think I got here?"

Andy hugged her. "It never crossed my mind." He grabbed the bag and started stuffing clothes inside.

"Where are we going?" she asked.

"Virginia Beach. I need to see what the police have. Then I'm coming back here. I'm not finished with J.T."

She stood up with her shoulders back. "And why do you think the cops are going to share anything they have with you?"

"Let's just say it's a gut feeling," he said. "Weaver knows I'm searching for a missing girl. Girls actually."

"What about Leon?"

He finished shoveling the clothes and zipped the bag. "He's the least of our worries right now," he said. "On the way back to the beach, I want you to tell me everything you know about Crystal and Paradise Island. There may be a connection. Now hurry up."

As they were about to leave, he turned and gave her the Beretta. "You might need this."

She hesitated before she took the gun. "Why?"

"I don't want any more surprises, especially with Beyer out there." He grabbed the bag and slung over his shoulder. "Here's the plan."

They stepped into the hallway and hurried toward the emergency exit.

"Stay close."

With his hand on the 9 mm tucked in his belt, he scanned the stairwell before they headed down to the garage.

Andy looked through the glass on the door. "After I leave, count to ten. Give me enough time to get into position, then go directly to your car. Remember, keep your hand on the Beretta." He saw her tense up. "Don't worry. You won't be out of my sight."

Her black Pathfinder was parked between a column and an Escalade, two aisles to the right, close to the exit. He stepped into the open and maneuvered between the rows of cars paralleling hers.

She started out from doorway and hesitated. *Come on, baby, don't panic now.* Her head turned nervously, searching the garage, then she moved toward the SUV.

He watched her through car windows. Another fifty feet, and she'd be there.

A dark blue sedan screeched out of a parking space and drove in her direction, two men in the front seat. She turned toward them, then raced for the Pathfinder, fumbling with her car keys.

When the car slowed, a large black male jumped out of the passenger side.

"Hey, fucker," Andy yelled. He stopped, turned toward his voice, then started to lunge at him until he saw the business end of the SIG.

"What the hell do you think you're doing?" the thug shouted.

"Walk back to your car nice and slow and spread your hands over the hood," Andy said. "Tell you buddy to get out." Andy motioned. "Sarah, get in the car and drive over here. Hurry." She stood frozen. "Hurry."

He stepped out from behind the SUV, heard a blast, then the weight of a sledgehammer hit him squarely in the chest and knocked him to the ground. The garage blurred, then went dark.

Chapter 16

Distorted sounds swirled, then Sarah's voice broke through. "Andy, Andy."

Steel girders and concrete came into focus along with her face.

"What the hell happened?"

He tried to sit up and fell backward from the pain in his upper chest. Whoever those thugs were, they knew how to find Sarah and him, and they weren't going away.

"Lie still," she said, the coolness of her hand against his face. "I called 911."

He touched the spot where it hurt, feeling for signs of blood, but instead, felt Pop's lighter. He pulled it out of his pocket.

"You're not bleeding," she said. "I already checked."

Flipping the Zippo over, he saw a copper slug imbedded into the smashed casing, a small caliber. Looked like a .22. Anything larger would have gone through.

"That stupid lighter saved your life," she said.

He tried to sit up again and shake off lightheadedness. "What happened to the guys in the car?"

She held up the Beretta. "When the driver fired at you, I opened up. Think I hit one before they took off."

"We need to get out of here before the police arrive." Pushing himself against the front tire took all he had. He grabbed his shirt and pulled it away from his body. Particles of gunpowder tattooed the cotton around a small, sooty hole in the center of the pocket.

Sirens wailed in the distance, coming in their direction. "Help me up." An ambulance screeched into the garage. He struggled to his knees. "The story is a guy punched me. That's it," he said. "We'll be here all day if you say anything about gunfire. Hurry, get the gun out of sight and help me with the shirt."

Before the paramedic jumped out, Andy took off the denim shirt, pulled down the V-neck, white T-shirt, then shoved the SIG into the back of his pants.

"Sir, where are you hurt?" she asked.

"My ego," Andy said, trying to smile.

"Don't be stubborn," Sarah said. "Show her."

He lifted the T. "See. No blood."

She probed his chest with her fingers. "Maybe not, but that's a pretty nasty bruise. Number one rib could be broken. You should have it X-rayed."

A police cruiser pulled in, then a second and a third.

He explained to the officers that a punk jumped him and nailed him in the chest. When Andy kneed him in the groin, the creep took off.

"Can you give us a description?" the officer asked.

"Shabby looking white guy about my size. Black Raider's T-shirt and jeans," Andy said. "Probably some junkie looking for money for his next fix."

After fifteen minutes of questioning, they finally let them go.

Sarah drove and filled him in on everything about Crystal, some of which he already knew. Both girls had ended up at Paradise Island for the same reason—fast money and a kick-start to a new life.

She recounted stories about Leon and his strong-arm tactics, something he had witnessed.

"Sinbad isn't like Leon," she said. "He's like a quiet storm off shore. Even when he explodes, it's controlled."

Andy thought he understood but sleep deprivation was getting the best of him.

They grabbed a few hours of shuteye in the parking lot of a strip mall, ate breakfast, then drove to the police station that sat nestled among municipal buildings. He needed to find out what the crime lab had uncovered, and Weaver was the key.

When Andy opened the front door, the female officer working the desk looked up. From her initial reaction, his appearance didn't help win points. He stepped to the counter, then leaned to the side to read her nametag.

"Officer Kim. It's urgent I speak with Detective Weaver," he said. "Tell him it's Andy Zartanian."

"You do realize this is Sunday, don't you? He isn't to be called in unless there's a homicide." She swiveled in the office chair.

"That's why I'm here," he said. "I have new information on the carnie whose throat was slashed." Shit, what information?

The officer turned back around. Sarah's knuckles hit his right thigh.

"Give me what you have, and I'll pass it on to him."

She was out of line. He stared back at her, then she turned away.

"We both know better," he said. "You're not here to screen information for Detective Weaver. Call him."

Officer Kim left the room. When she returned, she glared at him. "He said he'd be here in twenty minutes."

Weaver strode through the double doors dressed in a white, short-sleeve shirt with a button-down collar and khakis, no tie, same glasses. He wore topsiders without socks.

"Mr. Zartanian." He hesitated and squinted. "Ms. Walkovitz, correct?"

She nodded. "Sarah."

"Why don't we step into the conference room," he said and led the way. "Have a seat. I'll get the file."

The space felt like most meeting rooms, pale green, too big for one or two people, too small when all the seats were occupied. Framed pictures of city officials covered the walls.

Weaver reappeared with a large folder, slapped it down on the table, and sat across from them. He set a notepad and pen next to it, then folded his hands and leaned forward. "So tell about the new information you have."

Andy placed his arms on the oak, interlocked his fingers and mirrored his posture. "I think that guy up in Richmond, Leon, may have something to do with the murder."

Weaver studied him with a steady gaze. "And you know this how?"

"There was an incident that happened right before we came down here."

Weaver sat back and tented his hands. "Go on."

"It's a gut feeling," Andy said. "Sarah and I were headed to the car when his goons took a potshot at me in the garage."

"Do you know for a fact they were Leon's crew?" he asked.

"Who in the hell else would it be?" Weaver had started to piss him off. "They were going after Sarah. She was the target. I just happened to get in the way. It had to be his goons."

"You seem to have a habit of doing that." Weaver

wrote in the notebook, waiting for a response he never got. "I'll have one of my men bring him in again for questioning." He flipped back a couple of pages. "I spoke with Mr. Carlyle. Apparently, he doesn't care much for you. But he did confirm your story."

"I already told you that it's his granddaughter I'm trying to find. Who else have you interviewed?"

"I ask the questions here," Weaver said. "This is the Virginia Beach Police Department's investigation, not yours."

"There's a lot of crap going down that doesn't make sense. I'm sure it's all connected." Weaver's look was stoic. Andy couldn't tell if he was making any headway. "Working together, we could arrange the pieces so they fit."

Weaver leaned back in the chair. "Working together? What exactly do you think you bring to the table?"

"I bring military experiences most people couldn't imagine and I know the players in this swirl of crap," Andy said. "And I'm familiar with the carnie culture. No one else could blend in better."

Weaver closed the folder and shoved the notebook aside. "You better have more for me than that."

"I already told what I bring to the table. The carnies will talk to me, not the police."

Weaver's eyes locked onto Andy's and didn't waver. "Before I share information with you, I want everything you have," he said. "If I find you're holding back, I'll shove your ass in jail so fast, no one will find you until I want them to."

"What the hell are you talking about?" Sarah blurted. "Can't you see he's only trying to find a missing girl?"

Andy's hand grasped her arm and gently pushed her back in the chair. "The detective is only making a point." He turned to him. "Deal."

"There's a good chance these girls may be trafficking victims," Weaver said. "If so, they could be long-gone and almost impossible to find."

"That's all the more reason to jump on this now."

Weaver opened the folder. "I'm not the type who bullshits, so don't cross me." He pushed it toward him, then peeled pages back one at a time, explaining what they had.

Andy studied each page. Leon actually had a last name, Ney. His rap sheet went back to when he was a teenager in Atlanta. Petty crimes, then a bust for armed robbery had locked him away for hard time. Seven years in Georgia's Reidsville facility.

"This guy started young and kept going down the wrong road," Weaver said. "That said, looks like he's been clean for the past three years."

He'd also spoken with Joey Conner, Harley's boss. The only information that he had provided was payroll records that showed Harley's real name was Oliver Kowalski. His rap sheet included drugs, disorderly conduct, public intoxication, and several motor vehicle violations, all while riding with the Warlocks in Florida. No recent arrests on his record. He'd stayed straight for the last five years.

"This could be something," Andy said. "Harley's the person who signed the rental agreement for the bungalow."

"We're on it." Weaver turned over the page.

The next piece of information caught Andy by surprise. Fingerprints at the crime scene matched a photo of a missing girl. The soft-looking face and blondish, brown hair was Torrine Anne Lesley from Dayton, Ohio. She ran away from home a week after her seventeenth birthday. Weaver said it was an abusive situation.

Now Andy understood why she'd hardened. Self-preservation had surfaced in the form of a mask, a Goth lifestyle woven with dark lyrics. Tori needed him as much as Emily did.

Weaver flipped to the next page. "Found prints on the front porch post that match those of a Jackson Tindel." He handed him the photo. "This picture was taken when he was eighteen. He's twenty-nine now," he said. "Boy hails from Jupiter, Florida. Did two stints in juvenile detention for possession. Have you seen him around?"

Andy studied the mug shot, then tossed it back.

"I asked you if you recognize him."

"No. I haven't seen this guy," Andy said. "Any others?"

Weaver continued to scrutinize him. "We found three other sets of prints with no matches. Possibly females. They're much smaller than the others." He closed the folder and adjusted his glasses. "Emily Carlyle. The girl you're looking for."

"What about her?" Where was this cop going?

"I can't find that she ever existed," he said. "No birth certificate in Mass. No school records. Nothing."

Andy glanced at Sarah then back at Weaver. "She isn't a Carlyle. Well, she is on her mother's side. Her father's name is James Armstrong. I have someone trying to track him down. The grandfather said he's somewhere in Vermont, but so far the only thing I know is that he Carlyle fired him about a year ago. Can't find anything on him since."

Weaver slammed his fist on the table. "When in the hell were you going to get around to telling me?"

"Sorry. I forgot about him," Andy said. "Carlyle despises the guy and refuses to acknowledge his existence or any connection to the girl. I had to squeeze him hard just to get his name."

Weaver slid back the chair and stood. "One warning only. The minute you find anything, you let me know," he said. "We may be known for our hospitality down here, but our jails aren't."

Sarah slammed the passenger door closed. "Are you going to tell me what the hell that was about back there?"

"You mean not telling him about the father?"

"No," she said. "The look on your face when you saw that picture."

He didn't respond and inserted the key, then started the Pathfinder.

"Andy," she shouted. "Talk to me."

"Jackson Tindel is J.T.," he said.

Chapter 17

The tall man approached the house just before midnight. One of the guards raised his rifle above his head, acknowledging his arrival. He demanded respect from everyone who worked for him. Those who challenged his authority wished they hadn't. Angel was close to being taught a lesson.

The new bitch needed the same. A lesson she would never forget. It was only a matter of time.

"What took you so long?" Angel said. "You said you'd be here earlier."

He glared at the son-of-a-bitch. "Got tied up." Being questioned by this little prick pissed him off. He reached inside his shirt pocket and pulled out a Cohiba, ran it under his nose, and across his tongue. "Tell me about the girls. How'd they handle the drugs?"

"Blondie became real sluggish, but the other one got high and cocky. She's used before."

"Good. She won't be for long." He struck a match, put it to the end of the cigar, and drew it in. Gray smoke slowly escaped his lips in Angel's direction. "Have Rita bring them up. We'll see how much persuading they're going to need."

Angel's face tightened as he stood to leave the room.

"Wait. Bring me the bottle of that good shit. Asom Broso Anejo," he said.

His lieutenant returned with the dark tequila and two tumblers, filled the first, and waited.

He wasn't going to waste a two-hundred and thirty-buck bottle on this asshole.

Rita appeared with the girls in tow then whispered in each of their ears. "Here," she said and shoved them forward. "I did the best I could."

Emily wore the red thong and matching bra with black heels. Thick eye shadow and dark, red lipstick made her look hard, but a subtle look of naivety still shone through.

Tori stood dressed in the leopard pattern with black, stilettos, her posture upright and defiant.

"Nice," he said. "You with the dark hair, move your ass around the room for me."

Angel leaned over. "That blonde is going to bring top dollar. I still think we should keep her here."

He took the knife he'd been toying with and drove it into the wood next to Angel's fingers. "You piece of shit. Don't ever tell me what to do." His gaze held. A real man wouldn't allow someone to call him a name like that. "Rita, I'm waiting," he shouted without unlocking his gaze.

Startled, she took Tori by the arm. "Don't you understand English? Strut like I showed you. Now."

Tori hesitated, glanced at the man holding the blade in his hand, then moved to the other side of the room and back.

"Slower," Angel said. "This ain't no fuckin' horserace. Do it again."

"One leg in front of the other," Rita yelled.

Tori tilted her head back and swayed. "And I'll dig

you out, and I'll sit you up, for the fools to find you," she sang then stopped in the middle of the room. "This is bullshit." She crossed her arms and refused to budge. "Fucking bullshit."

Angel jumped up and started to move toward her when he grabbed his arm. "No. I'll take care of this."

He threw back the tequila, got up, and walked over to her. "Maybe another needle would help. What do you think?" He placed the cigar in his mouth, forced her chin upward with two fingers on his left hand, and held the knife in front of her face with his right.

"Go to hell." She jerked her head away. "I'm no whore."

"Call it whatever you want. *Puta,* hooker, or one of my girls," he said. "The latter has a much better life."

She stared back with widened eyes. "I don't fuck for money."

"That's right, you don't. But you'll fuck for my money." He wanted to cut her, make an example out of her, but knew it wouldn't serve any purpose. She was money to him. "Have them take her to the room and give her another shot, then get her ready," he said to Angel.

Two men came in and dragged her out, fighting and kicking.

He turned back toward the blonde. "You're Emily, aren't you?"

"Yes." Her voice trembled.

"You seem much smarter. Smart is good," he said. "Go back down with Rita and cover up. And wipe that crap off your face." He patted her on the arm.

He poured a second glass of Anejo. The man knew it pissed him off, but Angel had gotten cocky, and that led to mistakes. He needed to be reminded who was in charge.

"We'll move the three Ukrainians along with the

other one." He paused. "There's a lot of heat coming down because of the murder and the one who got away." He smiled. Emily would be his trump card. "We need to get them across the border quickly. *Comprende?*"

"Yes, but I thought you were going to move the blonde."

"I'll worry about her. Have you alerted Javier?"

"He's waiting," Angel said. "He'll meet us at the place outside of Santa Maria and escort us across the border to the Rio Rico house."

"Make damn sure our men are working the border," he said. "Once we get the other house cleaned out, we'll be moving close to thirty out of Mexico."

"You looking at the Far East, jefe?"

"For now unless I get higher bids," he said. "As soon as they arrive down there, I want portfolios on each so we can forward them to our clients." He jabbed his cigar close to Angel's face. "I don't want Javier laying a finger on any of the girls this time." He placed the cigar in his mouth and waved the blade in front of him. "And you stay away from Emily. I'll cut off the dick of anyone who disobeys my orders. Is that clear?"

"You know I don't fuck them without your okay, *jefe.*" He rubbed the side of his face. "I'll make sure he knows."

"Yeah, right." He walked over to the window. "I want the tractor purring. We can't risk any breakdowns like last time," he said. "The trailer will be here tomorrow."

"Garcia won't be back until the day after," Angle said.

"Bullshit." He turned back and grabbed Angel's shirt, then held the knife to his throat, drawing a faint line of blood. "Get him back here by the time the ride pulls into the yard. Is that clear?"

"*Si.*"

He pulled the knife back and let go. "The moment it arrives, I want him to start on the possum belly retrofit," he said. "And get one of the motor homes ready." He went back, stubbed out the cigar, and downed the last of the tequila. "No fuck ups with this shipment, or your *pelotas* are mine." Angel nodded. "What about the girl?"

"Should be ready by now," Angel said, straightening his shirt.

His heartbeat quickened as he walked down the hall. Stopping at the door, he glanced at the knife in his right hand, then pushed the door open with it.

Four posts had large steel rings screwed into each. Leather restraints held Tori's hands above her. Ankle clamps kept her legs apart. A red scarf tied around her head held a small rubber ball in her mouth. The attitude had disappeared and replaced by cold fear. She made guttural noises and squirmed as he ran his finger across the blade.

Her sounds and movements aroused him. "You'll do everything I say." He bent over her, slipped the blade under the strap between her breasts on the leopard bra and slit it open, exposing a pink butterfly tattooed on her left breast. He placed the cold steel against her skin, then slipped the blade under the black silk waistband and cut it, exposing a matching tattoo above her shaved mound.

Dread in her eyes intensified. She fought harder against the restraints.

"Nice. I like it a little rough." He unbuckled his belt, unzipped his pants, then dropped them to the floor. "*Puta la madre*. Just another whore."

The mattress gave way under his weight.

"You'll learn to enjoy this, bitch," he said as he thrust himself inside her.

Chapter 18

The unexpected twist of events changed the relationship between Sarah and Andy. They felt each other's pain. She had a calming effect and a way of ferreting out people and information. He had no choice. Soon she would enter the belly of the carnival world and meet his only connection, J.T. They'd squeeze him together and find out why his prints were at the crime scene and what he really knew.

The drive took longer than usual for a Sunday. Andy laid the seat back a few inches to relieve the painful bruise in his chest and listened to Marvin Gaye's "What's Going On?" They called it "Beach Music Sundays" down here. The Temptations, Drifters, O'Jays. No Beach Boys. He never understood the concept but liked it. His index finger found its way to the hole in the shirt pocket.

"We're almost to the coliseum," Sarah said. "When are you going to tell me what we're doing here?"

He glanced over. "I have to hook up with the pair of eyes who keeps me informed. Drive around to the backside of the lot."

She turned the corner and drove through the opened cyclone gate.

"Over there, next to that red pickup by the trailers. Back in."

"Why?"

He shook his head. "In case we have to leave in a hurry. That's why."

"Andy, why are you being so ugly with me?" she said. "I'm not the enemy. This detective stuff is all new to me."

"Leave it unlocked," he said.

They walked onto the midway. The lights weren't as visible during daylight hours, but the sounds of music mixed with whining motors and shrills of laughter were the same day or night.

"I can't risk running into Nick Pappas," he said as they hurried toward the cookhouse. "We're on his playing field, uninvited."

Thank God it was empty except for Rube. Andy tapped the counter. "Hey, old man."

Rube turned around. "I'll be damned. You back again?"

"Brought Sarah with me." Andy nodded toward her. "Meet Rube." He leaned over the counter. "Anything new happening?"

"You better not hang around here long," Rube said. "Old Nick's on a rampage. Had it out with J.T. earlier."

"Any idea what it was about?" Andy glanced around and made sure they were still alone.

"Saw them down by the office trailer," Rube said. "Right in each other's face. Damn hands flying everywhere. Couldn't hear a thing they were saying, but he looked like he was ready to take the kid out."

"Where's J.T. now?"

"Don't know. Came storming through here real testy." Rube shook his head. "Damn hothead. Said he'd taken enough of Nick's crap."

Shit, what if J.T. took off? The disappointment Andy felt must have shown.

"Boy'll be back. Got nowhere else to go." Rube leaned forward. "Besides, all his stuff is still here."

"Do you shut down at ten tonight?"

"Always on Sundays. Weather's the only thing that changes that," Rube said.

"What the hell's going on?" Nick's voice boomed from behind him.

His beefy hand clamped down on Andy's shoulder and twisted him around. He looked at him hard. "Andy? What the hell happened? You look like shit."

"Long story," Andy said.

His eyes landed on Sarah. "Nice. Real nice."

"Cut the crap," Andy said. "She's with me."

"Her loss," Nick said. "So why the big change?" He looked at her, then Rube.

Andy said nothing.

Nick widened his stance with arms folded. "When I ask questions, I want answers. You're on my lot."

"Screw you. Come on Sarah, we're leaving." Andy turned to Rube. "Catch you later."

"I'm not through talking to you," Nick said and gripped his arm.

In one swift motion, Andy spun and caught him with a left hook, that knocked him to the ground, then kicked him in the ribs. Nick rolled, trying to catch his breath. Andy stepped back.

Nick managed to get to his knees. "You'll wish you hadn't done that. You're fucking dead," he shouted as they walked away.

Time had come to go for broke. Either his plan would work, or he would find himself at the end of the road and never find the girls.

"Where did you learn to handle yourself like that?"

He smiled, slipped into the driver's seat, and headed north, twenty-plus miles to Doswell, then turned off on the King's Dominion exit.

"Do you mind telling me where we're going?" she asked.

"I have to think things through." His fingers tapped the steering wheel. "Besides, it's safe here. No Leon. No Beyer. No Nick."

He pulled up to the attendant and handed him a ten-spot.

"An amusement park?" she said. "We're going to a stupid amusement park? I thought we were going after the girls."

"We are. Trust me." He looked over at the miles of wooden and twisting steel tracks. "God, this place has some great coasters."

"Now I know you're losing it." Her frustration showed. "What do coasters have to do with any of this?"

"You'll see," he said. "Being in a park or on a midway is like listening to a symphony."

"Damn it. Cut the crap and tell me what we're doing."

"I'm serious. A true carnie can close his eyes, walk down the midway, and name every ride that's operating," he said. "Roundups, Paratrooper, Zippers, Pirate Ships, they all have their own distinctive sounds."

Sarah shook her head and said nothing.

He strode toward the Grizzly, a giant wooden coaster copied after Coney Island's Wildcat. After grabbing a couple of diet sodas, they settled in at a table that offered a clear view of the park. "Hear that clicking?"

"Yeah. So what?"

"That's the chain-dogs engaging into Rex Number 150 that carries the cars up the lift," he said, pointing to its underbelly. "Man, I love that sound."

"I don't give a damn about 150, 160, or whatever it is," she said. "Tell me why we're here."

"I have to get everything worked out in my head before we go back." He pulled out his wallet and opened it. "I never told you before, but I have a daughter close to Emily's age. She means the world to me." He placed the photo in front of her. "If I blow this, I may never see her again."

She furrowed her brow. "You're talking in circles. Blow what?"

He studied her face and measured his next words. "We're going to kidnap J.T."

Her mouth gaped open. "What?"

"Tonight after they shut down." He pulled out the cell. She started to say something. "Wait." He punched in Sprocket's number. "What kind of shape are you in?"

"Better than I thought. Actually getting around pretty good. Sorta following doctor's orders," Sprocket said. "Why?"

"I need a boat. Something with a cabin that can withstand rough waters twenty or so miles out."

"You gotta be kidding. But the sick thing is I know you're not."

"I'll only need it for a few days tops." The coaster rattled the structure as it passed.

"Where the hell are you?"

Andy ignored the question. "Lots of guys moor their boats at Rudee Inlet and don't touch them for weeks at a time, right?"

"A few." Sprocket hesitated then said, "Just finished an Ocean Alexander, forty-six-footer. Owner's in Europe for a couple of months."

"I know jack-shit about boats. You pick the boat. One more thing. I'll need you to come with me."

"Hell, there's always a catch, isn't there, Z? You

want me to steal a boat, then be the captain, too."

"Borrow one. I'll need it tonight. You in?"

"I'll have to figure out what I'm going to tell Gabby. Hell, that's my problem," Sprocket said.

"Call you back later with the details." When he closed the cell, Andy looked up at Sarah.

She bit her lower lip. "You're serious about what you said, aren't you?"

"Very."

After spending the rest of the day riding every coaster in the park, he was sure she'd set aside what they were about to do. It didn't last long and changed the minute they drove out of Dominion's parking lot.

"I'm not sure I can do this, Andy." She touched his arm. "I want to help but don't know if it's in me."

"We're beyond the point of having any other option." His comment silenced her.

On the way back to Richmond, they stopped at a Food Lion and purchased enough supplies to last several days. The deli had *domas*.

"These don't have meat," he said, examining one. "*Mamig* taught me to make them with a combination of beef and lamb."

"I never heard of them," she said. "Do you realize that you and William Saroyan are the only Armenians I know?" His head snapped to the right. "I meant know of. Read *The Laughing Matter* and *The Slaughter of the Innocents* in high school," she said.

"I'm impressed."

"Tell me they're all not as crazy as you."

"No. But we're a spirited lot. Usually tell it like it is."

She touched his shoulder and smiled. "I have to admit that I didn't know what an Armenian was, maybe still don't," she said. "And I have no idea where Armenia is."

He shook his head. "All my life I've answered those questions," he said. "Now when they ask where, I ask when, before or after the genocide when the Turks slaughtered over a million of our people and stole our land?"

Not having shown this side in a while, he let his boiling anger die down and thought about Pop and his friends. Thought about grandma, too and the mother he barely remembered. He and Emily had something in common, mothers they never knew.

He drove into the back lot, parked close to J.T.'s camper, then scanned the area. "Nick's truck is gone."

"What if he comes back?"

"I'll deal with him if he does." Andy grabbed her hand and led her to the midway. "Stay as close to the Himalaya as you can without being obvious and wait for him to close."

"And do what?"

"J.T. has a ponytail, braided goatee you can't miss, and a gold eyetooth. He should be working the control booth and on the mic." She took in a deep breath. "Calm down. You won't be out of my sight."

"You still haven't told me what I'm supposed to do."

"When he comes down off the ride, approach him. Tell him that you know where Tori is." She nodded. "He's probably going to ask a lot of questions. Don't answer. Just get him to come with you."

"You really think he's going to buy that?"

He squeezed her arm. "A hundred percent sure. Get him to follow you back to the car. I'll take care of the rest."

Several food joints had already closed. The thinning crowd made it easy for him to watch Sarah as she moved along the asphalt past the Roundup. Lot lice and a few marks hung around, wasting their hard-earned money to win a piece of worthless plush. Lights chased and strobes created a dizzying effect. She stopped across from J.T. where he gyrated with a mic in his hand.

After the riders exited, he yelled, "One more ride before we close. The last is always the sweetest. A real ball-buster. Only five tickets to really get down."

When the ride was loaded for the last time, he whipped the cars around, slowing them, then blasting them forward again.

The last of the riders staggered off yelling. Moments later, he locked the door to the control booth, then jumped down off the platform.

"Hey, you J.T.?" she called out.

He walked toward her. From the smile on his face, the little bastard was probably looking at her as another score.

"Yeah, who wants to know?" His wide grin flashed the gold tooth.

"A friend's looking for you."

His posture changed, then his face twisted into a cocky smirk. "Got lots of friends. You wanna be one?"

"No, but Tori does."

The smirk disappeared. "Who the fuck are you?"

"She needs to talk to you." Her voice didn't waver.

"Bullshit." It was obvious he knew something they didn't.

"Fine. I'll tell her you're not interested." She turned and walked away, playing him.

"Wait."

"I don't have time for this." She kept walking. "If you're interested in connecting with her, come with me."

He caught her arm. "Where the hell are you goin'?"

She pulled away, hurried to the end of the Roundup, and headed toward the back lot. He followed close behind.

Andy went around to the other side of the ride and came up on his back.

"Hey, I asked you a fucking question." J.T. spun her around. "I expect an answer, bitch. Where's Tori?"

Andy's arm wrapped around his neck. He shoved the barrel of the SIG into his back. "That's what you're going to tell me if you want to live."

Chapter 19

Words stuck in Andy's throat like cotton that day at the Santa Clara County Fair. He'd struggled to explain to Pop what went wrong. It was the last day of the run and what turned out to be the hottest day of the year. Billy Mathews had just finished greasing the Scrambler. Queue lines started to wrap around the ticket booth. He'd just loaded the ride when Andy hit the start button. It was still on the first revolution when one of the cars whipped around. Billy must have tripped and fallen backward into its path. No one knew exactly what happened, least of all Andy. He'd lived with Billy's death for the past twenty-four years.

He had learned in the military to detach himself emotionally from his target. J.T. was different. How far would he go with him? Did he have the right to make a life or death decision?

Even though it meant saving two lives, Andy didn't know if he could go through with it. He was in over his head and couldn't turn back.

J.T. lay bound and gagged on the back seat, fighting the restraints. Sounds came out as muffled grunts.

"Shut up." Andy's nerves felt raw as he swerved the

car off to the side of the road and threw open the back door.

"Andy, don't." Sarah reached over the front seat and grabbed him. Her nails dug into his arm. "Don't."

He jerked lose, pulled J.T. up by his collar, and raised his hand. "One more sound and you won't recognize yourself in the mirror."

J.T. quieted down.

Once they were back on the highway, Andy punched in Sprocket's number.

"Get off the line, Gabby," Sprocket shouted. Another phone slammed. "Where are you, Z?"

"Richmond. I'll be there a little after one." Andy glanced in the rearview mirror. J.T. lay there, staring back at him, eyes widened. "Can you meet me at the boatyard?"

"Yeah. When you get to the front gate, drive all the way to the back and park next to the old tug," Sprocket said. "Can't miss it. You'll see a white boat trimmed in black and gold at the end of the dock. Name's *Hard Work*."

Sarah started to say something. Andy held his finger to his lips. A tense silence fell between them until they reached the beach.

A series of light posts lit up the perimeter. Even at night, the tug's bright red paint stood out from the mostly white and blue weekend toys rocking in their berths.

Sprocket limped toward them. "Boat's ready. Twin screws are humming."

Andy opened the rear door. "Package is back here along with the supplies." He yanked J.T. out onto the asphalt.

Sarah came over and helped steady him. "Easy, Andy."

"I've got him." After cutting the tape wrapped

around his ankles, Andy gripped J.T. by the arm and lift-ed him up. "Come on."

J.T. fought him until they reached the edge of the dock. He looked down at the dark water then back at Andy.

"It's even darker twenty miles out," Andy said and dragged him below into the galley, then he handed Sprocket the SIG. "Watch him. Sarah and I'll get the rest of the things out of the SUV."

Once the boat was loaded, Andy untied the lines from the cleats and threw them onboard. Sprocket climbed up to the bridge helm, eased it out of the slip, then idled out the inlet into open water. He moved both throttles forward and met the force of the waves with the full weight of the forty-six foot vessel.

Andy glanced back to shore. Rusting bones of a Fer-ris wheel and coaster, the only remains of Virginia Beach's Pirate Cove, faded under the full moon.

Sarah sat back on the stern's cushioned seat with her arms stretched, white knuckling the rail.

The boat sliced through the water for several minutes, then cut sharply to the left, slamming Andy to the deck.

"What the hell happened?" He yelled and rubbed his arm. Sarah sat in the same position, calm replaced with fear. "Are you okay?" he shouted.

"Yes," she said, still gripping the railing.

He stood as the boat came to a stop and rocked in the rolling sea.

Sprocket scrambled down from the bridge. "Port side diesel died."

"Son-of-a-bitch." Andy jumped down the steps. J.T. was on the floor crumpled against the starboard wall. Andy pulled him to his feet, pushed him down on the chair, then ripped the tape from his mouth.

"Shit," J.T. screamed. Hair stuck to it. "What the hell are you doing?" He shook his head. "I trusted you, dude."

"My name's not dude." Andy hauled him up the steps, sat him down on the aft deck, and turned toward Sprocket. "Do you think we can make it on one engine?"

"Maybe. Give me a minute to check it out." Sprocket opened the hatch and slipped inside. "Have to figure out what's wrong," he said, scratching his head. "It may take a while."

"Damn it, we don't have that kind of time." Andy turned back to J.T. A sick feeling settled into the pit of his stomach. The image of Billy Mathews stood there behind him, staring. He closed his eyes and rubbed them to erase the memory, blot out the vision that had come back to haunt him.

Sprocket climbed back up, cranked the remaining engine, then eased the throttle forward. He struggled with the wheel. "We can't risk going out much farther."

"How about another thirty minutes or so?"

Sprocket nodded and put more distance between the city and them.

Andy didn't want to waste anymore time and grabbed J.T. by the shoulders. "You can make this short and sweet or take long enough for me to feed you to the sharks."

"Go to hell." J.T. struggled against the restraints, eyes glaring. "I don't know anything."

Andy slapped him across the cheek, not hard but enough to get his attention. "I haven't asked you any questions yet." Grabbing his ponytail with one hand, he yanked back. "What happened to Tori and Emily? Where are they?"

J.T. looked at Sarah then back at him. "Who the hell are you?"

"Shut the fuck up and listen." A rage was building

inside, and it wouldn't be hard to punch out this guy. "You know what happened to them. Now tell me."

"I don't know what you're talking about."

"Hey, Sprock." Andy pulled J.T.'s head back farther. "How many hours do you think he'll last out here?"

"Not long." His good eye started to twitch.

J.T. shivered. "It's fucking cold."

"It's even colder at the bottom."

Questions and short, nothing answers were all he got until they were ten miles off shore. Sprocket pulled back on the throttle and killed the engine. The sun would creep up on the horizon in a couple of hours.

Andy secured J.T.'s hands with line tied to cleats on the port and starboard sides, leaving enough slack to allow him to stand. He ignored his pleas.

"You're a crazy bastard," J.T. yelled.

"That's what people tell me. Now, are you ready to talk?" Andy grabbed him by the shirt and pulled him toward the rail until the rope almost jerked his arm from the socket.

"Shit," he screamed.

"Do you remember what I said back at the dock? Water's even blacker out here." The look on J.T.'s face told Andy that he didn't have the stamina to last. It was time to push harder. He'd spill his guts in a matter of an hour, maybe less.

Sarah started to pace. "Tell me what you're going to do."

"Stay back." Andy untied one of the ropes. When J.T. started to move to the other side, he knocked him down and tied his ankles to his wrists.

"Don't do this, dude," J.T. cried out.

She tried to shove him aside. "You're not going to throw him in?"

Andy glared at her and finished tightening the knots,

then lowered him onto the transom platform.

"This isn't what you said we were going to do. Kidnap him. Make him talk." She stepped back. "Not this, Andy. I won't be a part of killing him."

"We won't have to if he talks."

"You're crazy." She placed her hands in the front pockets of her jeans. "What if he doesn't?"

"Only three of us go back." Andy looked up at her. She held his gaze and didn't blink. "His choice," he said.

J.T. lay on the slotted wood, his body fighting against the ropes, while he screamed obscenities, then finally begged Andy to pull him back onboard.

"Sprock, start her up."

"What do you have in mind?" he asked.

"Our boy wants to have some fun. Shove it in gear." J.T. shrieked. The boat jerked forward. "I think he wants to go faster."

The wake's white, foamy spray doused him as they bounced across the rough sea. "Get me out of here." His shouts started to fade.

The boat slowed, then the engine quieted. Andy climbed over the stern onto the platform. Slipping off the ropes, he unwrapped the tape on J.T.'s hands and ankles then pushed him into the water.

J.T.'s arms flailed as he struggled to stay afloat. "I can't swim."

"Pull him out," Sarah yelled. "He's going to drown."

J.T. grabbed the platform, then his hand slipped off the wood, and he disappeared under the water.

Andy leaned over the side. "Shit, I can't see him."

"J.T.," Sarah shouted repeatedly. "Damn it, do something."

He kicked off his shoes, tossed her the SIG and Beretta, then dove into the water, surfacing several times for air.

A hand grabbed his neck from behind and pulled him under. Andy rolled over and dove, taking him deeper. J.T.'s grip tightened. Andy went deeper. His ears and lungs felt like they were going to explode. He was approaching his limit, the wall.

J.T. let go, then kicked his way to the surface. Andy followed. Breaking through the water, he wrapped his arm around J.T. from behind, then squeezed his throat until he went limp.

A large swell slammed their bodies against the platform. He held on with one hand and clutched J.T. with the other, gasping for air. "Pull him up," he yelled.

Sarah and Sprocket grabbed J.T. by the arms and yanked him out of the water. Andy pulled himself onto the deck, then dropped down to make sure he was still breathing.

Sarah shoved past him and rolled him on his side. After clearing his throat with her finger, she turned him over and gave him mouth to mouth. "You could have killed him," she said between breaths.

J.T. choked, then started to cough up water.

Sprocket knelt next to Andy. "The little bastard could swim after all."

Andy propped him up. "Had me fooled, asshole."

J.T. started breathing on his own and took in a raspy breath. "Okay," he said. "I'll tell you whatever you want to know."

Sarah grabbed Andy's arm. "Tell me the truth. Would you have killed him?"

"Depends." Andy paused and raised his eyebrow. "Still might."

∽∾

Minutes after midnight, the first black SUV approached the iron gate. High stucco walls on either side enclosed the estate's perimeter.

A heavy wooden door in the wall, a few feet from the gate, opened. Then a man dressed in black pants and a shirt that hung loosely over his trousers emerged. He nodded then spoke into a mic attached to his earpiece.

The gate opened, and the vehicle disappeared inside.

This happened two more times within the hour. All three were SUV's, less conspicuous than limousines normally used.

Three men, who represented the largest segment of the trafficking world, sat around a table in a windowless room. With their glasses filled with expensive liquor, the emergency meeting began.

"I know we met here a little over a month ago, but the Mexican connection has been floundering," he said. "We must shift our attention to buyers who can afford our girls in rich oil countries like Bahrain, Qatar, and the United Arab Emirates."

Borysko leaned forward, tented his hands, and smiled. "Then the Ukraine will become the major distribution point."

"Absolutely not," Yamada-san said. "The Far East is too big of a market for these girls."

"Stop, Borysko," he said. "We have the Russians to consider. The Ukraine is too close to Russia's hammer. Control will remain here."

"I agree," Yamada-san said.

He locked onto the Ukrainian's gaze. The man still had old KGB mentality. But he'd tolerated Borysko's insolence because he needed the supply of girls he provided from his country as well as those he siphoned from Russia.

"Yamada-san. I assume you have made arrangements for next month as we discussed?"

"Of course. Both men are quick and clean. No traces."

"What men?" Borysko asked.

"When we close down the Rio Bravo operation, we eliminate all links," he said. "The Mexicans first, then the Americans."

Chapter 20

Angel looked at the caller ID, then answered. "*Jefe'*."

"How's that girl, Tori, doing?"

"A lot calmer. Gave her some coke like you ordered."

"Remember, only her. I want the blonde kept clean, only light doses of GHB," he said. "There's been a change in plans. We're not waiting until Friday to ship the goods."

"What's up?" Angel asked.

"Call Javier and tell him the truck is leaving tomorrow," he said. "The girls will be there when the bar closes around three Thursday morning."

Why was he only getting bits and pieces, Angel wondered. And why was the boss treating blondie different than the others. Maybe she knew something.

Angel yanked Emily out of the bunk then dragged her upstairs and down the hall. "Too good to touch. Bullshit," he said, shoving her into the room. "How do you know *Jefe'*?"

"What are you talking about?" she slurred.

He threw her on the bed. "Talk, you little *puta*."

"Please, don't hurt me. I don't know who you're talking about."

He spat on the floor next to the bed then unzipped his pants. "You're worth something to him. Now, tell me, or you're going to be mine."

She shook with clinched fists held to her chin.

Angel dropped his pants. "One more chance." The door behind him flew open. He turned.

"You stupid animal," Rita said. "The boss will cut off your *pelotas* if he finds out."

He smiled. "Who's going to tell him? You?"

"Do it, and you'll see," she said. "The girls might be scared of you, but I'm not."

He stared down at Emily. "I'll find out. And if you're lying, it will be your last," he said, pulled up his pants, and stormed out of the room.

$$\infty$$

The time to get J.T. to talk was slipping away. The more distance that grew between the girls and Andy, the less likely it was that he would find them. He needed answers now.

Andy threw him a towel and shoved him below, then pointed to the banquette. "Sit, asshole."

Wrapped in the terrycloth, J.T. slid to the rear and slumped down. "Shit, aren't you going to let me change?" He shivered.

Andy stared at him while he wiped water from his face. "Do you see me complaining about being wet?" He sat in the black swivel chair across from him. Sprocket slipped in the banquette to his right.

"At least give me some water," he said. "I puked my guts up out there."

Sarah grabbed a bottle off the counter and tossed it

on the table. "Move over," she said then slid in next to him.

He looked at her hard then back at Andy. "I thought you were my fuckin' friend, Danny. Can't believe you sucked me in."

"Well, I'm not." He rubbed the SIG's barrel against his cheek.

J.T. started to chug the water then stopped. His eyes focused on the gun. "Hey, man. Chill." He took in a deep breath then let it out slowly. "Whadda you want to know?"

"Where's Tori and her sister?"

J.T. still shivered. "I don't know."

Sprocket's hand clamped onto his forearm and squeezed. "Wise up, you little punk, and tell the man."

Andy pointed the gun at him and smiled. His index finger twitched against the trigger.

J.T.'s eyes widened. "I swear. It's the truth. I don't know where they are."

Andy's gaze held his. "You know something."

T.J. looked away again.

Sprocket squeezed harder. "Talk, prick."

"Shit, you're hurting me," J.T. said. "I just made the calls. It's the fuckin' truth."

"What calls?" Andy asked.

"When I see a girl on the midway who might fit in, I call a number." Sprocket let go.

"What do you mean by fit in?"

"Young girls. You know, smokin' hot."

"Who do you call?"

"A friggin' number. A recording answers." He glanced down. "I leave a description of the mark and where they can find her."

Sprocket backhanded him in the chest.

"I ain't lying," J.T. said. "Never talked to anyone. Just the recording."

"Bullshit. You had to talk to the person who set you up. Give me a name."

He glanced away. "Just one time. Found a note in my camper that said I could make some serious cash if I called the number written on it. So I called and left a message. A man called me back and laid it out."

"And you have no idea who this guy was?" Andy asked.

"No. I swear."

Andy didn't believe him. "Tell me about this serious cash."

"Get anywhere from one to five hundred, depending on the chick. Cash only. Envelope's always left in my truck."

"What happens to the girls after that?" Andy stood, moved over to the banquette, and crossed his arms, the gun in plain sight.

"That's where my part ends. Straight up, I ain't lying."

"Why Tori and her sister if that's who she is?" He leaned forward so J.T. could feel his breath. "And what about Harley?"

Beads of sweat broke out on his forehead. "That girl with Tori ain't her sister."

"What's their connection?"

"After Tori hooked up with me, she connected with Emily somehow." J.T. paused. "Then something happened."

Andy reached over, grabbed his shirt, and shook. "That's a bunch of crap." He threw him back in the banquette. "You said Tori joined the show in Charlotte after Virginia Beach. Emily disappeared at the beach."

"Dude, I'm scared shitless. Got mixed up."

"What did you mean when you said something happened?"

"I don't know." J.T. dropped his head. "She wouldn't tell me. All I know is she was there with Tori, then they left. She said she was going back to the beach to help her."

"Then what?"

"I made a call. The chick was worth five hundred to me," he said. "Never thought Tori would get in the middle."

Andy ran his fingers over the 9 mm's grip. "How was Harley involved?"

"He was giving them a ride." J.T. started to squirm, began to fidget. "Don't know how he got cut."

"Bullshit. Your fingerprints were found at the house, Jackson Tindel." J.T. eyes widened. Andy glared. "My patience is running thin."

J.T. glanced down. "I was there a couple of times when we played Vah Beach. Hooked up with a girl who was crashing there."

"What girl?"

"Meg. She worked the show while we played there but stayed when we split," he said. "When Tori wanted to go back to the beach, I made a call and arranged for her to stay there."

"And you were there the day they disappeared, right?"

"No way, dude," he said. "I was in Richmond greasing my ride, getting ready to open. Ask anyone."

Something was missing. His answers about the girls were too pat. His fingerprints at the bungalow were too much of a coincidence. What was he trying to hide?

"Why was Harley taken out?" he asked.

"Don't know."

From the way he slouched, Andy knew he'd hit a

nerve. Was he involved in his murder? It was time to switch gears. "Tell me how Leon and Paradise Island fit into all of this."

"What the fuck are you talking about? I don't know anything about Leon."

"You know he manages the place. And he knows Nick," Andy said. "What's the connection?"

Sprocket moved closer to him and stared with his good eye.

J.T. shifted in the seat. "Word is Leon got behind, and Nick bailed him out."

"Nick doesn't have time to make book. Remember, that's what you told me," Andy said. "Besides, he moves around too much."

"No, but he has time for loans with some heavy interest," J.T. said. "I already told you Leon's into sports big-time. Bets on everything. I heard he was down a few grand. Nick stepped in and saved his ass from a local bookie. Mean fucking dude."

"Couldn't be much meaner than Leon." It made sense why he received preferential treatment at the club. "Nick's no dummy. He doesn't lay down cash without knowing he's going to get it back with some hard interest."

J.T. looked down again and tapped his fingers on the table.

"What was his collateral?"

He said nothing.

"I asked you a question."

J.T. hesitated. "Word was it was one of the girls at the club."

Andy glanced at Sarah. "Keep going."

"Not one of the dancers," he said. "One of the waitresses."

Sarah's hand flew up, and her nails caught J.T. on his right cheek. The other grabbed his neck.

"Crystal, you bastard," she said, shaking him. "It was her, right?"

Andy pulled her hands away. "Calm down."

"Am I right?" she shouted and tried to jerk free from his grip.

"Answer her."

J.T. sank back into the cushion. "Yeah, I think that's her name, but I wasn't involved."

"Don't stop now," Andy said.

"From the juice I heard, Nick wanted her, but she wouldn't give him the time of day. He worked something out with Leon who made it happen."

"That's bullshit," Sarah shouted.

"It's the truth. I heard she still wouldn't put out, which really pissed off Nick. Word was Leon took care of it somehow."

"Let's talk up on deck," Andy said and led Sarah by the arm into the fresh morning air. "Take it easy. What he's telling us is that she could still be alive."

"Get him to make the call. Use me as bait," she said. "I need to know one way or the other."

"There's no way I'm going to let you go under where I can't protect you."

"Andy, I'm tired of running." She grasped onto the railing and leaned against it. "This is the first time I'm able to do something. Maybe we'll get lucky and find Crissy and the other girls."

Seizing her by the shoulders, he spun her around. "Even if you get inside, they could break you. There's no telling how far these guys will go."

"I'm doing it. I'll get inside," she said. "You're not talking me out of this. I'm a hell of a lot tougher than I look. All you have to do is follow me, then call the cops."

"I'm not letting you risk your life with these bas-tards." He stepped back. "We'll find another way."

She grabbed his arm. "I'm doing this with or without your help."

Nothing about this felt right. Several months had passed since Crystal's disappearance. She could be any-where if she was still alive. Chances were they'd already moved her several times. What were the odds they'd even find her?

Andy's cell vibrated.

"Carlyle, what the hell do you want?" This guy had an uncanny knack for calling when things were in tur-moil.

"I've been trying to reach you," the man said. "We need to talk."

"Don't you remember? You fired my ass. Unless I hear something new, I'm hanging up in five seconds."

"Don't end play me."

"Five, four, three."

"Wait," Carlyle shouted. "Call me the minute you find her. I'll honor our original agreement."

Andy slammed the phone shut.

Two hours later, they idled into Rudee Inlet, then tied off in the berth. The place would be swarming with people by noon. The emptiness of the early morning hour served Andy well. With the exception of using the head, J.T. hadn't moved and remained sullen.

Andy slid in next to him. "If I find out you're lying to me about any of this, we're taking you back out and tying concrete blocks to your skinny-ass legs. Got it?" He grabbed a piece of paper and pen and set them down in front of him. "You're going to make the call, describe Sarah, and tell them she'll be at Raging Waters in front of Godzilla's queue line. Now write."

"No way, man. They'll kill me," J.T. said. "I told you everything."

Andy turned to Sprocket. "Your buddy, Mike. Think he'll help?"

"He's in if I ask. I'll call him."

They used most of the roll of duct tape on J.T.'s hands and legs, the last piece across his mouth.

Andy placed the SIG against the silver tape, then pushed. "You'll talk or swallow this barrel."

"Why don't we have Lil' Mike help persuade him when he gets here?" Sprocket said.

"Do it." Andy threw both packs over his shoulders and stepped onto the dock, then lumbered toward Sarah's SUV, totally exhausted.

"Going somewhere?" the clipped voice said.

He froze and knew he must have his piece aimed at him. "How'd you find me, Beyer?" Andy turned.

"Don't move," he ordered. "This time you're going to do what I say."

"You didn't answer my question," he said. "No one knew I was here."

"You disappoint me, Andy," Beyer said. "I thought you were smarter than that. You shouldn't have answered your cell."

Chapter 21

eyer's gun was pointed at Andy's head. Whatever information he and Carlyle thought he had could give Andy time to stall.

He dropped his arms. "You give me too much credit. I don't know any more about the girl than when I talked to Carlyle."

Beyer pointed with the gun's barrel toward the SUV. "Shut up and get in," he said. "We're going for a ride."

Behind Beyer, large tatted guns were raised and moving toward him. Lil' Mike.

"I said move." Beyer's hand tightened on the grip.

"Come on. You're not going to shoot me here." Lil' Mike was almost on top of him. "It's almost daylight. Lots of fishermen."

"You want to test that theory?" Beyer nudged the 9 mm toward him.

One of Mike's beefy paws sent the gun flying. The other knocked Beyer to the ground.

Andy pulled out his piece and stood over him. "Where did you say we were going?"

Lil' Mike stood with his arms crossed and feet spread. "Who's this dude?"

Sprocket appeared on deck and looked in their direction, then hobbled toward them. "Christ, what now?"

"This is the guy I was telling you about. Works for the old man," Andy said. "Any place we can keep him on ice for a while?"

"The maintenance building back there," he said, pointing.

Lil' Mike yanked him to his feet and twisted one of his arms behind his back.

"You don't want to piss this guy off, Beyer." He glared back at him. Andy grinned. "You and I keep getting into this same dance. You come after me, and I nail you."

"You son of a—" Beyer began. Lil' Mike shoved his arm upward.

The four of them walked past berths and metal buildings. Boat davits lined the dock. A blue, mobile boatlift with large tires was parked in front of a rollup door.

Sprocket unlocked the one marked "Entrance." He hit the light switch. The glossy, black and white checked floor caused Andy to blink.

After they bound and gagged Beyer, they wrapped a padded nylon strap around his upper torso. Another secured his knees.

Sprocket slipped the sewn loops over the hook on a hoist, then pressed "Up" on the remote control and sent Carlyle's goon toward the rafters.

"You guys go back to the boat," Andy said. "I'm going to throw the packs in the SUV."

When he opened the rear hatch, there it was. J.T.'s cell. He finally caught a break.

Rushing back to the boat, Andy went down into the galley and tossed the phone on the table. "I'll bet the number's programmed in there." J.T.'s eyes squeezed shut. Andy ripped the tape off his mouth. "What do you think?"

"Shit," he said, voice shaky.

Andy went to the stored numbers and scrolled. He must have used a code for the name. "I'm going to start with the first one and work my way down. When I get to the recording, I'll leave a message, saying that you've gone to the police."

"That'll never work," J.T. said. "They'll know it's not my voice."

"Is that something you're willing to bet on?" Andy chuckled. "After I make the call, I'm turning you lose. If they don't come after you, I guessed wrong and you're free." He picked up the cell and walked over to the galley counter. "But what if I'm right?"

He waited, then pressed the first number, and held it up for him to hear. Did the same with the next five.

"Okay." J.T. sounded like a beaten dog. "I'll do it."

৩৩৩

On the way to Raging Rapids, Sarah and Andy went over every scenario they could think of that had the potential of going wrong. She fit the exact description J.T. fed them in the message. Khaki shorts, sleeveless peach top, and wedged sandals.

They arrived at 11:30 a.m., thirty minutes before the park opened. Go-kart engines revved as employees moved them into position in five separate lines. Water surged down the fiberglass troughs of the coaster, sloshing over the sides into a recovery pool. The park was coming to life as it did seven days a week from May through September.

Andy parked at the rear of the lot where Sarah shifted some of her belongings into the backpack.

"There's a lot about you I don't know," she said. "Those years in the army. You're not telling everything."

He smiled, then glanced at the clock on the dash, and questioned his decision. "It's not too late. You don't have to do this."

"We've been over the plan a dozen times. Enough," she said, got out of the car, and closed the door. She reached through the window and touched his hand. "I've trusted you. Now, it's your turn to trust me. Believe me, we'll nail these bastards." She turned and walked across the blacktop until she blended into the crowd as they trickled through the gate.

Andy hung back in the car, waited until she was inside, and followed. Large groups of arriving school kids made it difficult to maneuver without losing sight of her. Damn it. Where'd she go?

He pushed through the crush of people and spotted her next to the queue line for Godzilla, the parks major attraction and largest vertical drop east of the Mississippi.

A woman approached Sarah. They spoke briefly, then both disappeared down the employees' walkway.

Andy hurried through the swell of people and followed the path to the maintenance area, where two men were loading PVC pipe on a cart.

"Did either of you see two women pass by here a minute ago?"

"Ain't seen no one," the man said. The red and white nametag on his blue shirt read, "Kip."

He shoved past them and ran toward the parking lot. There was no sign of her. How could he have been so stupid to let her do this? He scanned the area. Nothing.

An engine revved behind him. Smoke poured from the exhaust of a commercial van parked on the other side of the lot. He caught a glimpse of Sarah's peach top before the side door closed. Tires screeched. The silver vehicle sped across the asphalt, barely missing him.

Andy ran to the SUV, then tore out of the lot and headed in the same direction as the van. His heart raced as he floored the accelerator pedal, the dial on the dash moving clockwise. The vehicle hadn't turned down any of the side roads.

He was almost in Pungo, headed toward the North Carolina border when he spotted it. "Please, not now." His breathing eased after a state trooper passed in the opposite direction and kept going. With the back of his hand, he wiped sweat from his forehead.

They turned onto Route 603, then left on North Landing Road. Staying far enough behind, he jotted directional notes on a pad that rested on the seat next to him. When the van came to a junction at Route 165, it turned left and drove 5.2 miles onto Blackwater Road, then started to slow. The driver turned onto a dirt road and stopped. A man got out, opened a weathered wooden gate, then motioned the driver through. The property was fenced with posts and barbed wire like most farms in the area. Signs on posts read "Private Property. Keep Out."

He waited until the van disappeared down the road, under a cloud of trailing dust. His only choice was to enter on foot.

The cell vibrated.

"Are you okay, Andy?" Mia said.

"Could be better. Make it quick?"

"Why haven't you picked up my messages?" Her voice crackled. "I've been worried sick."

"Been busy. You calling about the girl's father?"

"No. We're still trying to track him down, but it's like he just disappeared," she said. "Something bad's happening."

"What do you mean?" he asked. How could it get any worse?

"Joey Conner canceled his order. So did Sammy Buhler."

Andy swallowed hard. Without those contracts, he'd go under. "Can't be. What did they say?"

"Just canceled. No explanation." She hesitated. "They also want their deposits back."

"That's not going to happen. They know that."

"What are we going to do?" Her voice sounded like she was about to cry.

"Leave me a message if anything else happens. I'm up to my ass in alligators."

"Wait," she said. "Losing those two contracts is pretty damn big."

"You don't understand. I don't have time now. I'll call you later." He clicked it closed. She deserved more of an explanation. Saving the business was important, but finding the girls topped it on his list of priorities.

Andy left Sarah's SUV parked on the opposite side of the road and walked about a tenth of a mile to the gate. The only way in was over the barbed wire. He pulled off his shirt and wrapped it around his arm, then carefully pushed back the wire. Jumping down on the other side, he tangled with metal in the underbrush that ripped into the flesh of his leg. "Damn it."

He stayed low and moved to the right of the road. Patches of scrawny pines offered some protection. The fallowed soybean field made the going rough. A cluster of healthy pines poked up about a quarter of a mile in from the road. Beyond that, was a row of Magnolias that lined both sides of the road leading to a circular driveway and the entrance to an imposing, tired mansion.

He crotched down and moved closer. Two men with rifles hung over their shoulders, and dressed in drab green T's and camo pants tucked into their boots, walked down the front steps and walked in his direction, then turned, their boots crunching against the gravel as they made their way toward the rear of the house.

Dropping to his stomach, he crawled with his elbows under the dead vines toward the peeling structure and listened. Their Spanish speaking voices faded.

There was enough cover for him to make his way around to the back. He scrambled through gnarled underbrush, trying to make as little noise as possible.

The ground gave way and sucked him down into an open culvert. Thank God it was dry. He lay there, feeling his way up the side, then shifted upright, and leaned against a large rock. All he could do was wait until nightfall.

Mudbugs swarmed him, hungry for his blood. God, he hoped that nothing that slithered inhabited the area. The humidity hung thick. He checked the Beretta and SIG to make sure they were clean. The sun burned red before it slipped behind the horizon. When darkness set in, a waxing moon cast more light than he wanted. Time had come to make his move.

Crawling out of the ditch, he stayed wide of the road and worked back toward the rear of the mansion. Cracks of light shone through shades on the upper floor, illuminating female silhouettes.

Parked next to an outer building were two motor homes, three pickups and the van.

Andy blinked several times trying to focus. Movement above caught his attention. A man on the main floor stood in front of a window, waving his hands. The shadow of what appeared to be a female, either short or sitting, was behind him. When he moved away, he saw it was Sarah.

He didn't have the firepower or an assault team to rush the place and couldn't do it alone. Worse yet, if they decided to transport the girls in the motor homes, he wouldn't be able to follow. His only choice was to do what Sarah had suggested, risk cutting a deal with Weaver, and deal with the tongue-lashing, but dreaded the thought of the detective going through with his promise to throw him in jail.

Chapter 22

S arah sat bound to a chair and looked around the enormous, empty room. How could such a large space make her feel so trapped? She began to second-guess whether she could pull this off. Fighting back panic, she knew she had to.

A thick-necked man approached and looked down at her, his eyes mean. He untied the rope, then ripped the tape from her mouth and wrists. He pushed her chin up hard with his hand. "Cooperate and things will go easy," he said. "How old are you?"

"Twenty," she lied.

His eyes swept over her body. Then he walked back to the table and picked up a cell phone.

Straining to listen, she only caught bits.

"She should work out—Okay, see you later." He returned, grabbed her arm, and squeezed.

"You're hurting me," she said, trying to pull away.

"Bitch." He spit through tobacco-stained teeth, then he turned and shouted, "Rita."

The woman who had kidnapped her came into the room with a needle in her hand.

"No," Sarah screamed and kicked him in the groin,

then shoved the chair back and ran toward the front door. Reaching for the knob, she felt a hand around her neck, snapping her backward. She fell, hitting her head hard against the planked floor. Pain erupted in her back and neck.

Her eyes blinked open to a throbbing head. How long had she been out? A different room came into focus, a cold, Spartan one.

She couldn't tell how many girls were in this rat infested basement, but each of their faces showed the dread these beasts had created. Any survival instincts they may have had were gone.

Someone touched her. She jumped. "Are you okay?" a female with an accent asked.

She turned her head and saw a young Hispanic girl. "Where am I?"

"They brought you down here about an hour ago," she said. "You were really out of it."

Sarah rubbed the back of her head then slowly sat upright. The room spun. "What did they do to me?"

"You were given what we all get. GHB," she said. "Maybe something else, too."

Sarah shook her head, stood with the girl's help, and looked around at the young faces. Fear and panic stared back. Her gut instinct told her to run. But where? She fell onto the bunk.

Another girl stepped forward and helped her. "Are you okay?"

"I think so," she said.

"I'm Emily."

Tori pushed her aside. "Is this some kind of fucking game?" she said. "That shit ain't that strong."

"What's the problem?" Rita said from behind.

"There isn't one," Tori said.

"Sit your ass down over there and shut up," Rita said then turned toward Sarah. "Let's go."

Sarah stood, reached for the woman's hand, then steadied herself with the railing as she ghost-walked up the steps.

On the other side of the room was a blurred image of a man pacing with one hand to his ear. His voice barreled through the fog. "Two drivers will have the packages there on schedule." He turned toward her. "It's time for your orientation."

❧

The conversation with Weaver went exactly as Andy had expected. Not well, and he hadn't told him everything yet. He needed to be fed the information slowly until Andy confirmed that Tori and Emily were in the house with Sarah.

A lone set of headlights approached, then the vehicle slowed, made a U-turn, and pulled in behind him. His passenger door opened.

"You sorry-ass, son-of-a-bitch," Weaver said and plopped down beside him. "I told you what would happen if you pulled shit like this."

"Don't threaten me," Andy said. "You know what I have to do. Either you're in or out."

Weaver stared hard, unflinching, then reached inside his jacket. "Here." He handed him a mini headset. "Keep me filled in on everything you see. Everything. Is that clear?"

Andy nodded and reached out. "The binoculars."

Weaver handed him a monocular style scope. "Night vision. Press the button on the side to activate it."

Andy fit the piece into his ear, got out, and did a com-check, then turned on the scope.

"Be careful. I don't want to have to explain this to the higher up," Weaver said. "If something goes wrong, you're on your own. Is that clear?"

"Got it." Despite the disclaimers, for the first time Andy felt Weaver might be on his side.

He retraced his steps back to the house and focused on the guards manning the front porch, their feet propped on the railing. He depressed the button and held the scope to his eyes. Automatic rifles lay across their laps. A dim light illuminated part of the first floor. Unfortunately, the angle to the upper floors limited his vision.

"Two guards like before," he whispered. "Looks like everyone is asleep."

"Daylight's around the corner. Make damn sure you've got good cover."

"Tell me something I don't know." Andy moved toward the rear and positioned himself behind the clump of bushes.

Men spoke in Spanish, interrupting the quiet. Their voices grew louder. The guards who'd been asleep rounded the corner, then made their way toward what looked like a garage or workshop. Tools, settling tanks, and scrap iron cluttered the area around it. Three rusted remnants of pickups with weeds growing through openings were scattered in the field behind.

"We've got movement," he whispered. "The guards in front are back by a shed doing something. Not sure what though."

Weaver acknowledged. Ten minutes later, Andy's earpiece crackled.

"Some kind of carnival contraption just pulled up at the front gate," Weaver said. "The driver's opening it now. He should be coming your way shortly."

The diesel engine grew louder with the groaning sound of metal against metal.

"What the hell's going on? A ride?"

"Talk to me, Andy. Whadda you see?"

"Hold on." The scope followed steady movements inside. A male passed by the farthest window to the left on the first floor. Several females moved in the basement. He recognized one. "Just spotted Sarah again," he whispered. "Wait, Tori's there, too."

"What about the other girl?" Weaver asked. "Do you see her?"

Andy scanned the other three windows, then moved back to the basement. "Can't tell for sure, but I think it's her."

The ride trailer eased toward the shed, an older model Hrubetz Paratrooper, tired iron often dumped south of the border.

"Stay where you are and relay everything they're doing. We need to buy time while we wait for SWAT and the warrants," Weaver said. "I'll make the calls now."

Weight on Andy's shoulders seemed to lift, and his breathing eased. The girls would soon be rescued, and the animals behind this sub-human operation would get what they deserved.

When the sun climbed above the horizon, the risk of exposure increased. What the hell was taking so long? His legs began to cramp in the small patch of underbrush.

"A pickup is headed your way," Weaver said.

Moments later, it pulled in front of the Paratrooper, and tall man dressed in jeans, tan shirt, and a short, leather welder's vest got out. He appeared pissed. Another short Hispanic man exited through the back door and walked toward him. The discussion became heated. They screamed at each other in Spanish, then the taller one stormed over to the ride and yanked open the doors to the possum belly. He vented his anger on the sections of railing and light-bars he tossed on the ground.

"Something's not right," Andy said. "Have you heard anything?"

"Hold on."

"Hold on for what? Tell me what's going on." Andy waited.

"We have a problem. You're going to have to stay where you are until dark."

"What are you talking about? Why not raid the damn place now and get them out?"

"It's bigger than that. You're not going to like it, but ICE and the FBI have a task force assigned to this. I have strict orders to stay out of it."

"Bullshit." He'd come this far and wasn't about to stop.

"I don't like the Feds' involvement any more than you, but it's out of our hands," Weaver said.

"Maybe yours but not mine."

⌘⌘⌘

Sarah adjusted the water temperature, turning it up as hot as she could stand. Her fingers touched the swollen lower lip where she'd bitten down. The hot shower and soap hadn't erased his lingering scent. He'd taken something from her and left her with this sickening ache inside.

"Make the smell go away," she said quietly and scrubbed even harder.

Later, she lay exhausted on her bunk, her back to the room. How long had they been locked up in this rat-infested basement? A hand touched her shoulder.

"I didn't mean to upset you last night," Emily said. "That bastard raped you, didn't he?"

Sarah felt tears burn against her cheeks.

Tori joined them. "Those fuckers," she said. "Those

monsters did it to me, too. That's their initiation. Who the hell knows what's going to happen next?"

Sarah turned toward her then looked back at Emily. "We have to stay calm and figure a way out of here."

"You've seen this place," Emily said. "There's frigging guards everywhere. They'll kill us."

"Got that right," Pilar said then faced the others. "Hear that? The bitch is leaving. Maybe we all should pack now so we can walk out together."

Sarah wanted to slap her and shake some sense into her. "That chip on your shoulder isn't going to help."

Pilar grabbed her arm. "And you gonna knock it off?"

Tori pushed her away then stood defiantly. "Touch her again and you're fucking dead."

Emily stepped between them. "Come on. One of us gets out of line, and we'll all pay."

Pilar stood there for a moment then walked away.

Emily sat next to Sarah. "You're serious, aren't you? You really think we can get out of here?"

"I know we can," Sarah said. "But you're going to have to trust me."

Chapter 23

If the Feds knew about the operation, why weren't they here? Asking Weaver to back off presented a problem, but Andy would work around them. He had the entire day to come up with a game plan.

What were they doing? Another man joined the first and helped torch racks out of the Paratrooper's possum belly.

"None of this makes sense," Andy whispered into the mic.

"What are you talking about?"

"They're modifying the ride's belly."

"This is your call. You know a lot more about those things than I do," Weaver said.

By the time the sun hung above him, the reason for the retrofit became clear. Thick, foam padding glued on all surfaces made the perfect compartment for moving the females, but the trailer's suspension was too stiff to expect anyone to travel inside the possum belly for any significant distance and survive.

The men laid furniture pads over the foam on the bottom, then threw their tools on the ground.

Andy caught only glimpses of people moving inside

the house. God, he hoped Sarah would be able to handle the situation.

Though the day dragged on, the plan never materialized. *Mamig* had told him stories about her family crawling in the bushes and hiding from the Turks, their destiny unclear. He wondered if they had felt as scared as he did now.

When night fell, Andy followed the path back to the road, then headed south a quarter of a mile to where Weaver was parked.

Weaver threw open the passenger door. "Get in."

"We've got to get those girls out of there," Andy said. "Sarah's there because of me. I can't just abandon her."

Weaver sat quietly and passed him a bottle of water. "I'm afraid I have some bad news."

"I thought you already dropped everything on me." Andy polished off the water. "Shoot."

"Stephen Beyer filed assault charges against you," he said. "He claims you brandished a weapon."

"What? He couldn't have."

"Well, he did. Filed them yesterday. I just got the information a little while ago."

"Those are bullshit charges," Andy said. "He's the one who pulled his gun on me. It just happened that I got the upper hand."

"It doesn't matter," Weaver said. "I have to take you in and book you. It shouldn't take long. Post bail, and you're out in a couple of hours."

Heat surged to Andy's face. He couldn't chance leaving and find out later that they'd moved the girls. "I know the drill, but I have other things to do." The SIG found its way into Weaver's side.

"Don't be stupid, Andy."

"Shut up." Andy grabbed the detective's weapon. "Any throw-down?"

"You're making a mistake," Weaver said. "Put the gun away, and this never happened."

"Pull up your pant legs. Now." He was clean. "Open your door and get out."

His fiery gaze held Andy's as he slipped off the seat onto the pavement. "It's not too late."

"Your cell," he said. "Keep the com set. You can take me in after I get them out."

"Think about it. There's no way you're going to pull this off." Weaver paused. "I'll cut you some slack, but you're going to have to compromise, too."

He was right. Even with Sprocket and Lil' Mike, it would be a tough go. "Talk," he said.

"I'll give you twenty-four hours."

Andy moved closer. "Like I said, those are trumped up charges. Beyer's an ex trooper."

"That doesn't matter. He still filed the charges. Besides, you can't rush the place alone," Weaver said. "You need me and a lot more."

He was coming back around.

"That ride came from somewhere. A show. An independent operator." Andy handed Weaver his piece. "I'll get back inside and give you a plate number. Run it, and ten to one, it'll lead back to Pappas."

"That in of itself doesn't connect him directly to the girls. We need more."

So much was missing. There had to be a common thread to all the players. "All this started when I was hired to look for Emily."

"That's a bunch of crap," Weaver said. "This is human trafficking, Zartanian. Porn, brothels, and international sales. The missing girl is a gnat in this operation."

"If the Feds are in on this, where in the hell are they? It doesn't make sense."

"The bastards are tightlipped," Weaver said and slapped the fender. "I'm as frustrated as you are. All they said was to stay away, and that they have a confidential informant in place."

Weaver's willingness to step outside the law and his opinion of the Feds surprised Andy. "The way those guys were working on the retrofit can only mean they're going to do something soon."

"I'm calling in my partner. We need more men," Weaver said. "If you're right, we have to be able to stay with them."

Andy had to talk to Sprocket. "I'm going back to my vehicle and check for messages, then I'm heading back inside."

"Don't cross me again. You know I don't like surprises," Weaver said. "All my chips are riding on you."

Andy punched in the numbers.

"Where in the hell have you been? I've left four messages," Sprocket said. "Beyer got away. The guy must be a fucking Houdini."

"How in the hell did he do that?"

"He must have had something sharp hidden," he said. "The way the strap was frayed, he cut through it a thread at a time."

"Damn it, did J.T. get away too?"

"No. He's with Mike. Kid ain't going nowhere."

The last thing he needed was for Beyer to be back in the mix. "I found the house where they're keeping the girls. It's an old place on Blackwater Road."

"About four or five miles off of 165?" Sprocket asked.

His comment caught Andy off guard. "Yeah. How'd you know?"

"Old soybean farm. The Garnet property. Used to ride bikes out there," he said. "Got some surprises on that land."

"I know. Found my way into a culvert. Is there any other road into the place other than the gate on Blackwater?"

"Yeah, but it's a dirt road riddled with potholes that could hide a new Fat Boy," he said. "So what do you want me to do with the punk?"

"Make damn sure he doesn't get away. Can you meet me out here later?"

"When?"

"I'll call and let you know when and where."

Andy retraced his steps to the pines. One of the motor homes had been moved to the front of the house. A guard leaned against it, smoking a cigarette. Andy waited until the man took his last drag and walked back into the house then made his way around the side of the mansion to the same spot behind the house. The possum belly doors were latched open and bore an eerie resemblance to the inside of a coffin.

The mangled license plate made reading it difficult. He called in the numbers to Weaver. "The last is either a three or an eight."

"I'll run it and get back to you."

Screams came from inside the house. Andy couldn't wait. He had to go in. His earpiece clicked.

"A white, Dodge pickup is headed your way."

"Damn it." Andy dropped back down and pointed the SIG toward the road.

Fifteen minutes later men's voices shouted in a mixture of Spanish and English. Loud shrills followed, then a bone-chilling quiet. Within moments, two men dragged a body down the steps and across the dirt to the shed. They propped him up against the building. Blood oozed out of the corners of his mouth, then his head flopped forward. Their message was clear.

"*Bastardo estupido*," the bearded guard said.

ͼ∋ͼͽ

The burning grew deep inside his gut as the large man drove manically down the road. How in the hell had he slipped past him? Time had come to take care of business. The motor home parked in front of the house had its interior lights on with one of his men inside washing the windshield.

Even though it was late, the interior of the house buzzed with activity.

"Angel," he shouted as he stepped inside the entry.

"Be right there, *jefé*," Angel said, then entered from the hallway. "Didn't expect to see you." He appeared nervous.

"I wanted to make sure everything was ready."

"The Paratrooper will leave two hours before the motor home. Just like you ordered."

He walked past him and down the hall then turned back. "So everything's okay?" he said. "No problems, right?"

Angel shifted. "Possum belly's ready. You saw the coach out front?"

"And the girls?" He walked up to Angel. "They'll be ready on time?"

"*Jefé*, what's wrong?" Angel said. "I told you they would."

He grabbed Angel by the neck and drove him back into the wall, forcing the air out of him, then whipped the switchblade out of his pocket, and snapped it open.

Angel's face was flushed, eyes bulged, and his protests choked.

"You fucking bastard," he said and moved the blade in a slow circular motion. "Not only did you touch the blonde, you leaked the operation to the Feds." He loosened his grip and pressed the steel point just below his Adams apple.

"No," Angel said, voice hoarse. "You're wrong, *jefé*. Believe me. Please."

"I'm rarely wrong. Especially this time." He pushed harder and drew blood. "One of them is on our payroll. Said the C. I.'s name is Angel." He toyed with his jugular, then shoved hard. When he pulled it out, blood squirted onto his shirt. He jammed the cold steel into Angel's stomach and jerked upward.

His mouth gaped open as he slid to the floor, back against the wall.

"Come and get this piece of shit out of here," he ordered, then bent over and wiped the blade on Angel's shirt.

With the operation compromised, he had to act quickly and couldn't risk losing everything. The females housed inside had to be moved to a new location.

He jabbed in the numbers. "Get your ass down here now. You're taking a quick trip across the border. Bring one of the guys with you." He slammed the cell closed, then walked out onto the front porch where two of his guards leaned against the dilapidated wood siding.

"Moreno, take the ATV out the back way and check the road," he ordered. "I need to know if the coach can handle it. Alonzo, get the rest of the men and form a perimeter around this place."

"What's going on?" Alonzo asked.

"Just do it." He slapped him on the back of his head with one hand and held the blade up with the other. "Now."

Rita stepped onto the porch with a thin robe overlapped in front. "Boss, why all the commotion?"

He liked her. She had a knack for transforming the girls, knowing when to come down hard and when to back off.

"We can't take any more chances," he said. "When the Feds don't hear from him, they'll know something's up and come down on us."

"Let's get out of here before they get here," she said. "The hell with the girls."

"Have you lost your fucking mind? That's several hundred grand," he said. "And the blonde is the key to a never-ending fountain of gold."

Chapter 24

Emily lay curled up in her bunk, blanket wrapped tightly around her. The darkness offered relief and helped her hide from the sights and sounds that brought her to this hellhole. She didn't believe Sarah when she said someone was going to help them escape. No one ever tried before.

The men in this house were dirty and smelled unlike those in the modern one. But both wanted the same.

Upstairs, garbled voices wafted in and out. Loud noises caused her to pull the blankets tighter. Her mind let her body float away. Then basement lights flooded the room.

"Everyone up," Rita shouted. "Get your clothes on. We're leaving now."

She tried to pull herself up but couldn't. Rita ripped the blanket off, then yanked her out of bed. "I said, now."

Emily started to say something, when Rita shoved her.

"Keep your mouth shut and get dressed."

Some of the girls started to cry. Others still dazed followed her orders.

"Rita, get them moving," a man shouted from upstairs.

Emily dressed, then made her way to the steps, and held onto the railing. A hand touched her shoulder.

"Do what they say," Sarah said.

Once the girls were gathered in the great room, Rita took a headcount. "They're all here."

He stood next to the door. "We don't have much time. Get them out now," he said. "The motor home's in front. I'll handle the rest."

Rita and one guard herded the girls toward the front door.

Emily was the last to leave when he jerked her by the arm. She gasped and looked up.

"Not you," he said. "You're coming with me."

⌘⌘⌘

Lack of sleep weighed heavily on Andy. Somehow, he had to keep his eyes open and not lose sight of the girls. This would all be over if it weren't for the Feds. Nothing had changed. He still needed to figure a way around them and not get bogged down in their bureaucracy.

Lights came on inside the house. People shouted as they moved past windows. A man ran down the back steps and jumped on an ATV, then tore across a field. Andy lifted the scope. It had to be the road Sprocket mentioned.

"A car is headed your way," Weaver said. "Black Mercedes. Looks like two men inside."

The odds stacked against him were mounting. "Did you get a make on the plate number?"

"Yeah, ID just came back. Ride's owned by Sanchez Shows."

"That guy's a mean bastard. Plays mostly border towns. His stuff's so bad, he can't operate in the U.S." The car pulled up in front, out of his visual range. "Is your partner on the way?"

"He's here now."

The man who'd delivered the Paratrooper left the house and walked toward the trailer, then closed and latched the doors to the possum belly. He climbed inside the cab and started the engine, then revved it to a high pitch.

"Looks like they're getting ready to move the ride," Andy whispered. "Driver's in the cab."

Moments later, the rig pulled around to the front of the house, lights heading down the road toward the gate.

"He's coming your way."

"I'll have Miller tail him," Weaver said.

Andy called Sprocket. "I need you at the rear entrance to the property now."

"You got it, man."

"If they send a vehicle in that direction, follow it," Andy said. "The main entrance is covered."

In front of the house, a diesel whined then kicked over.

He had to risk it and ran wide of the house, staying as low as possible. A dying magnolia tree offered some protection and good visibility. He hugged the ground behind it and kept his SIG pointed toward the front porch.

Female screams mixed with men shouting orders. Voices grew louder, then they were drowned out by the sound of the revving diesel.

One guard stood to the side of the motor home with his AK47 held close to his chest. Another in front mirrored his posture.

The door flew open. Females scantly dressed emptied onto the porch and were shoved down the steps toward the coach. The guard motioned with his rifle and shouted orders. Tori was the fourth to leave. Two more, then Sarah. An older woman with a canvas bag and AK-47 slung over her shoulder herded four more onboard, followed by another guard. The door slammed shut, and the vehicle lurched forward.

"The girls are in the coach and heading your way. The Mercedes is following. Keep them in sight until I work my way out."

"Copy that. I see the headlights," Weaver said. "Call me once you're in your car, and I'll give you my position."

Andy had spotted Tori and Sarah but not Emily. Either he'd missed her or she was still in the house. There wasn't time to second-guess himself.

The sound of a door slamming stopped him cold. Two men with their hands tucked under a girl's armpits dragged her to a white Dodge. He couldn't be certain, but it had to be Emily. Why had they culled her out of the group? The engine raced, then the truck tore around the side and out the back road.

As he rushed back toward the house, he heard an explosion and hit the ground. A fireball shot out the front windows and door. He crawled behind the Magnolia. The engine on the second motor home raced, then the vehicle jerked forward and followed the pickup.

Andy jabbed in Sprocket's number. "Stay on that white dually. He's got Emily."

A second explosion blew off the front part of the roof and sent flaming pieces of wood showering in all directions. The house went up like a tinderbox.

Panicked, he scrambled to his feet, ran until he reached the road, and jumped the fence.

His earpiece crackled. "Looks like the ride and motor home are headed in the same direction," Weaver said.

"Miller just crossed into North Carolina. He'll stay with them until the Feds take over."

"Thought they were already on it?"

"I did too. Looks like the only person they had in the area was their C.I."

"Shit. That must have been the guy they killed," Andy said. "Are you telling me that Miller's the only one tailing them?"

"It appears that way." Weaver paused. "Looks like the Feds really messed up."

"I hope the hell he stays with the coach. I'm going after Emily."

Chapter 25

Even though the night air inside was warm and stale, Sarah shivered as she fought to clear her head. She lost track of time, her mind fuzzy. Was it the third injection or more since they had left? She struggled to remember the events since being awakened in the middle of the night, then herded into a motor home.

Frightened, she leaned her head against the window and squeezed the cushion's edge. She could only see outlines of the other girls crowded into the small space around her. Someone slid in beside her and touched her hand.

"What do you think they did with Emily?" Tori's words sounded like a tape played at warped speed.

"I don't know," Sarah said, fighting to get the words out.

"Shut up." Rita came from the front, and Sarah felt the sting of her hand across the face. "You don't want to know what it's like to be thrown from this coach at 70 mph."

Sarah's lips moved, but no words came out. Then her head flopped back against the seat.

She didn't know how long she'd been out when her

eyes opened again, the sun glaring against the window. She stared out and tried to remember being free. The moment was fleeting and gave into the hopelessness. Tori sat curled up beside her. The other girls remained scattered and motionless in a drug-induced sleep.

The vehicle slowed then turned off the road. She strained to hear the conversation between the driver and one of the guards. When the coach stopped, the driver opened the door. An all-too-familiar voice shouted from outside. She felt a wave of panic and struggled to catch her breath. Her worse fear materialized. Leon stepped into the aisle.

୧୨୧୨

Andy ran down the dirt road focused on one thing, Emily. Once in the car, the needle on his speedometer hung steady at ninety-five. Based on landmarks Sprocket had relayed, he was gaining on him. This mess would soon be over.

He tapped the mic. Weaver was out of range. Andy called him on the cell and was told that he'd made some calls, then hooked up with a friend from ICE, and they along with the FBI, had caught up with Miller. There were five units tailing the RV and Mercedes. After hanging up, Andy prayed that Sarah was all right."

The lime-green Ford appeared on the steamy asphalt an eighth of a mile ahead. Andy pressed the pedal to the floorboard and pulled alongside. He shot Sprocket a thumbs-up as he passed.

The white dually slowed, exited the highway, and turned down a frontage road.

Andy punched in Sprocket's number. "Drop back. He'll make you with that paint job."

Sprocket's truck faded in the rearview mirror until it was a speck on the sunrise.

They were somewhere outside of Williamsburg when the truck pulled into a tired industrial complex, then stopped in front of the last rollup door on the right. The chipped, blue stucco hadn't been painted in years, and most of the faded signs were impossible to read through the graffiti.

Andy backed the SUV into a parking spot at the opposite end next to a dumpster, then relayed his location to Sprocket and told him to lose the truck.

❧❧❧

The passenger door opened. A sawed-off 12-gauge landed on the seat next to him, followed by his bearded friend.

Andy pointed. "They're down there."

Noise from a rumbling engine grew louder, then the RV drove past and positioned itself, ready to back in. The metal door rolled up, and the large vehicle disappeared inside.

The way the dually was parked blocked Andy's vision of the building's front door.

"Why don't we call the cops?" Sprocket said.

"We will once I get Emily out of there. Then I'm cramming this mess down Carlyle's throat."

The front doors of the car flew open. A hand grabbed his neck and threw him headfirst onto the pavement. He stared down the business end of what looked like a cannon.

"Who the fuck are you?" the man asked in broken English.

On the opposite side of the undercarriage, Sprocket lay in the same position.

The man moved to one knee next to him. "Talk asshole."

A fatal mistake. Andy grabbed the barrel, pulled the man over his head, and fired under the car.

The bottom of a sole hit Andy on the shoulder and threw him backward. The man fell on top of him and tried to jerk the gun away. They struggled, rolling on the ground. The weapon discharged. The man cried out then went limp.

Andy rushed to the other side. Sprocket grabbed on to the SUV and pulled himself to his feet.

The other guy lay on the ground, holding his leg. "*Cabron*," he shouted. "I'll kill you."

Shots erupted from the warehouse. Bullets pinged off the SUV's hood and building.

"Let's get out of here," Andy yelled, slipped into the passenger side, and crawled over the console. Sprocket climbed in and slammed the door closed. The engine raced, and the tires screeched.

Andy cranked the wheel to the left and punched it. "You okay?" he asked.

"Yeah. Thought they had us until you took that guy's legs out."

Andy jammed to the right, drove around the block, and pulled behind a building that offered a clear view of the street. "We'll wait here, then tail them when they leave. With all that gunfire, the cops will drop in here like flies on shit. Those goons aren't going to hang around and wait for them."

Within seconds, the dually flew past. "Looks like three or so occupants. We'll stay back where they won't spot us."

"My truck's around the block."

"No time to switch vehicles. We'll lose them if we do."

Fifteen minutes later, Andy was in familiar territory. Even though he didn't know Williamsburg that well, he knew the area where the Mega Drop Tower peeked over a building. The dually pulled into the back lot then parked behind a group of trailers.

"It looks like somebody with Joey's show is connected," Andy said.

"That's hard to believe. Seems like Harley would have said something."

"Maybe he did, but not to you, and that's why he's dead."

Joey had to be involved. The man Andy thought was his friend just became the enemy. That bastard had checked his reaction to Emily's photos, and he'd missed it. If he was protecting Nick, he'd go down with him. The truck had to be somewhere on the grounds.

Sprocket circled to the rear of the lot while Andy scoped out the living quarters, the obvious place to begin searching for Emily.

Turning to go back down the midway, he spotted Joey heading in his direction. Even though business was slower than usual, enough people milled around to allow Andy to sidestep behind a grab joint without being seen. He needed more time before he confronted him.

"Are you just going to stand there or order something?" the rousty asked.

Andy ignored her, kept his eyes on Joey, then moved back. Joey stood in front of the Yo Yo as riders' feet touched the ground. He waved his arms and screamed at the ride jocks then moved on with a hurried pace past the burger joint and Hoopla to the Starship. He grabbed the operator by the upper arm and pulled him until they were face to face.

After shouting at him, he let go, then he disappeared around the Wild Mouse. From what Andy remembered, it was where some of the upper scale motor homes were parked.

"Hey, mister, you deaf?" the girl asked.

Andy looked back at her then walked away.

The steel X-bracing provided minimal cover while he scanned the rear lot. Two small children kicked a soccer ball back and forth. A very pregnant woman sat on the metal step of a Jayco fifth wheel. She appeared borderline legal, a possum belly queen who had moved up in stature.

When he approached, she looked up. "You looking for someone, mister?"

"No. I've been thinking about hooking up with the show and wanted to see where the help bunked."

"Really, Andy?" He knew Joey's voice. "Nick told me you'd changed your appearance. He was right. You look like shit, even from behind."

Andy turned.

"Man, you really pissed him off. Said he's going to cut your nuts off the next time he sees you."

"I doubt that's going to happen."

"He's one tough dude. I'd stay away for a while," Joey said. "Let's go down to the office and you tell me what the hell's going on."

Andy stiffened. If Joey was in on this, Andy's odds were better outside. "We can talk here."

"Too many ears." Joey pointed. "Down there."

Andy walked toward the trailer with Joey next to him. His gut feeling told him to be careful. Andy knew firsthand how Joey dealt with tough guys. The old-fashioned way, and he'd always come out on top. The 9 mm tucked under his right arm gave him an edge, but since Nick had told Joey he'd changed his looks, Nick had probably let him know Andy was also carrying.

Joey pressed numbers on the security pad. "After you."

The .357 magnum wasn't in sight. Neither were the bundles of bills. Joey liked clutter, chaos. Andy's palms started to sweat.

"Have a seat," Joey said as he moved around to the other side of the desk.

"You're no clean-freak. Why the sudden change?"

"Tidying up. Tearing down tonight." That wasn't what J.T had told him. "So why the disguise?"

"Like I told you, I'm still looking for that guy's granddaughter. Have you seen her since we last talked?"

"I already told you I hadn't. Still haven't." Joey shifted behind in the leather chair. "Why's she so important? Another missing girl. So what? There's thousands with fucked-up lives who run away from home every year."

"I sure had you pegged wrong." Andy moved his hand closer to the piece. "She's somewhere on the lot. I saw her in a pickup. Who drives that white dually?"

"I told you she ain't here. You doubting my word?"

"I'm not sure yet. Is Nick involved?"

Joey leaned back, reached into his shirt pocket, then pulled out a cigar. "Involved in what?"

"Don't bullshit me," Andy said. "The operation out on Blackwater Road. Are you covering for him?"

Joey's jaw tightened. "You're way out of line. I don't cover for anyone. And I sure as shit don't know anything about whatever road you just said."

"The girl's here."

The .357 rose in his right hand from behind the desk. "Touch your piece and you're dead." Joey stood and stepped back. "You dumb-ass Armenian, I gave you every opportunity to back off. But no, you kept sticking that nose of yours in where it didn't belong."

"I never thought you'd stoop this low," Andy said.

"Shut the fuck up and slip out the steel. Nice and easy." Joey rapped the desk twice with his knuckles. The bowling ball head with the razor-trimmed beard came out of the back room. "Sinbad," Joey said. "He's all yours."

Chapter 26

The trailer door slammed shut then latched.

Andy kneeled in the cage made out of rebar that was positioned in the center of a trailer filled with plastic bags of plush. He grabbed bars with both hands and yelled. The muffled sounds stuck in the air. God, he hated small spaces. Darkness closed in like a trap. Focus. Keep your mind moving. A small motor whined, sucking humid air inside. He had to get out now.

"Breathe slowly." He counted, inhaled and exhaled. He repeated the process until he calmed down. It had been years since the tunnel rat syndrome had come back to haunt him. How in the hell had he gotten himself back in this dark hole?

Soaked in perspiration, he ran his hands over the bars and latch, then tugged on the lock. Measuring with his hands, the cage was approximately three by five feet and three to four feet high. He wanted to kick himself for telling Sprocket to wait for him back at the SUV.

Andy sat with his knees to his chest and dried his palms on his jeans. "Shit," he said. Sinbad's rush to lock him in here had worked on his behalf. He'd taken the SIG but not the Beretta.

Random thoughts occupied his mind. Where had they hidden Emily? How deep was Joey into this? And why was he so interested in Carlyle's granddaughter? What was Nick's role? He had to make the connections.

A tapping sound startled him. Three more came from under the trailer. He reached between the bars, pushed the plastic bag aside, then knocked on the floor. The screechy sound of metal against metal resonated.

"Z, can you hear me?" Sprocket whispered.

"Yeah."

"When you see the seam separate, grab and pull."

"It's pitch black. Can't see crap, and there's bars all around me with a padlock on the door."

"There's a big-ass lock on the outside, too. If I blast it, the whole damn trailer could go up in flames."

"We'll do it your way." Andy followed the sound with his fingers and felt movement. "Got it." He yanked. The jagged edge tore into his finger. "Damn." It burned like a raw paper cut.

"Hang in there," Sprocket said, his voice barely audible.

Andy ripped the plastic and pulled out a stuffed animal, then used it to grip the steel. It gave but not enough.

"Jerk on the son-of-a-bitch," Sprocket said.

"I'm trying." The metal moved enough for Sprocket's arm to fit through. "There's no way for me to get out of this cage and down through the floor."

His hand disappeared. "Take this." The 12 gauge came through. "When they come to get you, blast the bastards, then the lock," he said. "I'll be close by."

Andy grabbed it. "Take my Beretta."

"Don't need it. Have my own piece," he said. "It's 2:00 a.m. If they're going to move you, I'm betting it'll be before daylight."

"Got it." Andy reached out and pulled several stuffed

animals through the bars, then piled them up at the rear of the cage. He leaned back with the shotgun on his lap and waited.

It couldn't have been more than an hour when something clicked, and the steel lever that latched the trailer's doors squeaked. Shafts of light filtered between the plastic bags.

Andy raised the 12-gauge and steadied himself with his finger on the trigger. His heart pounded. He took in a deep breath as bags on the top fell away and exposed Sinbad's shinny head. Pulling the trigger was easy. A blast of pellets exploded into Sinbad's chest. His scream of pain was brief. He fell backward and rolled out of the trailer onto the ground. Andy racked the gun and fired at the lock, then kicked the cage door open.

With his back to the aluminum siding, he looked down at Sinbad gasping for air, then jumped to the ground.

"Over here," Sprocket yelled.

Andy reached down, pulled his SIG out of Sinbad's waistband, and tucked it into his. He pumped the shotgun, fired point-blank, and ran. The ping of a bullet hit the trailer next to him. Three more rounds followed.

Sprocket fired two shots. "Back here."

A Connor tractor gave them temporary cover unless Joey's men were flanking them.

"Jesus, man," Andy said. "I never thought it would go down this way."

"You got us in one hell of a bind."

They covered each other while they worked their way toward the side of the lot and back onto the midway. It wouldn't be long before cops swarmed the place. If they made it out the front entrance, Joey and his men wouldn't be stupid enough to follow. Lights in trailers, campers, and RV's came on like midway chasers. Several doors flew open.

"Everyone, back inside," Joey yelled.

As Andy ran past a wooden shed, a bullet whistled by his head and splintered its side.

Sprocket handed him a half dozen shotgun shells. "Looks like two, maybe three guys are firing."

"Can you make it on that bad leg?"

"Keep up with you any day."

They ran around the carousel and ducked behind a flat joint.

"One ride at a time, and we're out of here," Andy said. "The Hurricane's next."

They dodged seven or eight more rounds. The last one creased Andy's shoulder. "Shit." He grabbed it.

"You okay?" Sprocket asked.

"Yeah, only a graze. Stings like hell."

As the two ran along the back of the rides, they were peppered with a barrage of bullets. Sirens screamed in the distance, then closed in with a swirl of flashing lights.

"Let's get the hell out of here," Andy said. "It's his word against ours. He's probably greased the palms of half of the cops in town."

They slipped under the cyclone fence in back of the grab joint before the police cordoned off the lot. Sarah's Pathfinder was still parked behind the brick building where he'd left it.

"They'll be looking for this SUV," Andy said. "We need new wheels, but mine's parked at the Marriott in Richmond."

"The Ford's closer."

"No way. Besides, I have to get ammo." He had to think of something fast. Did driving to Richmond make sense?

Why was Emily separated from the others? Now it

made sense. It had to have been Joey who grabbed her.

Andy hung a quick right then left and pulled into a parking lot down the block.

"What the hell are you doing?"

"Where's the last place they'll look for us?" he said.

"You tell me."

"Back at the lot. Give me your cell."

He dialed Weaver and learned that the girls had been loaded into the possum belly and were headed toward a bridge that crossed into Nuevo Progreso, Mexico. The Feds wanted to take down the entire operation. His assurance they were on top of it didn't make Andy feel any better. They had certainly fucked up at Waco.

Andy turned to Sprocket. "I'd understand if you want out."

Sprocket shook his head. "If I had any common sense, I'd take you up on the offer. Let's cut the bullshit and get on with this."

Police still swarmed the lot, which meant that Joey wouldn't dare move her until they left. Andy drove Sprocket back to his truck.

"Wait for me behind that building," Andy said. "Keep your eyes open until I get back."

"You're serious about going to Richmond, aren't you?"

"We can't do anything until the cops clear out, and they'll be here for hours," Andy said. "I'll be back before they leave."

Once he got on I-64, he floored it and kept his eye on the Cobra sitting on Sarah's dash. If there were troopers looking for speeders, the unit would warn him.

When Andy pulled into the garage, he spotted a security guard walking down the far aisle where the Mustang was parked. Andy slowed until the guard disappeared into the building, then he pulled in next to the rental. Getting out, he popped the trunk, and stuffed the remaining magazines for the Beretta and SIG in his pockets. A car entered. He looked up and saw a patrol car at the far end heading his way.

"Shit." He'd forgotten about the phony warrant.

The cruiser stopped next to him. "Sir, is everything okay?" the cop sitting in the passenger seat asked.

"Fine, officer." Andy realized how scruffy he looked. Any good cop would question his presence in the Marriott's garage.

"Is this your vehicle?" He stretched and glanced past Andy into the trunk.

"No. Belongs to Hertz."

"Are you a guest in the hotel?"

His heart raced as he scrambled for the right words. "I just checked out. Headed to the airport now. Catching an early flight." The cop wasn't buying it. Andy dreaded the next question.

The officer opened the door and stepped out. "May I see some ID?" The radio crackled. "All units in the vicinity of 223 Foster Street. There's a two-twenty in process."

The cop jumped back inside, and the car screeched out of the garage.

Andy took in a deep breath, unplugged the Cobra from the Pathfinder, and connected it to the Mustang's cigarette lighter.

An early morning sun cast a blinding glare on the windshield. The horses under the hood were screaming when the alarm on the dash sounded. Eighty became sixty-five. A trooper's car sat in the grassy medium ahead. Andy flew past, then heard the siren scream. "Shit, not again." Flashing lights closed in. Andy pulled into the right lane, ready to steer onto the shoulder, when the trooper accelerated past.

When Andy returned, the midway was quiet. Only one patrol car remained in front of the entrance. He continued around the block where Sprocket's truck was parked, its passenger door cracked open.

With his SIG ready, he eased closer and nudged the door with the end of the gun. Where in the hell was he?

Hurried footsteps came from behind. Andy whirled around. "Sprock." Something was wrong.

"Z, I know where they're holding her," Sprocket said between breaths. "But our chances of getting to her are close to zip."

Chapter 27

The injection kept Sarah reeling. Her body ached with stiffness. How long had she been sitting in the same rigid position? She leaned her head against the cool pane of the window and watched the sunrise. How many had she missed? A knot tightened in the pit of her stomach. What happened to Andy? Why had he let her down?

"I have to use the bathroom," she said and struggled to her feet.

"Wait," the guard shouted as he moved toward her. He stood in front of the door for a moment then opened it. "Go," he said and pointed at the metal commode. He seemed to take perverse pleasure in stripping her of any dignity.

When she left the bathroom, she glanced out the front window and caught a glimpse of the highway, a barren road with insects pelting the windshield. Where were they taking them?

Not long after she returned to her seat, the RV slowed, turned left, and stopped.

"Everyone up. Now. Move it," Rita shouted.

Sarah crowded into the aisle with the others, shuffled

toward the front, and stepped down onto a gravel parking lot. An old adobe structure sat back from the roadway. Plastered on the wall were Mexican beer stickers that surrounded a rusted Coca Cola sign. Corona, Tecate, Dos Equis, and Carta Blanca. A dilapidated neon sign read, "Javier's."

The larger guard grabbed her by the shoulder and pushed her past the barred rear door. Inside the stale smell of beer and alcohol mixed with tobacco hit her. She managed to hold down the contents of her stomach as she hurried to the other side of the room.

The roar of a truck engine outside grew louder, then airbrakes hissed.

"We're ready," a voice yelled from outside.

"You, you, and you," a guard said and pointed to the first three girls. "Get your asses outside."

Sarah leaned back, her hands cupping the wall. Tori and Pilar slid next to her, their attitudes lost to fear.

He returned and pointed to them. "You three. Move."

The barrel of his gun hit Sarah's shoulder and nudged her forward. Outside an amusement ride trailer waited, doors to the possum belly propped open.

Already frightened, she started to shake when she saw Leon leaning against a Mercedes and talking to man dressed in dark slacks and a loose style shirt.

"Inside," the guard yelled. He grabbed her by the arm and forced her into the tight compartment.

"No," she screamed, arms fighting back.

"Shut the fuck up and get inside." He shoved the other two against her. Then the door slammed shut, and the latch clicked.

Sarah gasped for air in the tight space, where the foam had soaked up the musty humidity. A cramp built in her right calf. She tried not to panic as the air grew thicker. "Let me out of here," she screamed. For the first time in her life, she needed more drugs to wipe out this horror.

"No," Tori screamed. Others joined in.

Men spoke outside. "Quiet," Sarah said.

"I just called. He's on duty," a man said. "When we cross the bridge and reach the checkpoint, he'll wave us through."

"Okay. No fuck ups," Leon said. His voice sent barbs through her veins. "You said it's about two miles on the levy road?"

"Yeah.

"I'll lead. You ride with me," he said.

The trailer jerked forward, then bounced over the roadway as it picked up speed.

Sarah tried to calm herself then pushed on the door. It moved enough for her to see through a slight opening toward the front.

"Everyone turn and put your feet against the door. Maybe if we all push at the same time, we can break the latch."

"There's no room," Pilar said.

"Dammit, try."

They shifted and somehow managed to get their bodies into position.

"Press as hard as you can. Harder, dammit." The metal bent. The opening widened. "Wait." She twisted around and looked outside. The tractor's rear wheels slapped the roadway a few feet in front of her. As rocks pelted the steel cage, a new fear arose.

She turned and tried to push back the panic. "We need to break the latch now. Keep kicking." The truck slowed, then the noise from the road surface changed to a hum. She squirmed back around and looked out the opening. "We're on a bridge."

"Can you see anything else?" Tori asked.

"It's like a toll booth with orange cones. We're

crossing a river." The bar. The beer signs. It all fit. "The bastards are taking us into Mexico."

Pilar screamed. "Oh, God. No one will ever find us."

"Shut up," Sarah said.

The truck slowed. A man in uniform stepped out of a booth, stood on the pavement, then waved them through.

Moving past the border station, the truck turned left and bounced hard. Dust poured through the opening.

"There's a river on our left. I think we're on a levy," Sarah said. "Kick harder."

The truck slammed on its brakes, then a barrage of gunfire erupted.

Sarah looked out. The Mercedes squealed past in the opposite direction. Screams in the tiny space became deafening. The truck's rear tires spun and sprayed gravel, hitting her in the face. She shifted backward. The compartment started to roll. Legs and arms smashed against each other and into the sides. Then it stopped, rocking like a boat. The door was above her head, which meant the trailer was on its side.

"Help." Her screams joined the others.

The foam soaked up moisture like a sponge. Then water seeped in and began to fill the cell, swelling against their bodies.

"Shove with your hands," she yelled. "Don't stop." She struggled to keep her head above the rising water. Sounds of pounding metal renewed her hope. She shouted louder. Water rose to her chin, then covered her mouth. Her head moved up against the door. There was nowhere to go. She found a corner, took one last breath and closed her eyes. She didn't want to die. Her lungs ached as she tried to hold on.

Hands clamped around her arm and yanked her into the open water, then thrust her to the surface. She held onto one of the truck's tires and gasped, trying to catch her breath.

"Over here," someone shouted.

She swam to the bank, then inched her way up, clinging onto wild grass. The mud felt like quicksand. A hand clasped her wrist and pulled her up the slope. Exhausted, she dropped to her knees, breathing heavily. Police swarmed around her on the levy. A man emerged from the bank, his clothes drenched. A familiar face brought a smile to hers.

"Sarah, are you okay?" Detective Weaver shouted.

"Yes." She scanned the area and watched girls surface, fighting the current.

Pilar managed to reach the bank with the help of a rescuer.

"Tori was in the box with us. You have to find her. Hurry," Sarah said.

Weaver dove under. She waited with her eyes glued to the surface. "Come on." Seconds seemed like minutes. He finally surfaced, his arms around a body. When he got closer to the bank, she recognized Tori. "Is she alive?" she yelled and reached down. With help, he pulled her onto the packed dirt.

"Step aside," Weaver said, then checked for a pulse. "Nothing." He cleared her passageway then furiously began CPR, trying to resuscitate her. After several minutes, he stopped and checked for a pulse again. "I'm sorry."

"No," Sarah screamed. "I promised her that she'd be okay."

Chapter 28

The cinderblock was cold and hard against Andy's back, rough. He thought about what Sprocket had said. "I know where she is, but I don't think we have a chance in hell to get her." It set off a maelstrom in his head.

He had to think clearly and began filling in the pieces, running through the players. Joey was buried in this sick game, but Andy wasn't sure how deep. With what he knew about the operation, Joey couldn't afford to let him live. Maybe he'd been wrong about Carlyle, and the guy was a desperate grandfather who'd succeeded on being tough. Beyer was different. He'd stepped over the line more than once.

The vibrator surged on his cell. He checked the messages. One from Doctor Agopian and other from Mia. "Andreas, Vahan called and told me he was getting close to something. I'll let you know the minute he gets back to me," the doctor said.

"My brother-in-law just called," Mia said. "This is going to blow your mind. Nick Pappas's real name is Nick Papalini."

Now the tickler in Pappas's file made sense. Andy turned toward Sprocket.

"What's going on?" Sprocket said.

"We've got to get her off this lot now. Are you sure she's inside the Glass House?"

A puzzled expression stared back. "I spotted Joey coming out of his office then tailed him straight to it. There's two men guarding the front," Sprocket said. "He was inside for maybe a minute or two then hauled ass back down the midway."

Andy nodded. "Let's go." He was becoming accustomed to ducking and weaving behind food joints and rides. They wound their way to a spot across from the Glass House on the opposite side of the midway. Sprocket had called it, "close to zip," which meant there was still a chance. Guards sat on steps at each end. The bearded one at the entrance was one Andy remembered seeing at the house. The other, a skinhead, tattooed like a freaked out ex-con, looked much younger. He stroked the AK-47 as if it was a puppy.

"How much do you know about glass houses?" Andy asked.

"A little. Never been much into iron that doesn't spin or throw you upside-down."

"It's divided. The front space is used as a shop or living quarters," Andy said. "The back is where they store some of the glass sections."

"How do we get inside?" Sprocket asked.

The interior perimeters were faced with mirrors, and a series of glass panels formed a maze at forty-five-degree angles to the rectangular space. A deathtrap if you were caught in the middle with someone firing at you.

"There's an access door around back, but we've got to assume it's locked," Andy said. "They'd hear us if we tried to jimmy the padlock." He turned toward Sprocket.

"You're looking at our only option. I'll take the entrance. You get the exit."

Andy crouched low and took the lead until they were behind the house from hell.

"Signal when you're ready," Sprocket whispered then moved toward the right side.

Timing had to be perfect. They had to hit them hard, simultaneously before the guards got off a round.

Andy dropped into position on his stomach and took in several deep breaths. Even in the cool morning air, perspiration dripped from his face. He lifted the canvas skirt, held up his thumb, nodded, and let go of the cloth. He counted to three, bolted to his feet, and shoved the SIG into the guard's side. The man cringed.

"Not a word," Andy said. "Inside." He grabbed the man's automatic and slung it over his shoulder. Sprocket had the other guard's weapon in his hand and pushed the skinhead toward him.

Once the four of them were inside, Andy pushed the two against a wall. "Spread them," he said. "Sprock, make sure they're clean." He kept his gun trained on them.

Sprocket began with the first and ran his palms over the man's upper body, found two magazines and a switchblade, bent down, and pushed them toward Andy. His hands worked their way down to the guy's ankles. "Nothing else." He confiscated three magazines off the other guard.

"Face down. Hands out to the side," Andy ordered. "Shoot them if they even flinch."

He moved away from the maze of glass and found the inner door to the storage room then gently pushed it open with the tip of his gun. It was dark enough to develop film. "Emily?" He fumbled for the light switch, flipped it up. The fluorescents blinked on, then buzzed.

She lay motionless on a cot, covered with a thin blanket. He placed his fingers against the side of her neck and found a pulse. "Emily," he said, trying to shake her out of her sleep. "Wake up." She didn't budge.

He hurried back to where Sprocket had the guards splayed on the floor. "What did you bastards give her?" He kicked the one next to him in the side. The skinhead moaned. "Talk."

"I don't know," he said. "The boss takes care of that."

Andy scanned the space. "We'll tie them up in the storeroom, then get her to a hospital."

The one guard rolled over and held his side. "You cracked my fucking ribs." He struggled to his knees.

Andy lifted his leg, planted the sole of his left shoe on the guy's butt, and shoved. "Move, asshole.

The guard fell forward onto the floor, rolled, and let out another loud groan.

"Get up," Andy said and turned to the other guard. "Help him." Skinhead glared at him. "Do it." Andy waited until the guard's partner was on his feet. "Now get into the storeroom."

Once inside, Andy spotted two rolls of duct tape that hung from a hook on the wall. He sat the men back to back on the floor and taped their upper bodies to each other, then cinched their hands. The second roll covered their mouths and eyes, and finally their feet.

"Son-of-a-bitch," Sprocket said. "You've got enough damn tape on these bastards to hold down a 747."

"We don't have much time. Cover me."

He bent down and eased Emily up and over his right shoulder. Despite her small frame, the dead weight almost caused him to fall. Pain shot down his left leg to his toes, the same as it had that day during his final assault, and the reason for the discharge he'd never wanted.

Sprocket moved to the entrance, stood with his back tight to the wall, and looked around the corner. "Clear."

Andy fell in behind him and walked down the metal steps, then around behind the trailer. The air felt desperate and, in a crazy way, a calm victory.

"Over there behind the RV's," Andy said, running ahead of Sprocket. It didn't take long before he felt her weight slowing him down. Old trailers and equipment parked by the fence a couple of hundred feet across the field would give them cover.

"Go," Sprocket said. "Keep moving. I've got your six."

Andy's breathing and legs became heavy as he crossed the field. Burning grew in his lower back. He dodged a timber but not the pothole just beyond. The ground came up hard on his elbows and knees. Emily fell forward from his shoulder, her upper body landing on his hands, but her head hit the dirt. Skin ripped from his knuckles as he slid his hands from under her.

"Emily?" She lay there unresponsive. He ran his hand over the back of her head and felt a lump, then blood.

"Are you okay, man?" Sprocket said, helping him to his knees.

Andy stood, the pain more intense, but he had to push through it before someone spotted them. He lifted her back over his shoulder. "Come on." With a slower and shorter stride, he made it behind the pile of steel scaffolding, and lowered her onto the grass.

"Stay here. I'll get the truck," Sprocket said. "She's not looking too good."

"Make it quick. I'll meet you over there by the fence."

His cell vibrated. He couldn't believe the number that came up on the screen.

"Marie," he said. "What's wrong?" His ex-wife hadn't called him in over a year, never at this hour. It was always him calling.

"You son-of-a-bitch. Julie's been kidnapped," she said. "The guy said they'd kill her if I called the police or FBI. Someone is supposed to contact you and that you would know what this is about. How could you do this to your own daughter?"

"What time did he call?"

"A few minutes ago," she said. "You've got to do something."

"Stay put. I'll take care of it." He carried Emily the rest of the way and waited on the side of the road for Sprocket. The rumble of eight pistons grew louder as Sprocket coasted to a stop next to him and pushed open the passenger door.

"Hurry," he said. "Let's get the hell out of here."

"I'm staying."

"No way, man. Remember what he did to you last time?"

"They've got my daughter," Andy said. "Emily's my trump card."

"Are you nuts?"

"I've got to find Joey and press him. It may be my only shot." Andy shook his head. "Do you know where Sentara Medical Center is?"

"No, but I'll find it."

Andy laid her in the seat and fastened the belt. "It's down by Mooretown Road," he said. "Can't miss it. Check her in as Julie Zartanian." Sprocket's eyes widened. "Just do it and wait for me there." He eased the door closed then slapped the fender. "The bastard's mine."

Chapter 29

Sarah shivered despite the early morning heat that swelled up from the ground. She felt nauseous as her fingers touched the foil blanket that covered Tori's body. Images of her being sucked underwater couldn't be erased. She'd promised Tori that everything would be okay and she'd failed. If Rio Rico was where they'd taken Crystal, Sarah prayed that it wasn't too late to save her.

She stood in a silent crowd of girls next to a pickup with the flashing light-bar and watched, then she moved away and walked toward Weaver who was talking with a group of U.S. and Mexican agents.

"Can we talk?" she said.

"In a minute," he said then continued his conversation.

She wanted to grab his arm and jerk him away but didn't. What she'd been though had to have been a lot worse than what lay ahead.

He turned to her. "They're moving in on the ranch," he said. "You have to go to the hospital and get checked out."

"There's nothing wrong with me. I need to see if she's inside."

"The ranch?" he said. "That isn't going to happen. Agents will debrief you, then you'll be transported back across the border."

"I'm not going anywhere," she said.

"Like hell you aren't. Wait over there with the others."

"What about Leon?"

He shrugged. "Who?"

"Leon. The guy I used to work for. He was in the Mercedes."

Weaver remembered the rap sheet. "The car swerved during the gunfire and ended up in the river. Whoever was in there is probably dead," he said. "A team of divers are on their way here."

Sarah turned and hurried toward the females huddled at the rear of an SUV. Probably wasn't good enough when it came to Leon. She wanted to see his dead body. Spit on it. Kick it. "God, please let him be dead."

"I need your shoes," she told Pilar.

"Whadda you mean?"

"Give them to me. Hurry." Pilar unwound the straps, then shook them lose. She bent over and picked them up. "Cover for me if anybody comes looking for me."

She tugged on each of the short heels until they broke off, then bent the soles until they were almost flat. The laces were long enough to secure them to her feet to keep the rising heat from burning her soles.

The bank on the south side of the levy road was less steep than on the river. She slid down, then followed a narrow dirt path that bordered a cabbage field. From what she'd overheard, the ranch was about a mile east.

The packed soil gave way to mud that squished under her shoes, making each step more difficult. About a quarter of a mile ahead, a large adobe wall shimmered in the heat. That had to be it.

She glanced around and moved toward the wall, swatting insects that swarmed up from the low-lying foliage.

Sounds of boots pounding erupted on the road above. Three men dressed in camouflage fatigues jumped down the embankment and surrounded her. One placed his hand over her mouth and held his index finger to his lips.

"What are you doing here?" he whispered.

She couldn't get the words out to answer him.

He communicated to the others with hand signals. They nodded. "Lie flat on your stomach and don't move," he said. She hesitated. He didn't and forced her to the ground, then he ran toward the wall with the others.

She waited until they were about a hundred feet from her, jumped to her feet, and followed.

Popping sounds from a helicopter's rotor blades grew louder as it shot up over the roadway, stirring up blinding dust from the bank. She dropped to the ground. Cars raced on the road above. Gunfire crackled. Several large blasts exploded. Then everything stopped.

"Clear," someone shouted through a loudspeaker, the word echoed by distant voices.

She ran as fast as she could toward the wall, climbed back up the bank, and continued on the road until a large man stopped her, shoving a rifle into her chest.

"Let me through," she screamed." My friend might be inside."

He said something in Spanish she didn't understand. But the rifle against her chest sent a clear message.

She spotted him walking out the arched gate. "Weaver," she shouted. "Please tell him to let me by."

He walked toward her, his jaw tight and eyes narrow. "What in the hell are you doing here?"

"I have to know if she's inside," she said.

"There's twenty or more women and girls in there. You'll have to wait."

She grabbed the front of his shirt. "You have to let me see if she's one of them."

He pulled her hand away. "Stay next to me." His pace led them toward a woman who wore a black bullet-proof vest with bold gold letters. "ICE." She looked short next to Weaver but thicker. Hispanic.

"Is she the one you were telling me about?" Agent Espinoza said.

"Yes."

"There's no way anyone's going inside until the crime scene is cleared," she said. "It's going to take hours."

"I can't wait," Sarah said.

"Listen. The women will be led out shortly," she said. "If your friend's one of them, you can talk to her then."

About five minutes passed when agents escorted a line of females under the archway, their faces gaunt and lifeless. They moved in slow-motion toward a large bus, an official Mexican Police vehicle.

Sarah clinched her fists and bit down on her lip. One looked familiar but much too frail, and she could barely walk. Sarah shoved past the others, clutched her friend in her arms until she realized that her arms were wrapped around a limp body. She let go and stared in disbelief. Crystal's arms, face, and legs were covered with sores.

"My God, what have they done to you?" she screamed.

Chapter 30

Andy rushed down the backend of the midway to an opening between the Monster and Hammer, where he had a clear view of the office trailer. Not a soul in sight. Flags and canvas crackled in the morning breeze. The cold steel in his hand warmed under his grip. He fought back images of young girls being abducted from the midway, his daughter's the most vivid. When the office door swung out, Joey filled the opening.

"Keep coming, asshole," he whispered.

Joey stepped down, glanced around, and walked in his direction.

Andy waited, then fell into step behind him. "Just you and me," he said. The big man stopped and spun around. "What, no replacement for that goon, Sinbad? Who's going to cover your ass now?"

"Put down that piece, and I'll show you who needs protecting," Joey said. "Besides, what you did to him was real fucking bad, man."

"He got what he deserved, just like you'll get."

Joey laughed. "The cops are still looking for the guy who wasted him," he said. "Maybe I point them in your direction and see what happens. In this part of the country, they'll lock you up, and the only thing you will be doing is counting hash marks on the wall of your cell."

"Let's cut the bullshit and get to the reason why I'm here spending time with a piece of shit like you." Andy pointed toward the Glass House. "Do you see anything missing?"

Joey glanced to his right then back at him. "You must have grown a new set of stones. I've got enough grinders in here who can take you out." In spite of the bluff, he appeared nervous, less sure of himself, the cockiness gone. Maybe he was getting close to getting caught in his on con.

Andy held a steady gaze. "I did when you took the limit off all bets." He stared back with no emotion. "My daughter."

"What the fuck are you talking about?"

Andy took two steps toward him. "The ransom. My daughter for Emily."

Joey said nothing.

"I want you to call whoever's holding Julie and have her released." Andy guessed at the approximate time she'd been kidnapped. Still under twelve hours. The first twenty-four were the most crucial.

Joey cracked his knuckles. "Keep talking while you still can. Your daughter for what?"

"Not what," Andy said. "Who. The girl isn't missing anymore." Joey glanced back at the attraction. "That's right, Bozo. I have her. And those goons you had watching her won't be going anywhere soon."

"You told me your ex moved out of state. How in the hell would I know how to find your daughter? And why would I want to?"

Andy raised the gun. "Don't give me that crap. Tell where they're holding Julie."

Joey shook his head. "I'm telling you the truth. I

didn't snatch her and sure as hell don't know where she is."

"I never said you personally." Andy lifted the gun, gripped it with both hands and aimed. "But I'm betting you know who did."

"Let's take this inside and finish in private," Joey said.

"Sorry, not your playground this time." Andy motioned with the gun. "Behind the maintenance trailer in back," he said. "Move it. We're wasting time."

Joey took one step toward him with his fists clinched, then stopped when Andy's finger tightened on the trigger. He turned and headed to the back lot. Andy kept a safe distance behind with the barrel pointed at his back.

Joey stopped in front of a hoist that extended from the opened rear doors of a trailer. Hooked to the chain next to him was a black, fiberglass car off the Monster.

"This is as good a place as any," Andy said.

"I already told you I don't have her. But let's say I make a call and see if I can find out who does," Joey said. "What's in it for me?"

"A lighter sentence."

"Bullshit. You got nothing on me. My word against yours. I spread patch money wherever I play. That's my insurance." Joey folded his arms. "Hell, we both have something the other wants."

An eddy of wind swirled dust between them, distracting Andy for a split-second. A large pipe wrench came flying and hit his right arm. He spun around, then fell to the ground. Joey's boot landed a second blow to his left arm, dislodging the gun from his hand. As it skidded across the gravel, Joey dove for it. Andy pulled out the Beretta and fired.

"Fuck." Joey lunged at him again.

Andy rolled to the right and let the ground take the big man's impact. Even though Joey was larger, Andy was quicker. He leveraged his body and flipped him around, then yanked his arm behind his back, right wrist a millimeter from snapping.

Andy jammed the muzzle behind his ear. "Time's running out. We play it my way, or Sinbad's accident will look clean compared to yours."

"You're fucking dead," Joey rasped. "A ghost."

Andy shoved the muzzle deeper into his neck. "You've had your hand in the devil's pocket long enough. Last chance."

"I don't have your goddamn daughter."

Andy let go and jerked the cell from Joey's belt. "Make the call, asshole."

Joey sat upright, then stood on the packed gravel, and glanced down at his ripped flesh. A steady trail of blood dripped from his arm. He looked back at Andy. "This ain't over."

"Yeah. Now dial." Andy picked up the SIG, then slipped the Beretta back into the ankle holster.

Joey fumbled with the phone, scrolling through the list of addresses.

"Tell me something," Andy said. "Why is this girl more important than the others in the RV?"

"She's like any other commodity." Joey's neck stiffened. "This is much bigger than a piss-ant like you can handle."

"That's for me to decide."

"You just crossed into territory where you don't belong, Zartanian. You set yourself up, and now you're fucking dead."

"That's what Nick said. Now, dial." Andy rubbed the trigger, making sure Joey saw it. He wanted to empty the magazine into his gut and watch him bleed out.

Joey depressed a number, then spoke in a low voice. "Do you have the Zartanian girl?" He shoved the cell toward him. "They want to talk to you."

As Andy snatched it, Joey came around with a right hook and caught him on the side of the head, knocking him into the fiberglass car that hung from the hoist. He fell to the ground, then rolled away and shot to his feet. Joey lunged at him. Andy sidestepped, then kicked the bastard's feet out from under him. Stumbling backward, Joey landed on his back and let out a loud whistle of air. His body went limp.

Andy stared, sickened by the sight. A piece of angle iron protruded from Joey's chest. Panicked, Andy scanned the ground, looking for the cell, then punched "Redial." The screen was blank. The bastard hadn't called anyone.

Chapter 31

The sight of the crumbled body sprawled across the ground in front of him, eyes rolled back into their sockets, made Andy wretch. Not because of the angle-iron protruding from his chest or the blood that wormed its way down from red splotches on the Monster's black and gold fiberglass, but Joey was the only direct link to his daughter's kidnappers. Now he had no other option than other to wait until someone contacted him, new rules that changed the odds.

He ripped a piece from the bottom of his shirt and pressed it on his left temple, wrapped the cloth around his head, and cinched it tightly to slow the bleeding.

Andy raced to the Mustang, ignoring the pain. Julie was being held somewhere in Eastern Virginia or just over the North Carolina border. Anywhere beyond that perimeter wouldn't be feasible to make the exchange. What the kidnappers didn't know was that once the swap went down, they were going to die. When he left the Unit, he thought the killing would stop. He was wrong. It never did and only escalated.

He sped toward Mooretown Road and followed the blue signs to Sentara's Emergency.

A gray-haired woman sat behind the reception counter and looked up at him with a gentle smile that reminded him of *Mamig*. Unlike his grandmother's traditional black, she wore a powder blue and white striped dress. "May I help you?"

"I'm looking for Julie Zartanian."

She scanned the computer. "Take the first right past the gift shop."

Sprocket sat with his back against the far wall of the waiting room. "She's going to be okay," he said. "They had her drugged on GHB. Doc said it probably affected her short-term memory for a while."

"How long before she's awake?"

He shrugged. "Not sure. She's in E-3."

Andy pushed through the double doors with Sprocket next to him dragging his right leg. When he turned down the corridor toward Emily's room, an all too familiar odor of disinfectant mixed with alcohol slapped him in the face. The smell triggered unpleasant memories of the four weeks he'd spent at Walter Reed. The physical pain had been tolerable but not the torment of being discharged and forced to leave his family in Special Ops-Delta.

"What's wrong?" Sprocket said.

"A time I'd like to forget." Andy's cell vibrated. Caller ID showed, "Private."

"Yeah," he answered.

"Do you have her?" a stranger's voice asked.

"Yes, but first I want to talk to my daughter." Another hour clicked off. Eleven remained.

"Noon at Raging Rapids," he said. "You'll see her then."

Andy hesitated. Keep him talking. "How am I supposed to find you?"

"Just be there." The line disconnected.

He glanced down at his watch and concentrated on

replaying the man's voice to see if he recognized it. Nothing. Whoever he was had four hours to live.

"I've got to get back to Virginia Beach," Andy said. He shared what had happened to Joey and the phone call.

When he opened the door to her room, Emily moaned as she shifted in the bed behind the side rails. Her pale face stood stark against the white gown and blanket. Then she settled back down into a quiet sleep.

She had to stay here. He'd have to figure out another way to flush out the kidnapper and convince him that he had her with him.

"Don't leave her alone," Andy said, then scribbled a number on a slip of paper. "This is Weaver's cell. Call him the minute she starts to wake up."

"And tell him what?"

"That you're here with Emily," Andy said as he started to leave. "Have him get a hold of her doctor to verify what happened so they won't have you arrested."

"You need backup. She's safe here."

"You're staying."

"Wait." Sprocket reached into his pocket, pulled out a set of keys and tossed them to him. "You'll find what you need under the seat. Leave them on top of the right, rear tire."

თავ

The Mustang hugged the highway back to the beach. He kept it at the posted speed limit and fought back thoughts of what could be happening to Julie. With the addition of a sawed-off and Ruger .45 caliber, he didn't want to get pulled over and try to explain. Every minute, every mile was less time he had. He focused on the road and fought back the fear. Julie's life depended on him getting to Ragging Rapids on time.

He mentally mapped out the water park, recalling every detail of the layout. The attractions, arcade, food joints and the maintenance area. His gut tightened. He'd been so caught up in rescuing Emily, and now Julie, that he'd forgotten about Sarah. That single thought nicked into his conscience. She might be dead, and he was responsible.

When he pulled up, the front parking lot was empty. He circled the marked asphalt, searching for an open area to engage the kidnapper, then continued to the employee parking in the rear. A space next to the delivery entrance would give him a quick exit if needed. He backed in, checked the SIG and Beretta, clicked off the safeties, then slipped them into the holsters. The area appeared clear with only a few employees milling around the maintenance building.

Andy hurried to the rear of the car, unlocked the trunk, and arranged the other weapons, magazines, and shells inside. He eased the lid closed but not locked.

A large cyclone gate was chained open. Standing with his back against an unmanned guard shack was a familiar face, the maintenance guy, Kip. Andy walked toward him.

"Hey, this is for employees and deliveries only." Kip drew hard on the remains of a cigarette. "Public uses the main entrance."

"I can read," Andy said. "Just thought you might be interested in making a little cash on the side."

Kip threw the butt to the asphalt and squashed it with his black Brogan. "Long as it's legal," he said. "Ain't stealing nothing."

Andy waited until they were face to face then peeled off a hundred-dollar-bill and handed it to him. "You're hired. All I need you to do is create a little diversion, a few minutes either side of noon."

Kip stared at him with distrust. "I don't get it."

"Up there on the Godzilla platform where you can be seen and heard from the parking lot," Andy said and pointed. "Start shouting. Make it look like you're trying to get someone's attention."

"That's it?" he said.

"Yeah. If it works, there's another hundred in it for you."

Kip creased the bill lengthwise, then slipped it into his shirt pocket. "Deal."

"I'll be behind those bushes about a hundred feet inside the front gate," he said. "Do it when you see me wave."

As Andy walked toward the cluster of shrubs, he thought about the dozens of families who would be spilling in at noon, which meant he couldn't use firepower unless it became absolutely necessary and only away from the crowd. When he made his move, he'd have to assume Julie would be inside the car or trunk and not put her in harm's way. Damn shitty choices.

Go-kart engines started one at a time until they built to a powerful hum. Then the large pumps cranked up, pushing thousands of gallons of water up over a hundred feet to the slides' spillways. The park was coming to life.

Vehicles began filtering in. Andy scanned each, searching for anything that looked out of place, one without a bunch of kids. A river rock nestled in the landscape, about five inches across, was a good substitute for his handguns. The smooth stone felt comfortable in his palm.

It was five to twelve when his cell vibrated.

"I'm in the lot," the kidnapper said. "Where are you?"

"I speak to Julie first," Andy said. "Then we deal."

"Better yet, you can see her," he said. "Walk with the girl toward a black Chrysler just inside the main gate."

Andy had been through much worse, but nothing with as high a price to pay if he failed now. Clutching the rock in his left hand, he sucked in a breath, then signaled to Kip. The big man yelled, drawing attention from the crowd below.

Andy rushed the passenger side of the black sedan. Even though the windows were heavily tinted, he could see that only the driver occupied the front seat, the man's attention diverted to the waterslide. He hurled the rock through the front passenger window, then pushed the SIG in after it. The driver's door flew open, and a man rolled out onto the ground, firing under the car and creasing Andy's left ankle.

"Shit," he yelled as he stepped behind the rear tire.

The crowd that jammed the park's entrance erupted into screams, people running toward the rear of the parking lot. He looked under the car, then squatted with his butt against the wheel, both hands gripping the gun. The kidnapper had to be directly opposite him. Seconds later, the tall man came around the back. Andy shot to his feet.

"Beyer," he shouted as he grabbed his arm, dislodge his weapon, then flung him against the side of the car.

Beyer remained standing. "You'll never see her alive," he yelled, then grinned as he came at him again.

Andy thrust his left palm into Beyer's face and pushed upward. Cartilage crunched as it drove into his brain. He fell back, blood spurting from his nose and mouth, then the back of his head slammed against the asphalt.

Andy stood over him with his gun, wanting to empty the magazine. "You bastard."

He jumped up and pulled open the rear door. Empty. He pressed the button on the dash and popped the trunk. Nothing. No Julie, and the key to finding her lay dead on the blacktop in front of him.

Chapter 32

Even though most of Sarah's clothes were dry, the river's stench still clung to them. She stared at Crystal in disbelief and could only imagine what nightmares she must have endured during the three months with her captors. The once beautiful young woman was now skeletal and covered in sores. Patches of once soft, flowing hair were missing, and her beautiful smile was ruined, stained teeth and red gums. What had happened to her?

"Talk to me," she said. "It's me, Sarah." Her fingers traced the needle tracks across Chrystal's arms. "My God." This slow death had been her punishment. Why?

Crissy cocked her head, barely opened her eyes, then closed them and mumbled a few inaudible words.

Across from her, one of the officers was getting ready to put Rita into the backseat of a car. A growing rage exploded. Sarah tore after her, but another cop grabbed her just before she reached her.

"Goddamn you. You did this to her," she screamed.

Rita looked back at her with cold indifference as she was shoved into the car.

Sarah broke free and ran back to Crissy.

"We need to get her to a hospital," a female shouted at the paramedics. It was the same woman dressed in jeans and a black bulletproof vest with ICE printed on it. She reached down. "Stay put."

Crissy mumbled aloud. "I didn't."

Sarah gently clasped her face. "Didn't do what?"

Crissy struggled to keep her eyes open. "I wouldn't let them, so they raped me, and raped me so many times and..."

Sarah looked up at the woman. "I'm going with her."

"That's not possible, Miss. You need to be debriefed. After, you'll be transported back across the border."

"Look, the only reason I'm here was to find her. She's my friend, and I'm not leaving her side." A hand gripped her shoulder from behind.

"Listen to her," Weaver said. "I'll make sure you're taken to her after they talk with you."

Sarah wiped away tears with the back of her hand. "Where are you taking her?"

"Since we know she's a U.S. citizen, she'll be taken to the closest hospital across the border for initial treatment," the cop said. "There's going to be a lot of sorting out to do before we can move her to a rehab facility."

Sarah glanced back at Weaver.

"Don't worry. She'll be in good hands," he said.

Two EMTs approached with a gurney, eased the frail body onto it, and lifted her into an ambulance. She held clinched fists to her chin and shivered, then burst into tears.

Another woman came up from behind. "I'm Special Agent Ramirez," she said. "Come with me. We'll get through this as quickly as possible."

Sarah turned to Weaver.

"Go with her," he said. "I'll catch up with you later."

They approached a decaying adobe structure, surrounded by a high rock wall. An iron-barred gate was the only entrance. A large interior area was set up as an office. Computer monitors and filing cabinets lined the far wall. On the opposite side, a large map, colored with stickpins, dotted the various countries.

"Please, take a seat over there." Ramirez pointed.

"Is this where they kept her?" Sarah asked.

"This was their operational center. State-of-the-art. Behind that door is the dorm where they kept the girls, some of the most deplorable conditions I've ever seen."

"Can we get through this so I can see Crissy? Please." Her fingernails scratched the planked table. The memory of her captivity was all too vivid, every moment living on the edge of chaos.

"Why did they do this to her? She's of no value to them in her condition."

Ramirez pursed her lips. "One thing apparent is that she pissed somebody off. The other is she's quite a bit older than the rest of the females here," she said. "Revenge outweighed her monetary value."

"That someone is connected to Paradise Island," Sarah said. "Leon's the one."

Ramirez pulled back the windbreaker and removed the cell from its holder. "Ramirez." Seconds elapsed. "That's it? Just like that?" Color drained from her face. "Got it." She snapped it closed and locked eyes with Sarah.

"What?"

"Your friend went into cardiac arrest. I'm afraid she didn't make it."

Chapter 33

With one knee on the ground, Andy placed his fingers on the side of Beyer's neck and checked for a pulse he knew wasn't there. Thoughts of Julie racked through his head. He'd let his anger override her safety, taking out the only contact he had to find her. He would die before he gave up and needed to find another path to his daughter.

A security guard, wearing a tight shirt that barely covered his belly moved cautiously toward him. Stupid on his part since he wasn't armed.

"Stay back," Andy shouted. "Call the police."

"They're already on their way."

Three cars with flashing lights and sirens blasted through the entrance. More in the distance grew louder.

Standing with a gun in his hand and a body lying on the pavement next to him wasn't working in his favor. He placed the weapon on the car's trunk, then stepped back and clasped his hands behind his head.

The police cruisers screeched to a stop. Four cops jumped out with their weapons drawn. An unmarked car tore around from the right and positioned itself between the officers and him. This was becoming a habit for which he didn't have time.

A short, thick man bolted out and held up his hands. "Back down," he shouted. "Holster your weapons." He came around the car, then walked toward Andy.

Andy couldn't place the detective.

"You can put your hands down, Mr. Zartanian. I'm Detective Miller, Weaver's partner."

Andy sucked in a deep breath. He dropped his arms and let out a sigh of relief. "How did you know I'd be here?"

"Your friend called Weaver as he was about to board a military hop back to Norfolk." Miller nodded toward the body. "What the hell happened to this guy?"

"Name's Stephen Beyer out of Mass. He's responsible for kidnapping my daughter," Andy said. "This was supposed to be an exchange. My daughter for his boss' granddaughter. When he showed up without Julie, things got rough."

Miller turned. "Cancel the bus," he shouted, "and get SID and the ME out here."

"We don't have time to waste. Julie's life's at stake."

"Weaver already told me what's going down," Miller interrupted. "But this time we're doing it my way. Is that clear?"

"Fine as long as we pick up the pace," Andy said. "She's got to be somewhere in Virginia Beach."

"Do you think Beyer was flying solo?" the detective asked in a slow southern drawl.

"Not sure. What I do know is he's got my daughter locked up. We have to find out where." Andy reached down and slipped his hand inside Beyer's front pocket. He felt a hand grip his arm.

"My way. Remember? This is still a crime scene."

Andy stood and faced him. "Look, Miller, the

clock's ticking." Frustrated, he pulled out his cell and scrolled to the old man's number. "I'm going to start with Beyer's boss."

"The girl's grandfather?" Miller asked.

"Yeah." Andy started to pace. Why was Carlyle so slow to pick up?

"Mr. Zartanian, did you find her?" he asked.

"You get her when you tell me where you're holding my daughter."

Carlyle cleared his throat. "What are you talking about? I know nothing about your daughter. Now, tell me where you've got Emily."

"Your goon played me," Andy snapped back. "He's lying dead on the ground in front of me."

"An unfortunate loss," Carlyle said. "The only thing I know is Beyer called me and said he was going after her and that I'd have her back this afternoon."

"Bullshit. Tell me where she is, Carlyle, or I'll come up there and shove your balls down your throat."

The cell fell silent.

"Son-of-a-bitch." Andy slammed it closed. "We have to get to him. He has to have known about the kidnapping."

"I'll make a call and have him picked up for questioning," Miller said.

"We don't have that kind of time. I know someone in Boston who can get to the bottom of this quicker than any Bean Town cop."

The detective pulled a pair of latex gloves out of his pocket and snapped them on. "I'll pretend I didn't hear that," he said and began searching Beyer's pockets. He examined each item carefully, then placed it on the asphalt next to the left rear wheel.

"What about his wallet?"

The detective shot him a look. "Weaver warned me that you're a real pain in the ass," he said, then continued to scrutinize each item.

Andy walked over to the opened door and glanced inside the sedan in search of anything that might be a clue. With the exception of the broken glass, the car's interior looked as if Beyer had driven here directly from the showroom. Andy leaned forward, careful not to touch anything. The air held a new car smell laced with an acrid scent, an odor that was vaguely familiar. What was it?

"Detective, would you open the rear door?"

When he did, Andy peered inside, then moved around to the trunk, both equally as clean.

"Can't really tell much with a cursory glance," Miller said. "I'll have it towed in and let the lab guys go through it. If there's anything in here, they'll find it."

"There's got to be something in his pockets or wallet. Cards. Receipts. Scraps of paper?"

"Damn it. It's all right there on the ground in front of you," Miller said. "A cell, loaded magazine, handkerchief, Massachusetts driver's license, state trooper ID, and one lousy credit card. The wad of money in the clip totals nine-fifty. None of the bills are marked."

His frustration was building and so was Andy's. "Beyer picked this location, so it makes sense that he would stay close by. There must be a key or keycard."

"Look down. Do you see one?"

"Check the phone," Andy said. "Maybe the numbers he called will turn up something."

Miller snapped open the cell and accessed Recent Calls. "It's clean. The numbers have been erased. We'll have to get the records from the phone company."

"We don't have that kind of time. It's my daughter's life you're playing with."

"Calm down," Miller said. "I'll get someone on it

right away and also assign a couple of teams of uni's to comb all the local motels and hotels."

Andy shook his head. "Don't waste your time with hotels or any other place where he would have to walk through a lobby. The last thing Beyer would want to do is draw attention to himself. He'd need an isolated location where no one would see him drag in a young girl. End unit, single story's my guess."

"I understand your concern for your daughter, but I know what needs to be done and how to do it," Miller said. "Stay put until one of my men takes your statement." He turned and walked over to three SID techs who were working the outer parameter of the crime scene.

The parking lot turned into a sea of blue, cops everywhere. The FBI was already involved in the trafficking investigation and soon would become part of the kidnapping plot. Andy didn't have time to wait around on the sidelines when the jurisdiction battles began. J.T. knew more than he'd given up. If Andy could get him to crack, he was sure he could find a link to Julie. He had to.

Chapter 34

Andy slipped away to the Mustang and found the trunk lid still cracked open, all the contents intact. He pulled out the Beretta that he'd kept from the cops and placed it inside, then eased the lid down until it clicked. Rudee Inlet was only minutes away. He had to get there and back before Miller knew he was gone.

His index finger moved quickly over the numbers of his cell.

"I've been waiting for you to call," Sprocket said.

"Talk to me. I don't have much time."

"Weaver saved my ass and cleared things on this end," Sprocket said. "Emily's awake but doesn't remember a thing. Not even her name. Doc said it might be a while before she can tell us anything. Maybe never."

"Can you stay with her?"

"Sure. You still think someone might come after her?"

"Not sure. Just added insurance," Andy said. "With Joey and Beyer dead, I'm going to press J.T."

Miller had said to hold tight, so driving through the main gate wasn't an option.

Andy walked over to the maintenance area, glanced

back at the cops, and entered. The crush of attendees there earlier had disappeared. He worked his way back to the area where he'd first seen Kip.

Andy spotted him. "Hey, come here," he shouted. "I need to talk to you."

Kip walked toward him, his expression hard. "What the fuck was that all about?"

"The bastard kidnapped my daughter." Andy handed him another hundred. "You helped me out before. I owe you."

Kip snatched it without breaking a smile.

"There's two more C-notes if you'll help me," he said. "Nothing that'll get you in trouble."

"A guy doesn't hand out two-hundred-bucks without a hitch."

"I need a place to clean up. Shave, shower and a change of clothes."

Kip said nothing.

"And some wheels."

"Are you fucking nuts?"

Andy pulled out five more bills and fanned them like a hand of cards. "Five hundred. Either you're in or out."

The big guy snapped up the rest of the money. "Deal."

Before they entered the employee's locker room, Andy began to strip. When he pulled off the jeans, they reopened the wound on the outside of his right ankle.

"Damn it." Blood started to run down onto the floor. He showered, shaved, and slapped piece of wet paper towel over the wound. The gash on his temple was still mottled with blood, and he couldn't hide it. He slipped on his shoes, a park T-shirt, and red lifeguard shorts, then transferred everything from his jeans into the Velcro pockets.

Kip tossed him a set of keys. "It's the green Jeep

backed up to the fence. Bring it back in one piece." He looked at him with a hint of sympathy. "Hope you find her. If it was my daughter, I'd be doin' the same."

Andy rolled out of the back lot, turned, and headed toward Rudee.

He pulled into the marina, now a hum of midday activity. Lil' Mike's big, yellow truck was still parked at the far end of the boatyard, next to the repair shop.

Andy pounded on the door. "It's me."

When it opened, Lil' Mike's whole body filled the doorway. "Goddamn. Every time I see you, Z, you look different."

"What's up with our tooth fairy?" Andy said, pushing past him.

"The prick is scared shitless," Lil' Mike said. "Wonders what we're going to do to him next."

"Well he won't have to wait," Andy said.

The pathetic bastard sat in a tattered bucket seat, his writs tied in front of him, hair and goatee stringy. His expression lacked any emotion.

"This is going to be our last meeting," Andy said. "Your last chance to answer my questions. Is that clear?"

Despite the caved posture, J.T.'s face remained defiant. He ran his tongue across his gold tooth. "Dude, I told you everything."

Andy walked over to the steel workbench, grabbed a ball peen hammer, and slammed it down on the stainless steel top. "There's that word again, you stupid piece of shit."

Julie's image when she was seven, playing the piano, flashed in front of him. He blinked.

He glanced back at the pegboard. A pair of aircraft shears hung next to where the hammer had. Looking around, he picked up a wooden dowel, secured it in the vise on the bench, then took the shears and snapped off a small piece, then a second and more until he had ten. He gathered them in one hand, walked over, stood in front of J.T., and dropped them on the floor.

"Ten. Just like the number of fingers on both of your hands. Let's start with the vise. One finger at a time," he said.

J.T. looked away.

Andy jerked him to his feet and pulled him to the vice. "Lil' Mike, hold him in a bear hug." He placed one hand between the movable jaws and cranked the handle clockwise. "Tell me everything you know about Emily. Was she Tori's friend?"

"Don't," J.T. screamed. "I guess. They didn't know each other that long."

Andy turned the handle slowly until he heard a bone snap.

J.T. screamed out in pain. "You're one sick fuck."

"I guess doesn't work. Now talk. You're the bastard who gave her up."

"I told you how it came down," J.T. said. "I marked her, then the money showed up in my truck."

"Keep going." Andy loosened the jaws, placed the tip of J.T.'s left index finger in, and tightened the clamp. "Look at me, you little prick. I know there's more. Talk."

"Goddamn, don't break my fuckin' fingers."

"Just keep flapping those lips and tell me everything you know, and I won't."

"Just before we hit Virginia Beach, I found an envelope stuffed with a note and two bills. It said I'd get a big bonus for young and blonde." The carnie shifted his weight. "It spelled out what they wanted. Real detailed like," he said. "Talk about luck. First day we open, there she is. Then she's gone for a while until I see her again with Tori."

Andy released his finger, grabbed his collar, and

shook him twice. "What the hell does awhile mean?" he said and shoved him back in the seat.

J.T. moaned as he rocked with his taped hands against his stomach. "Okay. Three or four days."

"Keep talking," Andy said, grabbed the shears, and opened and closed them hard.

"Please, man, don't. The first time I saw her, she was with another chick." J.T. continued rocking. "Then she turns up back at the show talking with Tori. Never saw her after that. I swear."

Andy paced, then stopped in front of him. "And that was the first time you received a request for a specific type of girl?"

"The only time, man. I'm telling you straight up."

"I sure hope so for your sake," Andy said. "Who else on the lot knew what you were doing?"

"No one," J.T. blurted. "Nick would have had my balls if he'd found out. Doesn't want any heat coming down on the show."

"Nick Pappas innocent?" Andy had heard enough. He walked toward the door and motioned to Lil' Mike to follow him outside.

"Z, you're one amped-up son-of-a-bitch," Lil' Mike said, combing his beard with his left palm.

"My daughter's been kidnapped."

Lil' Mike's eyes widened. "That changes things. What now?"

"Make sure he's tied down, then split. Leave the door unlocked," he said. "I'll have him picked up. Let the cops along with the Feds squeeze him. He doesn't know it, but he's going down for conspiracy in kidnapping."

Andy drove away frustrated, not knowing if the tidbit of new information about Emily being a special request would help find Julie.

Then it hit him. The smell in Beyer's car. The hydraulics on amusement rides. Mystik oil, under pressure, powered pistons, and brake systems. It had an odor of its own. He'd caught the break he needed. Beyer had recently been on a carnival lot.

Chapter 35

Andy pulled away from Rudee Inlet, wondering if he'd been chasing shadows until he recognized the familiar odor as being Mystik oil.

He drove hard and headed back to Raging Rapids to see if Miller's men had uncovered evidence at the crime scene, something to lead them to where Beyer had been staying. If they'd turned up zip, the likely place to look was at the lot in Richmond. But before going there, Andy needed the firepower in the Mustang's trunk.

After parking the jeep, he spotted Kip and tossed him the ring of keys.

"Thanks. I appreciate the help."

The maintenance man smiled. "Man, I hope you find her soon."

Andy walked toward the gate, took a deep breath, and continued into the parking lot.

Miller had loosened his tie and appeared to be in a heated conversation with two uniformed officers, his left arm waving in all directions. Andy was a few feet away when the detective froze and stared at him.

"What the hell happened to you? I've had my men searching high and low, then you show up looking like some goddamn surfer," he said. His ruddy complexion reddened.

"How I look doesn't matter. Check the foot pedals in the car and the soles on Beyer's shoes. You'll find traces of hydraulic oil."

"Your point?"

"It's used in rides. Beyer's been stomping around the back lot of a carnival somewhere close by."

"How can you be so sure? The oil could have been there for days."

"That's a bunch of crap. It dissipates quickly. The stain, yes. The odor, no way."

Miller stared and said nothing, then he walked over to the sedan and stuck his head inside. "Smells like a new car to me. That's it."

Andy walked around to the other side, leaned inside, and rubbed his index finger across the brake and accelerator pedals.

"Zartanian, you idiot," Miller shouted and jerked his hand away. "You're contaminating evidence."

Andy yanked free, held his finger under his nostrils, and inhaled. "That's fucking hydraulic oil," he said and extended his hand toward the detective. "Smell, then tell me there's nothing there."

If a face could explode, Miller's was as close as any Andy had ever seen.

Andy had to back off if he wanted to get out of there without having to spend time in lockup. He walked around and met the detective in front of the opened trunk.

"I know what I'm talking about. I've been around rides all of my life with the exception of the time I spent in the service."

"Pull that crap again, and you're smart enough to know what'll happen." Miller paused. "The uni's haven't turned up anything at the motels yet, but they're still on it."

"Beyer was on the lot in both Richmond and Williamsburg," Andy said. "The oil had to have come from one of them. Somebody had to have seen him."

"The show in Williamsburg is sealed. No one gets in or out until the lab's finished." He relaxed.

"Then I'll hit Richmond."

"Weaver's scheduled to land at Norfolk Naval Air Station momentarily and wants to talk to you the moment his feet touch Virginia soil."

"He has my cell number," Andy said. "We're wasting valuable time. It's my daughter. I can't stand around and do nothing."

Miller got into his face. "Okay, but listen real good. You leave a pretty damn heavy footprint wherever you land," he said. "Beyer's dead. So is Joey Conner. Not to mention a black dude without a face, and a burly biker who was found with his throat slit."

"I never iced Harley. You know that," Andy blurted.

"But you were there. Now get the hell out of here. The Feds are on their way. If I get even a whisper on your daughter, I'll call."

One of the uniformed officers who stood at the main gate waved Andy through. Whatever he did, it had to be fast. Julie's life depended on it. A gut feeling told him Nick knew more than he'd let on. His past and arrogance fit the profile of someone who could be involved in kidnapping and selling young girls for profit. Next in line to take over Conner Royal Midways, he had the most to gain and possibly replace Joey in the slave trading syndicate.

Andy fell in with the flow of traffic on the highway, then punched in the numbers.

"I was just about to call you," Sprocket said. "The

girl's starting to fade in and out, but that fog's still pretty thick."

"Was she able to tell you anything?" A horn blasted from behind, then two punks in a red, Charger flew past. The passenger shot him a one-finger-salute. Andy glanced at the dashboard and realized that he'd slowed to forty-five.

"No. The doctor's aren't letting anyone near her." Sprocket sounded frustrated. "Even the two detectives here aren't allowed to talk to her, so they've spent their time questioning me."

"How are you holding up?"

"Me?" Sprocket said. His voice hit a higher pitch. "I can take care of myself. Anything on Julie?"

"Possibly. I'm headed to Richmond. I'll check in with you later."

Andy slammed the phone closed, tossed it on the seat next to him, and pressed down on the accelerator.

Early evening in Richmond meant the midway would swell with marks. As heir apparent, Nick would be there to watch over his newfound empire.

After getting out of the car, Andy popped the trunk, slipped the 9 mil between the waistband and small of his back and a spare magazine into the Velcro pocket. He pulled the large T-shirt down over the shorts, then closed the trunk and headed for the midway.

Nothing had changed. The rides went from zero to sixty, and lights flashed into streaks of shooting stars. He stayed focused, deaf to the sounds of the attractions and screaming crowds, and made his way toward the cook-house, keenly aware of any movement. No more surprises.

"Well, well, look who turned up in yet another getup," Rube said. "Got a new name, too?"

"Andy works. I'm looking for Nick."

"Ain't here. Ole boy ran down to Williamsburg." Rube partially filled a mug with Deadhead's Brew, topped it off with booze from a dented flask, then slid the cup across the Formica toward him. "Heard Joey got himself killed."

"That so? I guess that makes Nick the Man now."

"Looks that way. Don't it? But it doesn't much affect me one way or the other as long as I get paid."

Andy took a swig, then spit it out. "Geez, Rube. This stuff'll kill you."

"You ever find that girl you were looking for?"

"She's tucked away in a safe place. Right now I need to talk to that asshole boss of yours."

Rube looked past him. "Well, guess who just drove up? Ain't you the lucky one. He's parked over there in front of the office."

Andy turned and walked toward him. "Hey, boss man," he shouted, knowing that his best shot would be to confront him in an open area where there would be witnesses instead of inside an armored trailer.

Nick stopped, looked over his shoulder, and spun around.

"Yeah, it's me."

He moved toward Andy. "You stupid son-of-a-bitch. I told you what would happen if I ever saw you on my lot again." His voice boomed and caused heads to turn.

"Before you go off halfcocked, I came to talk not fight."

Nick grabbed him by his T-shirt. "Talk about what?"

Andy twisted his grip lose. "Do that one more time, and I'll make sure you'll never use that hand again."

"You're going down big-time. Some bastard killed Joey, and I pointed the cops in your direction. I hope they fry your ass."

"Joey was abusing young girls and peddling flesh."

Nick glanced away then back. "I don't know nothing about that, and I doubt you can tie him to that shit."

"The cops already have, but it really doesn't matter since he's dead," Andy said. "Where in the hell's my daughter?"

Nick looked puzzled. "What the fuck are you talking about? I don't know anything about your goddamn daughter."

A left hook came out of nowhere and caught the carnie square on his right jaw, knocking him to the ground. Andy reached behind, pulled out his piece, and covered it with his tee. Two ride jocks ran toward them. "Tell those guys to back off, or I'll use it."

"He's all mine," Nick shouted. "Get back to work." He slowly got to his feet, then brushed off his pressed jeans and starched shirt.

"I told you that I came to talk." Andy grabbed him by his arm, shoved him toward the far end of the cookhouse, and pushed him into a plastic chair. He sat in the chair across from him. "I know about J.T.'s role with the girls."

"J.T. and what girls?" Nick snapped back. "You're talking in goddamn circles."

"What was the heated conversation between the two of you about outside your office the other day?"

Nick glanced around, then locked on to Rube. "That old bastard's been talking, hasn't he?"

"I asked you a question. Answer it." Andy pointed the 9 mm at Nick's crotch. "I'm waiting."

"I was pissed that his girl wasn't there working," he said. "We spring at six so call's at five. She didn't show. The cocky, little shit was defending her. That's it."

"You spend a lot of time at Paradise Island. You're also tight with Leon and Sinbad. So you must know they worked for Joey."

"No way. He knew them because he'd been there a few times with me. That's it," Nick said. "The joint's owned by a group in New York."

"Bullshit. You've got ties in Jersey. I read your file, and the tickler screams Feds." Andy tightened his grip on the gun. "What's your connection to them, Mr. Papalini? And don't tell me there isn't one."

Perspiration started to form on Nick's brow. "So what, I changed my name and did my time."

"More bullshit. Less than a nickel for all the crap you pulled says there's more," Andy said, then stood. "Tell me what they're holding over you."

Nick shifted in the chair. "I guess it really doesn't matter anymore since Joey's dead."

"What the hell are you talking about?"

"They suspected Joey was skimming, building the cash side of his operation. They cut me a deal to report everything he did."

Another dead end. Nick wasn't stupid enough to be snitching for the Feds and have his hands mixed up in something that would put him away for life. Or would he?

Andy stepped back. "If I find out that you lied to me about my daughter, neither the Feds nor your Guido buddies will be able to protect you." He started to walk away.

"Dead man walking," Nick shouted.

Chapter 36

Sounds on the midway had changed from screaming teenagers and blaring music to metal against metal and revving diesels. Four carnies gathered at the base of the Ferris Wheel, dismantling fencing that surrounded the ride. A sick feeling churned in the pit of Andy's stomach. Nick was pulling slough and leaving town.

Andy couldn't let that happen. Julie had to be somewhere on the lot.

A thick arm wrapped around his neck from behind, then lifted his feet off the ground. "Nick told you to stay away," he said.

Andy shoved an elbow into the guy's gut and broke the chokehold, then he jammed his instep with the heel of his shoe.

"You son-of-a-bitch," the carnie yelled. He steadied himself, came at him, and swung a wrench toward his head.

Andy stepped into him, grabbed the end of the steel, and twisted it free. Coming around, he slammed it against his kneecap.

He screamed in pain, fell to the ground, and rolled in oil-soaked sawdust. "Bastard."

Andy took several deep breaths, then tossed the wrench under the trailer. He leaned around the popcorn wagon to make sure no one else was coming. Now that Nick had spread the word to his goons about keeping him off the lot, he couldn't let anyone see him. How had he let this happen? First Sarah, then Julie. Marie was right. When had his job become more important than his daughter?

"Hey." A voice from behind startled him.

Andy whipped around. "Geez, Weaver. What are you doing here?"

"Miller gave me a heads up. Told me where you were going," Weaver said and pointed. "What's with bozo?"

"One of Nick's thugs. He's tearing down and moving. We've got to stop him. I'm sure Julie's here."

Weaver paused. "I think our best bet is off the lot. We're still searching motels at the beach, which makes more sense."

"Damn it," Andy yelled. "I've been so caught up in this that I forgot to ask you about Sarah. Is she okay?"

"She's a train wreck emotionally and physically. But she's a fighter. She'll heal in time."

"Thank God."

"Not so quick," Weaver said. "You can't undo the call you made. Those bastards almost killed her, and you were the one who sent her inside."

"Come on," Andy yelled. "I know what I did. How do you think I feel making her a target?"

"Settle down. Let's get back to your daughter."

"Nick has to know something. I'll beat it out of him if I have to," he said, then started toward office. A hand gripped his upper arm.

"You aren't going anywhere without me. Consider us joined at the hip until I say different."

"Fine. Nick's trailer's at the other end of the midway."

The whine of a small diesel grew louder. Behind them, a 350 pickup was backing up to the hitch of a Dippy-Dog joint. Andy's mind raced with a sense of urgency. Was Julie hurt? Had Beyer drugged her to keep her quiet?

"We have to do something now," Andy said.

"There's nothing I can do legally if they aren't breaking the law," Weaver replied as they walked toward the office.

"Legal or not, we've got to stop them."

"I told you before you're too close to this to think clearly," Weaver said. "I'll do the talking."

"He needs more than a damn conversation."

"Let's try it my way first."

Several concessions were buttoning up, and teardown was well underway. In less than eight hours, the lot would be empty.

"Over there." Andy pointed. Nick was a few yards away when he felt Weaver's hand again.

"Keep your trap shut."

"I don't believe my eyes." Nick cracked his knuckles. "You don't know when to stay away, do you? Think your dickhead friend here is going to help?"

"Can the crap." Weaver flashed his badge. "Detective Weaver with Virginia Beach P.D. I need to talk with you now."

"You should be arresting that crazy bastard next to you." Nick shook his fist in Andy's face.

Weaver stepped between them. "Right now I need your cooperation. Got it?"

Nick stepped back and taunted them with a smirk.

"I'd like you to hold up on moving your show until I've had a chance to look around," Weaver said. "We believe there's a missing girl on your lot."

Nick laughed. "You have to be kidding. There's probably a half dozen lot-lizards that follow us around."

"We're only looking for one," the detective said.

"One sorry-ass girl isn't going to keep me from tearing down."

Andy rushed Nick, grabbed his throa,t and slammed him against the office trailer. "That's my daughter you're talking about," he shouted.

Weaver grabbed Andy from behind and tried to pry them apart. Andy struggled free, caught Nick with a left hook, and dropped him to the ground.

"Arrest that bastard now," Nick screamed.

Weaver looked down at Nick. "I asked politely to take a look around. Now, I'm taking all your options off the table."

"Fuck you," Nick said. "I'm filing assault charges."

"I don't see any witnesses." He turned to Andy. "What about you?"

"All I heard was you asking him if you could look around."

"Spin it whatever way you want, but I'm tearing down until I see a piece of paper that says I can't," Nick said as he stood. "You got one of those?"

"Not yet."

"Come back when you do because that piece of tin you're holding doesn't mean shit." Nick punched in the code on the panel next to the door, pulled down the handle, stepped up into the trailer, and slammed it shut.

Andy looked at Weaver and said nothing. By the book was taking too much time.

The detective pursed his lips, then pulled the cell out of his pocket. "Weaver." He listened. "Got it."

Andy felt a rush. "What? Did they find her?"

"Not yet. That was Miller. He said the lab boys confirmed that it was hydraulic oil."

"Yeah, yeah. We already know that. Did they turn up anything else?"

He held up his palms. "Hold on. I'm not finished," he said. "The oil was on the accelerator and brake pads but not the emergency brake pedal."

"So?"

"Jesus. Would you just listen?" Weaver told him that the lab guys had matched the oil on the sole of Beyer's right shoe to the pedals. "But here's the kicker. It was only trace, which means it was put there by someone else."

Andy stood speechless. Another person had driven the rental. It splintered his theory about Beyer working alone.

"We know he hooked up with at least one other person," Weaver said.

Andy shook his head. "Beyer had no intention of making the exchange. If this person finds out he's dead, he may or may not want to negotiate. She's got to be worth something to him." He could barely get out his next words. "If not, and Julie can identify her kidnappers, he'll kill her."

Chapter 37

The clock ticked like a slow time bomb. Each second lessened Andy's chances of finding Julie alive. He needed to detach himself from Weaver and go at it alone. No more rules. His daughter was the highest value target he'd ever gone after, and he wouldn't fail her.

"You know how I operate," Andy said. "Target. Isolate. Kill. I get the job done."

Weaver picked up the pace down the midway. "Have you ever asked yourself why I've given you so much slack?"

Andy hesitated. "Not really."

"You should have because you've pulled enough crap for me to charge you on numerous felonies, not to mention obstruction of justice, and destroying evidence," he said. "And that's just the stuff I know about."

Andy said nothing and kept walking.

"Your military career. That's why," he said. "Your records stop at a remote area in Fort Bragg where Delta's based."

"Get to the point."

"We aren't so different. I spent most of my twenty

years as a Navy SEAL," Weaver said. "That's our bond, Andy. Mutual respect and a way of life most people can't imagine."

Weaver wasn't a tough, play it by the book cop after all.

"Then you know whoever has my daughter has a bull's-eye on the center of his forehead."

"I didn't hear that."

"Another thing," Andy said. "Being conjoined isn't working. We did it your way and got squat from Nick."

"You're wound too tight right now to cut loose."

"We split, communicate, and cover twice the ground."

Weaver shook his head. "Not going to happen."

"There's a pair of eyes in this show who trusts me and will talk," Andy said. "If you're with me, he'll clam up."

Weaver paused and stared at him. "I'll wait over there by that entrance to the coliseum," he said. "I'm going to call in a couple of favors and see what I can do to expedite a search warrant to stop Nick."

When Andy approached the cookhouse, he found it empty with the exception of Rube, who was busy fastening down equipment.

The old man looked up. "Damn, boy, you sure stir up a hornet's nest whenever you're around."

"I don't have much time. Tell me what you know about Beyer. Did you ever see him hanging around with one particular carnie or leave with anybody?" Andy tapped his fingers on the counter.

"You seen him here yourself," Rube said. "He talked to a lot of us. But no one special. Never saw him walk out with anyone either."

"Are you sure? Think hard because it's damn important."

Rube hesitated. "Well, I seen him at the sugar shack a couple of times."

"No way. Beyer's not the type looking to make a buy."

"Probably not. Maybe he was just poking around." Rube secured the oven with a bungee cord. "The candy on the lot's mostly for the crew. Can't trust no townies sniffing around."

Andy glanced over at the fried dough joint. A heavyset woman was cranking down an awning. He pointed. "With her?" She looked like anyone's mom, not a drug dealer.

"Maybe." Rube paused, as if he was picking at his memory. "Either her or the girl who works for her. I told you. The man showed that picture all around the lot."

Another dead-end. "Listen, Rube," he said, "you've been pretty straight with me."

"So? Get to it. Don't have a lot of time to sit around and jaw."

"I need a straight answer," Andy said. "Do you think Nick played me when I questioned him about seeing the missing girl?"

Rube cocked his head, and his lips curved into a smile. "Can't say. I don't know if he really ever saw her. She wasn't here that long."

Out of the corner of his eye, Andy spotted Weaver rushing toward him.

"We need to talk," Weaver said out of breath. "Looks like we caught a break. I'm headed down to the courthouse. The judge wants to see me in person ASAP."

Finally, Andy was about to get cut loose. "I need to work the lot to see what I can dig up."

"Keep whatever you do close to legal until I get back," Weaver said. "We're going to do this one according to the book." He turned, headed back down the midway, and disappeared around a large tractor moving into position.

Some of the equipment would leave the lot within the hour. Legal or not, Andy had to move. A large clang from behind startled him. He spun around. Rube continued to drop a cache of pots and pans into a storage box.

The lot swelled with drivers, flatties, and roughies breaking down. Andy walked toward the first joint, trying to stay out of their way and not draw attention. He glanced inside the Fairy Floss trailer, then stepped onto the chrome step of the 350 hitched to the front end. Nothing. He worked his way down the midway and poked around five other concessions. This was going nowhere. Whoever had her wouldn't keep her in plain sight.

"Hey, Z," Sprocket shouted.

Andy turned. "You're supposed to be with Emily."

"I tried to stay, but the detectives questioned the hell out of me, then gave me the boot. Said she's a material witness."

"That doesn't make sense. You're the one who brought in the cops."

"Tell them," Sprocket said, "not me."

"How's she doing?"

"Still in and out of consciousness. Mumbled something about a big house with a wall by the water," Sprocket said. "I tried calling you, but your cell kept going to voicemail. Got a little worried, so I split and came up here to see if I could find you."

Andy checked his phone. "Damn, it's dead." He'd been so emotionally involved that he'd forgotten to charge it.

Sprocket's expression soured. "What if someone other than me tried to call?"

"Toss me yours." He punched in numbers and accessed his mailbox. Three from Sprocket and the fourth from Carlyle who demanded to know where his grand-daughter was being held.

"Nothing about Julie," Andy said. "Just yours and one from the old man. Sounds like he's unraveling."

"Why wouldn't he? After all, it's Emily's his grand-daughter. Just tell him."

"I was ready to before I learned Beyer was the one who'd snatched Julie. He doesn't get Emily until I'm certain he wasn't a part of it."

"So, what now?" Sprocket asked.

Andy was sure Beyer would pick an area where there were several exits. "We check out the living quarters, tractors, and pickups before they pull out of here."

"Wait," Sprocket said and stopped. "Easier said than done. If she's in one of the tractors, the doors are going to be locked up tighter than a gnat's ass."

"That's why we check out the equipment when the drivers pull them into position."

Sprocket shook his head. "Come on, Z. Be real."

"We don't have a choice. Weaver was here and left to get a search warrant, but there's no way he'll be back before some of the equipment starts pulling out of here."

"I know she's your daughter, but I also know that no carnie is going to let you paw through his truck or joint," Sprocket said. "I sure as hell wouldn't. The LQ's are buttoned down even tighter. Right now, that search warrant's your only guarantee."

"Maybe not. Let's keep moving. We have to assume whoever Beyer was working doesn't know he's dead."

"Does the girl's grandfather?"

"Yeah. I threw it in his face, hoping it would force him to make a move."

"If the old man's in on it, he must have passed that info onto the person holding Julie," Sprocket said.

Andy paused for a moment. "If that was the case,

there would have been a message from the kidnapper." He paused. "I don't think Carlyle even knows this guy exits."

"Then that's your answer. He wasn't part of it," Sprocket said. "Even if he's a piece of crap, you should let him know where his granddaughter is."

"Later. Right now we have to we have to draw out the guy holding Julie. Let me use your cell again." Andy pulled a slip of paper from his pocket then punched in the number.

After two rings, Miller answered.

"Anything from the phone company?"

"I was just about to call you." Miller paused. "What's going on? This isn't the number you gave me."

"My phone died. You can reach me on this one from now on."

"Beyer made five calls from midnight on, the last to you minutes before you killed him."

"Who were the others?"

"One to Carlyle. One to you earlier. Another to one of those prepaid phones. And one to a Marie Rosetti."

"What the hell?" Andy dropped the cell to his side, then put it back against his ear. "That's my ex. She goes by her maiden name now. Are you sure it was after midnight?"

"Yes. The printout shows it was made at 10:07 a.m.," he said. "Do you have any idea why he called her?"

"No, but I'll find out."

"I'll do what I can to track down the person who purchased the prepaid cell."

Miller was doing his best, but it wasn't good enough. "I've got an idea. Give me the number."

"Don't do something stupid, Zartanian."

Andy made a writing motion with his right hand. Sprocket shrugged. Andy glanced around, picked up a rock, and dropped to one knee. "The number." He scratched it on the blacktop and folded the cell closed.

Sprocket walked over to him. "Are you going to let me in on whatever the hell you're doing?"

"We split up in the LQ's but not out of each other's sight. I'll punch in those numbers." Andy pointed. "When I signal, you listen for any sound that could be a cell going off."

He shrugged. "I don't understand."

"Beyer called this number. There's a good chance the person is here on the lot and so is Julie," Andy said. "Start over there by that Airstream. I'll stand by those two pickups with camper shells."

Sprocket moved into position while Andy took a less direct route to the trailer with a torn aluminum skin, a step above possum bellies. Andy waved then punched in the number. He pulled the phone away from his ear and blocked out the white noise. After two rings, he ended the call.

They moved to two other locations and got the same results. Nothing.

"Damn it." Andy motioned to Sprocket to join him.

"What now, Z?"

Fiberglass cars and steel arms folded into position on trailer bases. Carnies moved like trained pit crews, performing tasks they did weekly. Tearing down and setting up in the same day was a way of life. The first ride pulled out of the lot and headed toward the turnpike.

"Whatever we do better be damn quick." Sprocket said.

The cell rang. Maybe Miller found something. Andy looked at the number. "It's him." He flipped it open.

"Back off now if you want to see her alive," a man said. The phone went dead.

Andy looked at Sprocket. "It's Rube. The bastard tried to disguise his voice, but I'd know it anywhere," he said and took off toward the midway. The cookhouse was still there. But Rube was gone.

Chapter 38

The son-of-a-bitch had conned Andy from day one, made him a mark. Now there was a bullet in his 9 mil with Rube's name on it. Find him, and he'd find Julie.

He looked at Sprocket. "He can't be too far. Search the back lot," he said. He slipped the gun out of his waistband. "I spoke with him just before you got here. The bastard's got to be somewhere close by."

"Wait," Sprocket shouted as Andy started around back. "What does the guy look like?"

"Old man with thinning, gray hair and a couple of front teeth missing," Andy said, then continued to the back lot. His mind raced as he scanned the area for something, anything. He didn't know what Rube drove or which trailer was his.

Sounds grew louder as carnies started their trucks and revved the engines. He caught a side-glance of a male jumping into the driver's side of a beat-up, white pickup. Rube.

"Drop the piece nice and easy," Nick ordered. "I told you to stay off the lot."

Andy placed the weapon on the ground, raised his

hands above his head, then turned. Sandwiched between two henchmen, Nick stood with a shotgun aimed at the middle of his chest.

"You're letting Rube get away," Andy yelled. "He's got my daughter." He looked back as the truck pulled onto the roadway.

Nick glanced at his goons and laughed. "Hear that. The professor is real dangerous." The two followed and mimicked him like oversized puppets.

"He was working with Beyer, and Beyer's dead," Andy said. "There's no telling what he'll do. I've got to stop him."

"You took out one of my guys," Nick said and nosed the barrel closer. "Busted him up pretty good. Bastard's going to be off my payroll for a while."

"I don't have time for your crap," Andy said.

"You're history, Zartanian."

"Shoot me and Weaver will be down your throat." Andy was trying to decide which one to take out first. The bearded one had a large gut and huge hands that looked like they could crush a skull with little effort. Skinhead was as wide as he was tall. He cracked his knuckles.

"Oh, I'm not going to shoot you, but you'll wish I had by the time we're done." Nick's look hardened. "He's all yours boys. When you're finished, drop him in the James River off of Pear Street."

Both thugs came at him with clenched fists. The shaved head on the left launched a right hook. Andy sidestepped the punch, grabbed his arm and used the momentum to yank him to the ground. He kicked the bearded carnie in the stomach. As he fell forward, he kneed him in the face. Skinhead hesitated.

"Come on," Andy prodded. "You aren't done, are you?"

"Get him," Nick shouted.

The goon lunged forward. His face collided with Andy's forehead. He staggered. Blood bubbled from his nose and dripped to the ground. He came at him again. Andy landed a foot to the groin. The guy folded like a tired pillow and made a sucking noise as he hit the ground.

Sprocket stepped out from the side of a motor home, his .38 pointed at Nick.

Andy stared down the barrel of the shotgun. "You aren't stupid enough to use that."

"You just gave me good reason to," Nick said. "You're trespassing and started a fight with my boys."

"That'll never fly. Weaver's not going to buy that load of crap."

Nick mouth twisted into a smirk. "But your detective buddy isn't here to protect you now, is he?"

"No, but I am," Sprocket said, "Hand him your gun, stock first."

Nick tensed up and started to turn then stopped.

"You're not as dumb as you look," Andy said, picked up his gun, and walked toward him. He pulled the Remington from Nick's hands and flung it on top of the motor home. "Come on. Rube just pulled out of the lot."

They ran down the backside of the midway to the Mustang, jumped inside, and screeched onto the street.

"He went north," Andy said. "White mid-eighties pickup."

"Did he have Julie with him?"

"I don't know. Barely caught a glimpse of him." Andy came to an intersection, glanced over at Sprocket, and cranked a hard left. "I'm gambling that he didn't take the turnpike."

"Driving up and down these streets doesn't make sense," Sprocket said. "We're wasting time."

Andy jerked the car to the curb. "You're right. We need to toss him a carrot, give him a way out." He punched in the number and waited. It went to voicemail. "Beyer's got the money, and I've got Beyer. A hundred big ones for the girl." He flipped the cell closed.

"Do you think he'll bite?" Sprocket asked.

"He's in this for only one thing. Money," Andy said. "Beyer was too smart to tell Rube about the big casino. So when he hears the amount, he'll bite hard."

Five minutes had passed when the cell rang.

"Yeah," Andy said.

"Let me talk to Beyer."

"He's out of the equation, Rube." Trying to control his anger, Andy said, "It's you, me, Julie, and a hundred Gs. That kind of money will buy you a lot."

"Where's the cash?"

"I've got it," Andy said. "You get it when I get my daughter."

"Wait at the coliseum's entrance." The line went dead.

Andy made a U-turn and drove back to the parking lot where the carnies were in the final stages of tearing down.

"He's going to want to see the yard-notes," Sprocket said.

"I know. Give me all your bills." Andy jumped out of the car, popped the trunk, and opened the canvas laptop case.

Sprocket handed him his cash. "What's the plan?"

Andy took what he had and laid them in neat rows on the computer, careful to put the C-notes on top. "He'll see double zeros and think it's all there."

He removed the guns from the trunk and laid them on the floor behind the driver's seat, then powered the windows down.

"Get inside and stay low. If things start going sideways, I'll say she's a Zartanian," Andy said. "That's your signal to shoot but not kill."

Andy set the case on top of the trunk, leaned against it, and waited for the white pickup to drive in. He checked the time on the cell. Minutes dragged on. Where was he?

"Looking for me?" Rube said from behind.

Andy spun around. The carnie stood next to the opened gate with a long-barrel revolver in his right hand.

"You were the last one I figured who would stoop this low," Andy said. Rube wasn't smart enough to pull this off alone.

"I'm not cutting jackpoints for the rest of my life," Rube said then spat on the ground. "And I sure as hell ain't going off a carnie lot horizontal like. That money's my ticket out."

"Where's Julie?"

"The money first."

"It's in that case on the trunk," Andy said. "I want to see my daughter, and she better not have so much as a scratch."

"No one's touched her. This is just plain business," Rube said. "Nothing else. Give me the money, and I'll tell you where she is."

"Bullshit. I see her, and you get the hundred Gs." Andy opened the case, tilted it toward him, and closed the canvas. "It's all here. Now where's my daughter?"

Rube licked his lips and grinned. "You were an easy mark. Led you like a puppy."

"You bastard."

"Put the briefcase down on the pavement away from the car."

Andy zipped the case, trying to buy a little time. He walked about ten feet away from the passenger door, placed the canvas on the ground, then backed up and leaned against the rear panel. Sprocket was directly behind him.

"I held up my end. Now, it's your turn," he said.

Rube walked toward the case, eyes fixed on it. He dropped to one knee, then struggled with the zipper.

"She's a Zartanian, old man."

"I've got him," Sprocket whispered from behind.

Rube had the case almost open when the gun fired. The bullet hit him in the shoulder. He screamed as he fell on his side, getting off one round.

Andy kicked the pistol out of his hand then put one knee on his chest. "Where is she?"

Rube struggled.

"Talk."

"Go to hell."

Andy backhanded him across the face, reached inside his front pockets, and threw the contents on the ground. A room key with a plastic tag attached stuck out from the folded cash, the number 104 barely legible.

"The Webster. It's the flophouse where I stayed."

"What do we do with him?" Sprocket asked.

"Give him to Weaver when he gets back," Andy said.

Rube's eyes widened. "Don't turn me in. Beyer'll kill me. I wasn't in on it until after he snatched her. That's the truth. He paid me to throw you off."

Andy ignored him. "The place isn't far from here." He jumped inside the car and tore out of the lot.

Two turns and three blocks later, he spotted the dilapidated neon sign that hung in front of the hotel and slammed on the brakes. The car's right wheels landed on the sidewalk.

Andy threw open the front door, jarring the residents in the lobby. The same clerk behind the counter jumped out of his chair. He shook his head, either half-asleep or more than likely drunk.

"What are doing?" the man slurred.

On the wall, 100 to 108 was painted with an arrow that pointed toward a hallway.

Andy ran down the dingy corridor. His heart beat faster and hand shook as he stood in front of Room 104. He prayed she wasn't hurt as he inserted the key, twisted the knob, then shoved open the door.

"Julie," he said as fumbled for the light switch. Musty air hit him like a wall. A small light bulb in the center of the ceiling dimly illuminated the little space and the bed below.

The room was empty.

Rube had told the truth. Never had her and didn't know where she was.

Chapter 39

Weaver drove into the coliseum's parking lot with ADA Dominic sitting next to him and two squad cars close behind. What the DA's office had dug up on Nick would shut him down. The search warrant wasn't necessary to make the case, but it might help find Andy's daughter.

Sprocket was holding a gun on the cook. "Jesus," Weaver said and jerked the wheel to the right, stopping in front of both men. He jumped out of the car. "Tell me what went down here, and it better be good."

"Z went after his daughter," Sprocket said. "This bum's been holding her."

"What's his connection?"

"Rube's the missing link," Sprocket said. "Z bated him with some serious cash. When we took him down, he found a key for a room at the Webster in his pocket."

"And this guy got shot in the process?" Weaver asked.

"I only grazed the old geezer after he'd pulled this piece." Sprocket handed him the gun.

"What the hell's going on?" Nick shouted.

Heads turned.

"That's the guy. Serve him," Weaver said.

"I'm Assistant District Attorney Dominic," he said as he slapped a piece of paper into Nick's hand. "This warrant gives us the right to search the premises. Not another piece of equipment leaves this lot until I say so."

Nick scanned it. "This is bullshit. I've got a show to run and schedule to meet. You're already putting me in the red." He glanced down at Rube. "Who in the hell shot you?"

"I did," Sprocket said. "You know damn well why. Andy told you before you unleashed your goons on him."

"He's too stupid to be involved in a kidnapping. The old man's just a cook, and not a very good one."

Rube pointed a finger at him. "You're the stupid one. Who do you think I worked for?" he said. "Sure as hell wasn't you."

"Shut up, old man."

"Joey never trusted you. He knew you were skimming and lining your pockets with his money," Rube said. "He's the one who paid me to watch your sorry ass."

Nick turned to Weaver. "The bastard doesn't know what the hell he's talking about."

"It doesn't matter. We'll settle this downtown," Weaver said, then faced Sprocket. "You said the Webster, right?"

"Yeah. It's the old flophouse a couple of blocks east of the Marriott."

"The boys here know what they're doing. He'll talk."

Dominic stepped forward. "I'm going to get the uni's started."

Weaver looked at Nick and grinned. "Great. I'm willing to bet that it won't take long before they put the bracelets on you," he said. "The sugar shack's a start."

"You're blowing smoke, detective. I ain't going

down for a little weed. My connections will laugh in your face and make anything you find disappear," Nick said and walked away.

"Wait," Rube shouted. "I saw the missing girl in his trailer. The one Beyer and Andy were looking for."

Nick stopped.

Weaver looked at Sprocket then at Rube. "Keep talking."

"Cut me a deal, and I'll give you enough to put him away."

"I'll make that decision. Tell me what you've got."

"The old man's out of his mind," Nick said. "He ain't got jack-shit on me."

"Watch." Rube cleared his throat. "I told Andy that Nick was pissed at J.T. because Tori took off. But I lied. J.T. went off when he found out that Nick had forced her to stay with him in his LQ overnight."

"That's bullshit. He's playing you."

"Hook him up," Weaver said to the officers.

"Wait," Dominic said and pulled him aside. "Let's make sure whatever we have on him is solid before we make an arrest."

Nick smiled. "At least one of you is thinking. I'll be in my office." He turned and walked away.

"These guys are going to take you in for questioning," Weaver said to Sprocket. "I'll track down Andy and cover his six."

৩৩৩

Andy ran back through the grungy lobby, then slammed open the door. A decision had to be made. Go back and squeeze Rube or try and talk to Emily. But he'd need Weaver's help to do that.

An unmarked car with flashing lights in its grill, screeched to a halt behind his rental.

Weaver jumped out. "Did you find her?"

"No. Goddamn Beyer used Rube as a decoy."

"I know this isn't what you want to hear this," the detective said. "There isn't much more we can do until someone contacts us."

"Bullshit." Andy slapped the car's hood.

"I questioned Rube before they hauled him away and got zip. The poor bastard did all this for a thousand dollars."

Andy shook his head. "I think Emily's our only other lead."

"I just got word on my way over that Boston PD has tried to contact Carlyle at his office and residence," Weaver said. "Seems he's just disappeared."

"That doesn't make sense." What was Carlyle trying to pull? He'd spoken to him only hours before.

"His secretary hasn't seen him since yesterday."

Andy thought for a moment and tried to remember his last conversation with Carlyle.

"Have them check the JFK Suite at the Copley Fairmont," Andy said. "That's where he stays when he wants to get away."

Weaver opened the cell and punched in a number.

Andy started to pace. Just when things seemed to have come together, they started to unravel.

The detective closed the phone and looked at him. "A team's headed there now," he said. "Something else. Sarah's on her way back to Virginia. She's still in pretty bad shape." He stopped.

"Don't leave me hanging," Andy said. "Talk."

"The girlfriend, Crissy, was so far gone that she didn't make it," Weaver said. "Flat lined on the way to the hospital. It was hard news, along with the fact Sarah was told that Leon got away."

"Damn it."

"You're the only one she trusts right now. She wants you to meet her at the airport," he said.

"That's impossible. I'm focused on finding Julie. Nothing else matters," Andy said. "Do you get that?"

"Calm down. I'm a father, too. Miller's taking care of that."

Even though Andy was the one who'd gotten Sarah into this mess, his first obligation was to his daughter. "Weaver, I need your help," he said. "I have to talk to Emily."

The detective started to walk toward his car. "Are you coming?"

"I'll be right behind you in this pony."

Weaver's cell rang. He didn't say anything, just nodded. When he finished, he said, "Wait. Carlyle isn't at the hotel."

"That's the only place that—"

"Hold on. Let me finish." Weaver paused. "You wouldn't happen to know a man by the name of Vahan Manoogian?"

Andy swallowed hard. "He's Doctor Agopian's right-hand. They've been running down info on Carlyle for me," Andy said. "Vahan was close to finding something."

"Not anymore. Manoogian was found dead in the suite."

Chapter 40

When Sarah stepped into the jet-way, heat and humidity wrapped themselves around her, making it difficult to breathe. Despite the high temperature, she shivered and fought back the images of the Rio Grande. She needed to get to Andy and tell him what she'd discovered.

Nerves frayed, she clutched the small carry-on and moved through the crush of passengers into baggage claim.

"Ms. Walkovitz," a voice said from behind.

She whipped around. A tall policeman with a friendly smile nodded.

"I'm Officer Davis."

She stepped back. "I thought Detective Weaver or Miller was going to meet me."

"Sorry, but they're tied up on another case," he said. "Mr. Zartanian's daughter is missing."

"What? When did it happen?

"It's complicated," he said. "I'll tell you what little I know on the way to Virginia Beach."

"Please, it's important. I need to talk with Andy."

"My orders are to escort you to Virginia Beach," he

said. "Detective Weaver will be there shortly. Talk to him about it."

She hesitated then walked beside him to the black and white parked in the "No Parking Zone."

As they pulled away from the curb, she glanced out the passenger side window, then screamed. Leon leaned against the concrete column and gestured with a finger across his throat.

Davis slammed on the brakes. "What's the matter?"

Sarah faced him. "It's him, Leon, next to the column." She turned back and pointed. He was gone.

❧❧❧

Andy followed Weaver to Sentara Medical Center, hoping Emily would remember something that would lead him to where Julie was being held.

After double-parking in the loading zone, they pushed open the glass doors, ran through the lobby, and ignored shouts from a security guard.

"Room number?" Andy asked."

"302."

They bypassed the elevators and headed for the stairwell, taking two steps at a time to the third floor.

When Andy shoved open the door, the hallway was clear. No guard. Her room was down to the right. 302 was open, but the room was empty. Blankets and sheets were strewn across the bed.

"Damn it, Weaver. Where in the hell is the guard?"

"May I help you?"

He turned around. A nurse stood in the hallway with a perplexed expression.

Weaver held up his hand and pointed to the badge on his belt. "Where's the girl that was in here?"

"You just missed her," she said.

Andy glanced up and down the hall. "What happened to the officer who was on duty?"

"A detective told him to leave because he and another gentleman were taking her to her grandfather," she said. "They left a few minutes ago."

Andy shook his head and turned to Weaver. "We have to catch up with them."

As they approached the lobby, Andy hesitated. "Take the front entrance. I'll check the rear."

He elbowed through the automatic doors before they fully opened and ran to the parking lot. Catching his breath, he scanned the perimeter.

With his weapon drawn, he took off to the left and rounded the corner. Ten yards ahead, two men moved past a barrier wall. The shorter one dragged Emily with her arm twisted behind her.

"Hold up," Andy shouted.

The first guy stopped and faced him.

"Miller?" Weaver had told him that he was picking up Sarah.

He grabbed Emily from the other guy and pulled her in front of him. "Back off."

"You're the leak," Andy said. He steadied his hand against the cold metal. "You're also a coward."

Miller had one arm around Emily and his weapon in the other hand.

"Let her go," Andy shouted.

"You know what happens to dirty cops," Weaver yelled from behind.

Emily struggled to jerk free. "You're hurting me."

"Shut up," Miller snapped. "Both of you back off, or she's dead. Kinji, get his weapon. Weaver, slide yours away from you."

In one fluid motion, the small, muscular man moved toward him.

Kinji was a step away when Andy extended his right arm with the butt of the weapon facing away, his finger over the trigger guard. The man grabbed it. Andy pulled him forward and came around with a left hook to the jaw. As he fell to the ground, Miller fired a round and took off running with Emily as a shield. He disappeared behind the barrier.

"Come on," Andy yelled as he ran to the concrete wall.

Weaver stood next to him, both with their backs against the cold cement. They worked their way to where Miller had disappeared, then inched around the corner.

The building's door eased close.

"Never picked Miller for a bad cop," Weaver said. "The bastard's mine."

Andy cracked open the door. "There's power equipment to the left and crates to the right. I'll take the crates."

Once behind the wooden boxes, he shot Weaver a thumbs-up then panned the building's interior. One of the two diesel generators hummed in the large space. Other noises came from two large boilers and switchgear. Large and small pipes covered the ceiling in an iron grid. He pointed the muzzle toward the steel girders above.

"You've reached a dead-end, Miller," Andy shouted. "It's over. Let the girl go."

"Stop him," Emily cried out.

Miller said nothing.

Where was he? "Give it up." A round missed the barrel and pinged off the concrete wall behind him.

"Like I said, she's dead if I don't get out of here."

Keep him talking. Create a diversion. "Let me guess, you were working for Joey then went on your own once he was killed," Andy said. "Am I close?"

"You're way off," he said. "I never talked with or met Conner."

Andy picked up a bolt and lobbed it at the barrel. Miller fired another round.

"You're one sick twist." Andy blocked out the plant's noise and focused on movement. He couldn't stay there much longer.

"The clock's ticking," Miller said. "I hate to waste a pretty young thing like this." His voice wavered, lacked confidence. "I want an answer, or Emily gets the next bullet."

"No," she screamed.

"Emily, stay calm. Nothing's going to happen to you," Andy said. "Miller, you know my daughter's missing. Emily might be able to help find her."

"Then do what I say."

Andy had to play along until he could separate Emily from Miller. He'd heard enough to pinpoint their location, the best place to take him out.

"Deal."

"Throw out your weapon, then come out with your hands above your head."

"Sure. So you can shoot me?" Andy said. "I've got a better idea. Have Emily walk out half the distance between us."

"You don't seem to understand. She's the reason I'm here."

A commotion erupted. Emily screamed then bolted out from behind the boiler.

Andy fired to cover her. "Over here," he yelled. Weaver fired several rounds. Andy zeroed in on a steam pipe he guessed was somewhere above Miller. He fired. A blast then a deafening hiss filled the room. Steam shot down behind the boiler.

Miller screamed out in pain. "I can't see."

Andy grabbed Emily and pulled her behind the generator.

A gunshot blasted.

Miller's screams stopped.

"Got him," Weaver yelled.

"It's going to be okay," Andy said and squeezed Emily's shoulder. "We'll get you back home."

Her sobs softened. "I can't go back. You don't know what my stepfather is like. He'll hurt me."

"What do you mean?" he asked. "I thought your mother was dead. Don't you live with your grandfather?"

She stepped back with a puzzled look. "No. I don't have a grandfather."

Chapter 41

Andy sat with Emily and Weaver in the conference room at Virginia Beach PD. His only lead to finding Julie sat across from him in a fragile state of mind. Tangled memories needed to be unraveled, then set in order, something a professional could do in time. But time was something he didn't have.

He twisted the cap off the plastic bottle of water, poured it in a glass, and pushed it across the table in front of her.

Weaver leaned forward. "You know that you're safe now."

Emily stared back at him and said nothing.

Andy adjusted the yellow pad of paper in front of him, tapped it with the tip of a pencil, and held back the questions he wanted to ask, per Weaver's suggestion.

"You mentioned a big house with a wall on the water and some men," he said. "Take your time and tell me what you remember about your time there. Anything at all."

Emily took a sip of water, her hands shaking. She pursed her lips and looked away.

"Please. My daughter's your age." He tried to quiet

the urgency he felt. "It's likely the same people that had you have her."

"It was awful. They hurt me." She lowered her voice. "I don't want to talk about it."

"Try and stay calm, "Weaver said. "Just tell us what you remember now. The rest will come later."

She folded her arms on the table then laid her head on top.

Andy glanced at Weaver, not sure what they should do. He heard a knock on the door and turned.

An officer stood in the opening. "Ms. Walkovitz is here."

Sarah stepped around him, ran toward Andy, and wrapped her arms around his neck.

"Leon's out there," Sarah said, choking back tears. "I saw him at the airport."

"If he's out there, the police will pick him up," Andy said. "I'm so sorry about what happened to you."

Emily lifted her head. "Sarah?"

Andy stepped back and watched the connection between the two. It clicked. If anyone was going to help Emily remember, it was she.

Sarah rushed around the table and pulled the frightened girl to her. She eased back and held her face as if she was trying to read her expression.

The two stood holding each other for several minutes while Andy and Weaver watched.

Sarah gently broke the embrace, placed her arm around Emily, and looked at Andy. "Tori told me what Emily had shared."

He nodded.

Facing her, Sarah said, "The big house had walls around it with an iron gate. Right?"

"Yes, and men with guns." Emily's voice quivered.

"Do you remember anything else about the place?

The area surrounding it?" Sarah asked. "Tori said there was water, and your feet were cut on some rocks."

Andy interrupted. "There aren't any rocks on the ocean front, only sand. It has to be where the water flows inland."

Weaver stood and pulled down a map from a tube above the blackboard. Virginia Beach and the surrounding areas were in colors that defined each of the districts. He picked up a pointer.

"Here, here, and here are the closest inlets."

Emily squinted. "I crawled in sand. I remember whitecaps and foam."

Andy walked over to the map. "The yellow bungalow is here and the beach there," he said and pointed. "Two blocks." He circled the area with his index finger. "The closest banks with rocks are at Rudee Inlet."

Weaver placed the tip of the thin, telescoping metal on the map. "There are houses on both sides of General Booth," he said. "Also beyond the restaurant and down the inlet."

Andy shook his head. "Can't be many with large walls and an iron gate."

Weaver's expression changed. "We'll need a reason for a search warrant," he said and glanced at his watch. "I have a meeting with the Task Force in ten minutes. They might have something that will help us locate the house." He sucked in a deep breath and locked eyes with Andy. "Even if we find it, there's no guarantee Julie is there."

Another crushing blow of reality flashed doubt but only for a moment. "I've got an idea," Andy said. "Would you have a problem if I take Sarah and Emily with me and drive the area to see if something jogs her memory?"

Weaver hesitated. "Two conditions. Stay in the car and keep you cell on so I can reach you."

"Got it."

Weaver stood. "I need to talk to you outside."

When the door closed behind them, Andy said, "What now?"

"You really got to Beyer. He was desperate," Weaver said. "Remember the second call to your ex?"

Andy nodded.

"He told her to push you, because if you lived, Julie would die," he said.

"Marie's been pissed at me since she moved here. Thinks all this is my fault. For once, I have to agree with her."

"One more thing. If you find something, no one-man commando assaults. Got it?"

Andy held the gaze. Once he found the house, he was going inside with or without help. Before that, Emily had to identify it, a heavy burden for a young woman who had just been rescued from the bowels of hell."

❧❧❧

Andy spread the map in the passenger seat, with Emily and Sarah in the back. The Mustang's roofline made it difficult for anyone outside to see them. It had taken over thirty minutes to convince Emily that she would be safe. Even with all the coaxing, she'd only agreed because she trusted Sarah.

They worked their way through streets north of the inlet. Nothing jogged Emily's memory.

Andy looked up at the rearview mirror. "Does something look familiar? Even if you're not sure, tell us," he said softly. "Maybe, could be, not sure, anything works."

She nodded.

"That's okay."

He drove down every street with homes having water

access. Nothing, but a gut feeling told him he was close.

"The houses here are too small. No walled estates," Andy said. "We're wasting time."

"I remember some large homes at the north end of the beach," Sarah said.

"Too far. She wouldn't have made it back to the bungalow." Stay calm, he reminded himself. "It has to be down at this end."

Weaver had mentioned something about building new houses on the other side of General Booth.

Andy turned onto the roadway and headed South.

"Over there," Emily shouted. "I remember that sign."

Andy's heart raced. The billboard showed children splashing down Godzilla at Raging Rapids, their faces with ear-to-ear smiles. He glanced in the rearview mirror at Emily.

"Anything else?" he said, took the first left past the sign, and pulled to the side of the road in front of a gray and blue house. The inlet with rock-covered banks was visible on both sides. Docks dotted the waterway with boats bobbing to the rhythm of the tide.

"Nothing looks familiar," Emily said. "It was dark. We were going to the carnival."

Andy turned back and faced her.

"Someone grabbed me from behind." She squeezed her eyes shut. "Then I felt a needle in my arm."

Andy knew she was at the edge of remembering. *Keep her talking.*

She took in a deep breath. "Three men in a smoky room."

The sound of an approaching vehicle grew louder. Then an SUV drove past.

Emily screamed. "That looks like the car or one like it."

"Stay calm. No one can see you." He eased onto the

road and followed the black Suburban. It turned left out of sight.

He reached the corner, following at a safe distance behind, until the SUV stopped in front of a large iron gate between tall stucco walls.

Julie was behind those walls. Andy knew it as much as he felt it. Emily had found her, and it was up to him to rescue her.

Chapter 42

Andy convinced Weaver that Emily and Sarah would be safe and more comfortable at Sprocket's house than they would have been at the police station. What he didn't tell him was that Gabby would watch over them with Lil' Mike as security while he and his friend as backup went back and rescued Julie.

He and Sprocket sat in his car at the same place where they had spotted the SUV parked in front of the gate and waited for nightfall. Though it had been a while, his training was still fresh in his mind. He had been in situations like this before. Whenever possible, good surveillance before an extrication assault like this provided the best result. Know your enemy. Understand him. Think like him, all part of his training.

"Keep your cell phone on," Andy said. "I'll do the same so you'll be able to hear what's going on. Don't talk unless it's absolutely necessary and then in a whisper. Got it?"

He nodded.

"Tap once if you copy my transmission," Andy continued. "Twice if there's a problem."

"Z, you're not even sure she's in there."

Andy ignored his friend and grabbed a spool of white kite string. "I'd guess that wall's about ten feet high." He reeled off the cord, measuring it from the center of his chest to the tip of his fingers eight times, cut it, then shoved it in his front pocket.

Sprocket shook his head. "What if you're wrong?"

"I'm not wrong," Andy said then faced him. "In or out? Your call."

"Shit, man. That's one dumb question," Sprocket said. "Where do you want me?"

"Right here. You're my eyes on the outside."

Three hours had passed after sunset, and no one had entered or exited the compound.

Andy picked up the cell, punched in Sprocket's number, then placed the SIG, penlight, and phone inside a large Ziploc. He tucked the Beretta inside the front of his jeans and slid out of the car.

"Wait, Z, take this." Sprock handed him a knife in a sheath. "Ka-bar seven-inch blade. Sharp enough to shave with."

Andy smiled as grabbed it, pulled the blade out of the black nylon, and held it up to take a closer look. Razor-sharp steel, ripteeth above the quillion and a non-slip grip made it the perfect weapon for an up-close fight. "I owe you big time." He attached the sheath to his belt. "Thanks again. I'll let you know if I need you."

☙❧

One by one, lights in nearby houses went dark with only a few remaining, none closer than fifty yards from the iron gate. Once he passed that point, he would blend into the darkness.

Andy chose the right side of the property because it faced east toward the Atlantic and was the darker of his two options. The left side faced General Booth Boulevard, where lights skipped across the water and splashed the white stucco.

He maneuvered on the rocks, steadied himself against the wall, then came across something he hadn't anticipated. The rock underneath him dropped off into the water, but the wall continued.

Andy pulled out the string, tied one end to the Beretta's finger guard and the other to a small rock. He tossed the rock gently over the wall, eased it down until the tautness stopped, then placed the gun on the ground.

Holding the Ziploc'd weapon above his head, he scissor-kicked to the end of the wall. Inaudible voices on the other side warned him of a potential problem.

Easing around the end of the concrete, he saw a large dock on the opposite side. Tied to it, at the stern and bow, was an expensive black cigarette boat, similar to the ones used by Navy SEALS on covert missions. Between him and the rear of the house were an expansive lawn and a patio with teak lounges, tables, and chairs. Two men stood at the edge of the concrete, one Asian, the other Russian or Ukrainian with a barrel chest, strong jaw, and arms like pontoons. Both were dressed in black and wore pancake shoulder holsters.

"I need to hit the head," Asian said and went inside.

Andy removed the penlight and cell from the Ziploc. He shoved the light into his right front pocket and cell into the other. Removing the weapon, he approached the lawn and stopped short of a light beam emitter mounted to side of a rock planter. After examining it closely, he flopped over onto his back and inched his way under the thread of light. Staying in the shadows, he moved to within two feet of the stocky man.

Andy tucked his weapon into his jeans. Then in one fluid motion, he raised up behind him, grabbed his chin, and snapped his neck. He gripped the body, dragged it to the edge—short of the emitter—and let it slip into the water.

He moved back toward the glass door, stood with his back against the wall adjacent to it, and readied himself. The door opened. "Oleke," Asian called out.

Andy stepped in front of him and jammed his palm into the base of his nose, then thrust upward. Ignoring the spurting blood, he pulled the body to the edge and dumped it into the water to join barrel chest.

He slipped out the cell. "Two down in the rear," he whispered. "Click," answered back.

With the backyard clear, Andy stepped inside and heard voices talking at the other end of the house. An even greater sense of urgency consumed him. He couldn't risk another confrontation.

Cigar smoke clung to the air as he made his way down the carpeted hall. He checked the first room with two unmade beds. The guests had checked out and wouldn't be retuning.

"They've got the girl," a man said. "We need to get her back. Is that clear?"

The voice sounded familiar.

"Yes, I heard two of Yamada's men are flying in from Texas tonight," another replied."

"Where did you hear that?"

"Oleke. He said they're supposed to be here sometime before midnight."

"Oleke talks too much."

Andy cleared the last room downstairs, backtracked, and moved up the side of the stairway. When he reached the top, he looked down the hallway. There were four closed doors and one open, a bathroom. She had to be behind one of them.

The first was empty. As he made his way to the next,

a door slammed and startled him. He paused then inched open the first door. Clothes were scattered on the bed with an open suitcase at the foot. He wiped sweat from his brow, moved to the next, and did the same. Two more to go.

With his back against the wall, he took in a deep breath, glanced at the stairway, turned the handle, and slipped inside. Stale air hit him, and drawn curtains kept moonlight from filtering in.

With the penlight next to the SIG in his left hand, he clicked it on. The beam landed on someone tied to a bed, gagged and blindfolded, too.

"Julie?" he whispered and moved toward her. She moaned. It had to be her.

Wide strips of silver tape covered her mouth and eyes. He laid the gun and flashlight on the bed, then gently pulled back the piece covering her eyes. She moaned louder. Adhesive stuck to her eyelashes, eyebrows and hair tossed over her ears.

Julie's eyes blinked rapidly then opened and stared at him.

"It's me, sweetheart," Andy whispered and placed his index finger to his lips. "You have to stay quiet. Understand?"

She nodded.

"I'm going to remove the tape from your mouth." He lifted it slowly."

"Dad–"

He cupped her mouth with one hand and held the index finger of the other to his lips. "Whisper."

"I'm scared." Tears streamed down her cheeks.

"I'll get you out of here." He peeled away the remaining piece of tape.

Andy pulled out the cell. "Got the package," he said to Sprocket, then freed her hands and started on her ankles. Light spilled in from the hall, then the chandelier illuminated the room.

"Who the fuck are you?" the familiar voice said.

Andy spun around. The bald head with a small patch of hair under his lower lip stood in the doorway, blade in his right hand catching the light. Tattooed on the forearm was a severed serpent's headed with a saber in between.

"I've seen you before," Leon said. Light continued to bounce off the steel he gripped.

"My daughter leaves with me," Andy said with the SIG in his hand, aimed at Leon's head.

Leon laughed. "You think that gun's going to get you out of here? Ten men will be here five seconds after you fire the first shot."

"Then I guess I won't use it." Andy set the weapon on the foot of the bed.

"Daddy," Julie said. "Please, no."

"Don't worry," he said, not taking his eyes off Leon. He stepped forward, positioning himself between Leon and Julie, and pulled the blade from its sheath.

Leon's grin widened as he hunched over into an attack position. "That' ain't going to help. I'm going to cut you so nobody will recognize you." He took a wide swipe and missed.

"Come on. You can do better than that," Andy prodded. He knew the man's strength was his weakness. His gaze held steady with Leon's as he shifted his weight back and forth.

Leon's eyes signaled before the blade came at him from his left side. Andy stepped forward, pushed Leon's arm aside, and shoved his knife into Leon's throat. Blood gushed out. Andy jerked it back and plunged it into a spot just below his chest bone, twisted, and pulled down. Leon's guts spilled out as he crumbled to the ground.

Andy reached down, wiped his blade on the man's

pants, then rushed over to Julie. "We're getting out of here now." He cut the rest of the tape. After tucking the knife into the sheath, he picked up the gun, and helped her stand. "Take a second to steady yourself."

With the cell to his ear, he said, "One more down." It clicked back. "Leaving with package." Another click.

Even though she was a little wobbly, Julie gripped the back of his jeans' waistband, her other hand on his shoulder. It wouldn't be long until they were in the water, then back at the Mustang with Sprocket.

Once Julie was safe, Andy would return and dispose of the remaining kidnappers.

Chapter 43

The safest way to get her out of the house was through the back. Julie clutched his arm as they made their way down the steps then out the French doors in the rear.

Weather conditions had changed. Wind picked up and blew whitecaps in the inlet.

"We have to get into the water and make our way around that wall," Andy said and pointed.

She nodded.

He stopped just before the emitter. "Lie on your back and scoot down." A puzzled look stared back. "Watch me. It's a threadlike beam. Stay flat on the grass, or you'll set it off."

Once they cleared it, Andy waded into the water with Julie behind him and followed the shoreline to the end of the wall. Though difficult to hang on, a weight lifted from his shoulders. The Mustang was less than two hundred yards away.

"We're almost there," he whispered. Chest-deep, he held the gun and cell above the water.

Julie hesitated. "I'm scared."

"Keep moving." Andy inched his way toward shore.

He had to reach it before someone discovered the missing guards and Leon.

A pair of headlights rounded the corner and blinded him for a moment. "Don't move," he said and held the gun above the waterline, pointed at the approaching beams.

The car slowed, made a U-turn, backed up toward the gate, and stopped to the side. Two doors slammed, and the beams faded.

"Click, click."

Andy held the cell to his ear. "I saw it."

"Two men," Sprocket said. "One's headed your way. The other's standing by the car, packing what looks like an AK47."

Andy heard the side gate latch. With their escape route comprised, Andy weighed what options he had. Tackling the rough water with Julie to the shore across the channel was out of the question, which left only one.

"Honey, you're going to have to trust me," he whispered. "I have to go back inside."

"No." Fear in her eyes changed to panic.

"Just listen." He moved closer to her ear. "There's a place under the dock where you'll be safe."

"But—"

"We have to do it now before they start looking for us." Andy nudged her back toward the end of the wall, then eased around it. With no guards in sight, and Julie hanging onto him, he gripped the edge of the end-wall and pulled them toward the other side.

Julie screamed.

"What the hell?" He whipped around and kicked one of the bodies, then turned and aimed his handgun at the French doors and waited. There was no way of telling if anyone had heard her.

He moved behind her. "Hang onto the wall and work

your way to the dock," he said. "I'm right behind you."

Andy kept his gun trained on the doors until he reached the cigarette boat. Then he moved around the bow that pointed away from the house. The hull bobbed in the water along with the platform.

"What are we going to do?" she said.

"Hold on." He peered through the X-braced sides where the sections were connected. There appeared to be adequate space between the deck and the water.

"Duck under, then come up inside." Her eyes widened. "Do it."

Julie hesitated, then took in a deep breath, submerged, and popped up under the wooden planks.

"You'll be safe here. Hold on to these pipes so you don't hit your head."

✸✸✸

Andy eased the French door closed. There were at least two men in here, possibly more. Any disturbance would bring the man with the AK47 inside.

Voices from the room at the front of the house grew louder, an escalating exchange of angry words. He moved closer and guessed three.

A sound like a blast of air came from inside. A silencer.

"What the hell are you doing," a man shouted.

Andy recognized Carlyle's voice.

"A message from Mr. Yamamoto," a male with a heavy accent replied.

"Your cleanup does not include my bodyguards."

Andy sidestepped with his back against the wall until he reached the door, then he peered through the crack between it and the frame. A well-built Asian male had his gun pointed at Carlyle. Another man lay sprawled on the floor next to a bookshelf, his head in a pool of blood.

"Open the safe, and I will make it painless."

Carlyle shifted in his chair. "How dare you threaten me." He wheeled the chair around the table. "Yamamoto will hear about this."

"Who do you think sent me," the gunman said. "The safe, or I'll start with the knees first and work my way up."

If Andy left now, the gunman would finish the job for him. Andy grinned, then backed up toward the French doors with his gun trained on the room.

"Open it," the man yelled. "Now."

"Damn it," Andy whispered, then inched his way back to the room and peeked through the narrow opening.

Carlyle faced the shooter, almost taunting him. "Everything about our operation is in there," he said. "I will double what Yamamoto is paying you."

The man pulled up his sleeve and exposed a tattooed forearm. "Yakuza honor. My allegiance is to Yamamoto-san."

"Triple."

The man pointed the muzzled automatic at Carlyle's knee and fired, the suppressor muffling the explosion.

Carlyle screamed out in pain as he fell forward and out onto the floor.

Not wanting to alert the other guard, Andy shoved the SIG back into his waistband, then rushed into the room and in one fluid motion jerked the gunman's arm to the right as he slit his throat but not before two rounds discharged.

Another man rushed in through a side door and caught Andy by surprise. He stepped away and barely missed the sharp steel.

He pointed the gun. "One more step and you're dead."

The pocked face said nothing. The man's body tensed, and his face turned red, ready to burst. Seconds passed.

"That's better," Andy said.

Pock face's grimace widened to a grin, and then he lunged forward.

Andy fired, but it didn't stop him. He got off a second round, then felt an intense burning in his thigh. The man fell to his knees and rolled over onto his back, the knife still in his hand.

"Carlyle, get under the table," Andy said. "There's another one outside."

Andy glanced at the door then the one to the side where his recent victim had entered.

"Down a hall to the laundry and hired help's entrance," Carlyle said as his upper body scooted his lifeless legs toward the opening under the desk.

Andy thought for a fraction of a second and decided to meet the enemy head-on instead of getting trapped in an unfamiliar space. He pulled the door open, crouched, and stepped into the hall with his eyes focused on the front of the house.

A barrage of bullets splintered the front door.

Andy returned two rounds then ran toward the rear. Another blast answered back. He ducked into a doorway, fired two more rounds, then continued through the shattered French doors. Gunfire followed every move.

He glanced at the water, then decided he'd be a sitting duck. More important, Julie was out there, and he needed to draw gunfire away from her. He opted for the rock water feature next to the wall. All he had to do was hang on a little longer. He got off another round, then a click. "Shit."

The man stepped into the yard, leading with his AK47 and spraying a round of bullets into the water.

The stone tied to the gun was only a few feet away but in full view of the shooter. Andy grabbed a stick, slid it toward the stone, and eased it back to him. His opponent focused on the water, scanning left to right and back.

The Beretta slid up the stucco. With only a foot to go, Andy glanced back. The bastard was on the dock above Julie. Andy gave it one final yank and caught the gun. Bullets riddled the wall above him.

He crawled to the opposite end of the stacked rock and tossed a stone on the ground at the opposite end. Another barrage riddled the wall, then a click.

Andy stood and aimed as the guy ejected the magazine.

"No time, asshole." Andy fired three times, all in the kill zone.

❦❦❦

The street in front of the house was a blur of flashing red and blue lights. It looked as if every emergency vehicle in Virginia Beach had to be there, including a black armored SWAT vehicle.

Julie sat next to him on the back bumper of one of the rescue vehicles with a blanket wrapped around her. A female officer stood in front of them, trying to be sensitive with her questions.

Andy's eyes darted right. Two EMTs wheeled Carlyle out of the house on a gurney and placed him in the back of an ambulance. If what Andy had heard earlier was correct, the contents of the safe would put Carlyle behind bars for the rest of his life.

Andy flashed back on the first time he'd heard the old man's name in front of the Big Dipper on the Santa Cruz Boardwalk. "Mr. Carlyle's head of Carlyle Precious Metals out of Boston," Beyer had said. "Fifth Generation." Now he would be known worldwide as, Carlyle, the pedophile who had been instrumental in the trafficking of young girls to feed his sickness.

Sprocket tapped his shoulder. "Damn Z, it sounded like Chinese New Year in there."

Andy stood and gave him a brief hug. "I owe you big time."

"Do me a favor," Sprocket said with a smile. "Let me know next time you're coming to town so I can make sure I'm not here."

Andy caught sight of Weaver, followed by several men and one female, as they walked toward him, DEA, ICE, and FBI on their vests and windbreakers.

"Did you have that looked at?" Weaver said, nodding toward his thigh.

With all that had happened, Andy had forgotten about the pock face's blade that had grazed him. "I'm okay."

"You made the Task Force look bad," Weaver said. "You'll have a lot of explaining to do."

"I did what I had to."

"I don't know whether I should lock you up or nominate you for a medal," Weaver said.

Andy looked at Julie then back at the detective. "Now that she's safe, either one works for me."

Watch for

Death
Drop

Another Andy Zartanian thriller

Coming Soon

from

Robert O'Hanneson

About the Author

With over twenty years in the amusement business, selling rides to carnivals and parks worldwide, Robert O'Hanneson writes what he knows, the amusement business and his Armenian heritage. He and his wife Carol wrote *BLOODY SOIL*, a historical fiction novel that captures the pain of the Armenian Genocide. Though never published, portions of it were read on Fresno's NPR station.

Capturing tense moments during the Cuban Missile Crisis, O'Hanneson also wrote *INSIDE THE SILOS OF DOOMSDAY*, an article that was published in *Military History Magazine*. As one of two men responsible for launching megatons of nuclear weapons, he tells what it was like as a young man to serve in that position when the U.S. and Russia were at the brink of a nuclear war.

A native Californian, born in San Francisco, O'Hanneson later moved to Santa Clara Valley at a time when the major product was agriculture and not computer chips. He now resides in Modesto with his wife.